It wasn't one emotion, but *all* of them.

One minute she'd envision throttling him with her bare hands, and in the next, hugging his hurts away. Thirty seconds later, an egotistical comment would send her right back plotting his demise... or kissing him mute.

There was absolutely no rhyme or reason for the draw she felt toward the infuriating man, and the more she tried figuring it out, the more confused she got. The only thing she'd deduced with one hundred percent certainty was that emotions were damn addictive... and she didn't want it to stop anytime soon.

She'd gotten way too good at living her life on autopilot, never detouring from the normal route. She'd plateaued, fearful of all the pitfalls that came with risk taking, but if the last few days have taught her anything it was that following the straight path also meant never soaring high above.

That's what Isa wanted right now. She wanted to soar... even if it was temporary.

Shifting her hands beneath Roman's T-shirt, she trailed her palms up his rock-hard abs and across his chest, her nails catching on his hardening nipples.

A growl rolled from Roman's chest. "You're playing with fire, Doc."

"Good."

Acclaim for April Hunt's Novels

Lethal Redemption

"Fast-paced and action-packed, this swoon-worthy nail-biter is sure to keep readers hooked."
—*Publishers Weekly*, starred review

"Hunt's pace and tension are spot-on. High-stakes, sizzling romantic suspense."
—*Kirkus Reviews*

"Fans of military and private security series with brave and vulnerable men and women will enjoy this gritty romantic suspense."
—*Library Journal*

Deadly Obsession

"Expect masterful storytelling interwoven with sizzling tension and high-stakes suspense."
—Cristin Harber, *New York Times* bestselling author

"*Deadly Obsession* is a page turner full of sizzling passion, gritty action, and thrilling danger!"
—Rebecca Zanetti, *New York Times* bestselling author

"With a spunky heroine, a hero to die for, and thrilling action, *Deadly Obsession* is a keeper!"
—Paige Tyler, *New York Times* bestselling author

Hard Justice

"4 stars! Entertaining and satisfying."
—*RT Book Reviews*

"All kinds of romantic suspense goodness with a side of sexy alpha male."

—HerdingCats-BurningSoup.com

"Intriguing, passionate, sexy, suspenseful, and at times angst-ridden and funny, *Hard Justice* is April Hunt at her best. A wonderful, well-written, and addictive romantic suspense read that pulls you in and doesn't let you go. Excellent characters, entertaining plot, stellar romance."

—OkieDreams.com

Holding Fire

"Passionate chemistry and nonstop drama drive Hunt's second book in the adrenaline-charged Alpha Security series."

—*Publishers Weekly*

"4 stars! The suspense is ever-present...and the heat between the hero and heroine is intense."

—*RT Book Reviews*

"April Hunt has me hooked!"

—HerdingCats-BurningSoup.com

"April Hunt has quickly become one of my one-click authors. Her daring heroes are so damn charming. And with sassy, take-charge women by their sides, it makes for one hell of a ride."

—NallaReads.com

Heated Pursuit

"Smartly balances slow-burning passion and explosive high-stakes danger. This book kicks off an adventure-packed romance series, and readers will eagerly anticipate the next installment."

—*Publishers Weekly*

"4 stars! Fast paced and intriguing."

—*RT Book Reviews*

"Fun and sexy."

—SmexyBooks.com

"April Hunt creates a sexy, thrilling, action-packed story with *Heated Pursuit*. I could not put this book down."

—JoJoTheBookaholic.blogspot.com

"A fantastic, fast paced, and well developed debut! A hot alpha saving a feisty woman . . . what's not to love?"

—Sidney Halston, *USA Today* bestselling author

"Heat, humor, and heart-pounding action! I couldn't turn the pages fast enough!"

—Annie Rains, *USA Today* bestselling author

ALSO BY APRIL HUNT

Heated Pursuit

Holding Fire

Hard Justice

Hot Target (novella)

Deadly Obsession

Lethal Redemption

FATAL
DECEPTION

APRIL
HUNT

FOREVER
New York Boston

Copyright 2020 by April Schwartz
Excerpt from *Deadly Obsession* copyright 2019 by April Schwartz

Cover illustration and design by Elizabeth Turner Stokes. Cover copyright © 2020 by Hachette Book Group, Inc.

Forever
Hachette Book Group
1290 Avenue of the Americas, New York, NY 10104
read-forever.com
twitter.com/readforeverpub

First Edition: June 2020

Forever is an imprint of Grand Central Publishing. The Forever name and logo are trademarks of Hachette Book Group, Inc.

The publisher is not responsible for websites (or their content) that are not owned by the publisher.

The Hachette Speakers Bureau provides a wide range of authors for speaking events. To find out more, go to www.hachettespeakersbureau.com or call (866) 376-6591.

ISBNs: 978-1-5387-6341-4 (mass market), 978-1-5387-6339-1 (ebook)

Printed in the United States of America

OPM

10 9 8 7 6 5 4 3 2 1

To all my fellow nurses...
"Live life when you have it. Life is a
splendid gift—there is nothing small
about it."

—Florence Nightingale

ACKNOWLEDGMENTS

With every book I write, it only becomes clearer that I can't do this alone. The support my family gives me on a daily basis makes it possible for me to live my dream of putting happily-ever-afters into the hands of the readers.

Sarah E. Younger, agent extraordinaire...I've called you many things in these acknowledgments through the years: my cheerleader, my sounding-board, my therapist, and my wing-woman to name just a few. Every single one of them still holds true today, and there isn't a day I'm not thankful for having you on my side. #AgentJackpotLottery

Madeleine Colavita, editor elite...there's no one I'd rather write books with than you. I can't put into words how thankful I am for you sharing all your wisdom with me through *seven* books. And to Estelle, Monisha, and everyone on the Forever team... *Thank you!* I'm so lucky to have amazing people helping me each and every day.

Tif Marcelo, best friend and critique partner aficionado...I really did hit the jackpot during that three a.m. frozen dinner (wink). *Fatal Deception* never would've happened if it weren't for you nudging me along the way.

And to my readers—I'm so appreciative of each and every one of you. I'm able to do what I love because of you.

FATAL
DECEPTION

CHAPTER ONE

Focused on the petri dish in front of her, Dr. Isabel Santiago steadied her hand and applied a drop of the FC-5 virus to the latest batch of microscope slides. The task was easier said than done, and it had nothing to do with her bulky biohazard suit and rubber gloves and everything to do with the noise filtering into the lab through the speakers.

"I think I diagnosed the source of those headaches you've been having. It's your...music." Isabel shifted her gaze to the wall of windows, the protective glass that separated the basement Tru Tech lab—affectionately called the Legion—from the clean room.

Maddy Calhoun, a doctoral student and her best friend, sat in the other room, fingers tapping as she performed the role of Isa's safety spotter. "Don't be hating my playlist. The Psychotic Zombies are all the rage right now—something you'd know if you went out with me more than once in a blue moon."

"If they're the kind of education I get on girls' nights out, I'm kind of glad that I stay in as often as I do," Isa joked.

Maddy leaned into the two-way mic. "Isabel Santiago,

you *owe* me. Do you have any idea what I could be doing on a Saturday night? Or *who*?"

Beneath her headgear, Isa chuckled. "That neighbor who lives on the floor above you? What's his name? Clint? Carson?"

"Cody." Maddy wrinkled her nose. "And, no. Been there and not doing that again. Don't get me wrong. He was drop-dead gorgeous, and the things he could do with his tongue? *Have mercy.* But afterward? There was nothing. I shit you not, Is, we were looking up at the stars and I commented on the Milky Way, and he thought I wanted to drive to the nearest 7-Eleven for a candy bar."

Isa swallowed a laugh as she safely tucked the FC-5 samples back into their spots in the biohazard fridge. "It couldn't have been that bad."

"It so, so was. But stop trying to change the subject. I expect payment in full for Saturday."

"I let you play your music."

"Not cutting it. I had a big night planned for the two of us. I'm talking slinky dresses, drinks—and did I mention that the place was owned by brothers? *Brothers*, Isabel. Hot gods all derived from the same gene pool." Maddy fanned herself with a stack of papers. "I need an ice bath just thinking about them."

"Sorry to kill your plans of debauchery, but I really need to assess this latest batch of samples and start new ones with Tony's recommendations. He had an interesting thought about changing the class of antivirals."

"*My* interesting and your and Tony's interesting are *way* different from one another. And just so you know, mine is the one that's spot-on and, if luck's on our side, the one that could potentially lead to multiple orgasms. Sharing hobbies with a man who's triple your age isn't exactly a cause for bragging."

Isa chuckled at the image of a ninety-some-year-old Anthony Winter, but her one-time mentor, now an epidemiologist with the Global Health Organization, wasn't a day over sixty-four and traveled to far-off places most twenty-year-olds wouldn't venture.

"I'm ready to step into decontamination now," Isa announced. "Maybe we can forgo the slinky dresses and hot gods and grab a quick drink on the way home."

Maddy pouted. "Not the same thing."

It wasn't.

As sad as it may be to someone with Maddy's active social life, it was viruses that took up most of Isabel's waking hours. Ebola. Smallpox. She worked on all of them and a lot more in the name of the United States government. Most researchers waited their entire careers to be given the opportunity Tru Tech Industries had given her—her own basement lab equipped with all the latest cutting-edge tech. But all that responsibility came at a price.

Her personal life.

Isa stepped into decon, and the second the airtight door locked her inside, a mixture of foaming germicides blasted from the wall-mounted nozzles. She lifted her arms and let the liquid run over every inch of her suit, while Maddy, watching from the corner video monitor, directed her on which areas needed an extra dose.

Fifteen minutes and a change of clothes later, Isa

stepped into the clean room. She had just opened her mouth to give in to her friend's need for hot god brothers when the light above the lab's private elevator came on, alerting them they were about to get a visitor.

Only a select few personnel had the clearance to visit the Legion, so when Frank, the Legion's soon-to-be-retired security guard, stepped out, Isa wasn't surprised.

"Perfect timing." Isa smiled, always loving the time of the night that the older man made his rounds. "Tell us how the retirement party plans are coming."

Frank's wide, panicked eyes shot her way. "Doc! Ru—"

Someone pushed him from behind. As the older man crashed into the table against the wall and hit the ground, four additional figures stepped off the elevator.

Isabel's brain didn't register the intrusion until the one nearest her aimed his gun at the center of her chest.

"Going somewhere, Dr. Santiago?" His clear blue eyes locked on her through the slits of his black ski mask.

The intruders fanned out. The one nearest Frank grabbed him by the uniform and dragged him along the floor to the other side of the room while his friend did the same to Maddy.

Isa's gaze instantly snapped to the panic button a good twelve feet away.

"Don't do anything you'll regret, Doc. And trust me, if you touch that alarm, you *will* regret it." Blue Eyes shifted his stance—and his gun—closer. "Turn around."

Isa's nerves froze her feet to the ground. She trained for spills, exposures, and the occasional equipment breakdown. Armed men in her lab wasn't part of Tru Tech's annual continuing education.

"I don't know what you're doing here, or how you got inside, but this is a secure building," Isa's warning fell flat even to her own ears.

"Yet my friends and I managed to get in just fine. And I should think what we're doing here would be pretty obvious...or maybe you're not as smart as I've heard. Now fucking *move*."

He dug the muzzle of his weapon into her back and nudged her across the room.

Maddy sobbed into Frank's shoulder as they both sat huddled on the floor, a trickle of blood dripping down the older man's forehead. His small taser—if he still had it—couldn't compete with assault weapons.

Blue Eyes yanked Isabel to a stop in front of the lab's sealed door. "Let me inside."

"No." She lifted her chin in staunch defiance and ignored the tremor in her voice. "You have no idea what's in there."

"Actually, I do. Last warning." He aimed his gun at the center of her chest. "Let me inside the lab. *Now*."

No way in hell was Isa giving them access.

Maddy released a loud wail, the sound temporarily pulling Blue Eyes' attention away from the door. Isa leapt for the panic alarm. She flipped open the cover, fingers brushing over the button at the exact time a hand fisted in her hair.

"I don't fucking think so." Her assailant swung her face-first into the wall.

Pain exploded behind her eyes, dimming her vision. She barely registered Frank lurching to his feet, rushing the man. A shot rang out, echoing in the basement like an exploding bomb.

Isa watched in horror as Frank jerked backward, his white uniform shirt blossoming red before he dropped to the ground. "No! Frank!"

Blood seeped through the security guard's fingers at an alarming rate, pooling on the floor beneath him. "I'm...fine."

In a few minutes, he'd be anything but fine.

For a split second Isa was transported back to her med school emergency medicine rotation. In the aftermath of a mass shooting, casualties rolled in, one immediately after another. People shouted for her help—or for her to help their friend. Hospital staff ran from one patient to the next, quickly triaging and assessing, and like the others, Isa had kept pace next to her attending...until suddenly she couldn't anymore.

People had looked to her for help in their scariest, darkest time, and she'd failed them.

"No. No. No." Isa dragged her focus back to the lab.

She hadn't been able to save some of those people at Virginia Hospital Center, but she sure as hell wouldn't lose Frank.

Isabel whipped off her lab coat and dropped to her friend's side in an attempt to stanch the flow of blood.

"You can go to hell," she threw at the man holding

the gun, "because I'm not opening that door. Those viruses are locked up for a *reason*."

Blue Eyes aimed his gun at her head. "You have to the count of three to open the lab door, or your blood will mix right along with your friend's. One. Two. Thr—"

"I'll do it!" Maddy struggled with her captor as she attempted to step forward. "I'll do it! Just don't hurt anyone else. Please."

"Maddy," Isabel warned, shaking her head. "No."

They didn't handle simple strains of influenza. A single small mishap could jumpstart the worst pandemic the world had ever seen—and it would've happened on her watch.

Tears poured down her friend's face. "I'm sorry, Isa. I—I have to. Frank's already...I'm not letting something happen to you, too."

Maddy's brute walked her to the control panel, and after an eye scan and entering her personalized code, the airlocked door slid open with a *whoosh*.

Blue Eyes nodded to the two men standing off to the side. "Get what we came for and make it quick."

"I don't know how you think you're getting out of here. There's one way into the Legion and one way out." Isa glared.

"You let me worry about that, sweetheart."

Isabel's throat dried. He didn't seem worried about *anything*, and that made *her* worry. The men ransacked her lab, purposefully toppling empty beakers and tipping wheeled carts as they made their way toward the back of the lab. One of them stopped in front of the cryo unit where she kept her samples of

FC-5...and pulled out what looked to be his own travel case.

Her heart leapt to her throat. "No!"

Isa lurched to her feet. She'd made it two steps when Blue Eyes shoved her face-first against the glass wall.

His masked mouth brushed against her ear, making her cringe. "You really must have a death wish."

Isa squirmed against his grip, and it tightened. "*Please* don't do this. You have no idea the people that virus could hurt."

"Sweetheart, I don't care who it can hurt. I care about who it can help—*me*."

His men stepped out of the lab, the one with the case announcing, "Got what we need." He nodded toward Isa and Maddy. "What do we do about them?"

"Leave them. For now." Blue Eyes' mouth brushed against her ear as he leaned closer. "Until next time, doctor."

He released his hold on her, and the men backtracked the way they came, guns trained on the women as they retreated to the elevator. Isa wasn't telling them the fault in their plan.

The elevator only had two stops.

Upstairs security wouldn't let them strut across the lobby and breach the exit.

Isa dropped to Frank's side as they disappeared into the elevator. "Maddy! Hit the panic button, and then call security. We need an ambulance. Now."

Frank released a wet cough that ended on a wheeze. "I'm okay, Doc. Just a little flesh wound. I've gotten worse scrapes yanking the weeds in the garden."

Isa smiled wanly and applied more pressure to the wound. All too quickly, her coat soaked up the older man's blood. "I'm sure you have, Frank."

The day she'd left bedside medicine, she'd vowed never to put herself in the position where she'd have to lie to a patient again.

And yet here she was.

"You're going to be fine, Frank." Isa lost her fight against brewing tears. One drop fell down her cheek, quickly followed by another. "Stay focused on the hammock waiting for you when you get to your Caribbean bungalow. But you should know that I wasn't kidding about going with you. I may stow away in your luggage."

"The more the merrier." Frank sucked in a sharp breath, the effort making a shrill whistling sound. "We'll all be just...fine...Doc. Just...fine."

Isa knew better. Anyone willing to break into a government-sponsored lab wouldn't give two thoughts about the kind of destruction their actions could cause. If those men released FC-5 into the general public, *no one* be would fine.

CHAPTER
TWO

Visiting Tru Tech Industries wasn't on the list of things Roman Steele wanted to do today. Or tomorrow. Or next week. Or at any point in time in the near—or far—future. Yet there his dumb ass stood at the police checkpoint for the last twenty minutes with no sign of being let through any time soon.

Roman slid his two younger brothers a sharp glare. "You assholes hauled my ass out of bed for this?"

Liam, the baby of their four-man band, smirked. "Come on. It's not like you had anything happening."

"*Sleep*. I had sleep happening. And how the hell do you know that I didn't have plans?"

"Because the day ends in a *y*, big brother."

Next to him, Ryder laughed.

Liam wasn't wrong. His big plans had consisted of whaling on the heavy bag until his left leg either locked up or gave out. Not the healthiest exercise regime for an amputee, but it'd worked for him for the last few years. He wasn't about to change it now.

Keeping in shape and running Steele Ops with his brothers and the ever-growing collection of military elite they employed took up most of his time.

They'd officially opened their doors last year, converting the historic Keaton Jailhouse in downtown Alexandria to house both of their business ventures. Iron Bars Distillery & Beer Garden took up the first three floors and had quickly gained a reputation within the community. But beneath the feet of their vanilla-vodka-loving customers, Steele Ops ran like a well-oiled machine.

Anti-terrorism. Covert extractions. They got shit done the government couldn't do thanks to bureaucratic red tape or lack of manpower. Only a select few knew of their existence, one of them former Army chief of staff Hogan Wilcox.

His teammate's Cade's father, Wilcox was the one who'd raised tonight's alarm, which meant that whatever happened here at Tru Tech wasn't insignificant. As much as he didn't want to be here, it was probably a good thing they were.

Ryder cleared his throat as they took another step to the front of the security line. "I have one request. Just a little thing really. I wouldn't even call it a request...more like a *suggestion*."

"You two are just full of demands today," Roman muttered.

"Let *me* do the talking. We both know when you open your mouth, chances are high you'll piss someone off."

True. Of his brothers, Liam and Ryder were definitely the most personable, with Knox, the eldest, a close second. Roman had never been much of a people-pleaser, and after his years in black ops and working at the kind of CIA installations that *don't exist*, he saw even less need for roundabout politeness. Manners only got in the way of progress.

"I'll keep my people skills on the down-low," Roman agreed. "At least until someone says something that's too stupid to ignore."

From deep inside the security perimeter, one of the plainclothes cops ended her conversation with what looked to be a lab employee and headed their way. Natasha James eyed each of the brothers warily as she motioned for the perimeter guard to let them pass through.

Finally.

"I should've known when Roger Carmichael said he'd hired outside help who it would've been. Why is it that wherever there's trouble there's usually a Steele?"

Liam grinned. "Come on, Nat. Admit it. If we all hadn't come back home, you would've been bored sitting in that squad car."

Nat dropped her gaze to the detective badge on her hip. "Actually, I've graduated from beat cop—which means that this clusterfuck is all mine. Please tell me you won't make it any worse."

"It's definitely not on our agenda." Ryder nodded toward the building behind them. "Can you tell us what happened?"

"Long story made longer? At nine last night, four masked men stepped off a private elevator and right into the basement lab. They threatened the workers, shot the security guard when he tried intervening on the doctor's behalf, stole a nasty virus, and then, believe it or not, hopped back on the elevator as if nothing happened."

"And no one thought to stop them from leaving the building?" Roman asked.

"Yeah well, that's just it. They *didn't* leave the building…and yet they're not here." She guided them to Tru Tech's front entrance.

"How the hell does that work?"

Nat shrugged and led the way through the police chaos and into the building. "Wish I knew. There's only one way to get down to the basement lab where the virus was stolen and there's no video footage of anyone stepping *onto* the elevator. Just off of it when they reached the lab."

Liam grunted and said exactly what Roman was thinking. "Then someone's messing around with the surveillance images."

"If they are, we sure as hell can't tell."

"*I'll* be able to tell."

Liam wasn't boasting. It was the honest truth. There wasn't much the former Navy intelligence officer couldn't do when a computer was put in front of him. If someone tampered with the security feed, Liam would know. If no one did, and these assholes really did disappear into thin air, then they did it while carting around brass-plated balls and fucking magic wands.

"You said something about a doctor?" Roman asked. "People were in the lab at the time of the theft?"

"Three of my best employees." Dressed in a suit that probably cost more than Roman currently had in his bank account, an older man crossed the lobby, headed their way. "Roger Carmichael. Tru Tech CEO."

"Your three employees?"

"Dr. Isabel Santiago, her assistant Maddy Calhoun, and the Legion's core evening security personnel, Frank Hutchins."

"Core?" Roman asked.

"Not every staff member is permitted into the Legion, for obvious safety reasons. Those who are undergo rigorous security clearances and specialized training in the event of—"

"Something like this happening?"

Ryder cleared his throat and muttered under his breath. "Down-low."

Carmichael frowned, obviously unhappy with Roman's retort. "Actually, no. I can't say we've ever trained for this eventuality, because it shouldn't be possible." His eyes narrowed on each of them before falling on Roman. "I can't stress the importance of finding my missing virus enough. As it stands, I'm sure the government will use this as another reason to gift our deserved funds to another undeserving cracker-jack box lab."

Carmichael's tone rubbed Roman the wrong way. "*That's* why you want us to track down your virus? Because you won't get your bonus check in the mail?"

Ryder cleared his throat, playing referee. "We'll find your virus, Mr. Carmichael. Where are the employees who were present at the time of the break-in?"

"In quarantine until their bloodwork comes back clean, which will hopefully be sometime tomorrow."

Roman cocked an eyebrow. "Was there an actual exposure?"

"It doesn't appear so. According to Dr. Santiago,

despite the fact that the thieves stole the virus, they did so with great care. The quarantine is a standard precaution. I'm guessing you want to talk to them?"

"You guessed right."

Nat nodded. "That's a good idea. Maybe repeating the story will jog something in their memories. I'll get in touch with you later to compare notes."

Liam nodded and shook her hand. "Thanks, Nat. Congrats on the promotion. We'll try not to step on your toes too much."

"We both know that promise will fall a few miles short. Just don't do anything I'll have to arrest you for." Nat reached for the phone on her hip and walked away with a small wave.

Carmichael took them the roundabout route, dropping Liam off at security before taking Ryder and Roman up to the third-floor quarantine level. He stopped in front of two sets of doors. "Miss Calhoun is in the room to the right, and Dr. Santiago the left."

"They weren't placed together?" Ryder asked.

"It's to minimize risk in case one was exposed and the other was not."

Ryder glanced nervously at the door. "And we're okay strutting in there?"

Roman smirked. "Nervous, little brother?"

"Of contracting a highly lethal disease and watching my dick rot off? Hell yeah, I'm nervous."

Carmichael waved off the concern. "Miss Calhoun and Dr. Santiago are in separate air-pressurized rooms within those doors. You'll simply be stepping into an observation suite a lot like medical universities use for surgical teaching purposes. There's no chance of contact or contamination."

On his hip, Carmichael's walkie screeched to life and he blew out a frustrated breath. "If you'll excuse me, I have more fires to put out. When you're done, Eddie will see you to the lobby." He nodded toward the lone guard standing at the edge of the hall.

When Carmichael disappeared from view, a familiar shit-eating grin slid onto Ryder's face as he reached for the doctor's door. "Guess I'll take the doc—"

Roman knocked his brother's hand from the knob. "Yeah, I don't think so."

"Why the hell not?"

Roman studied Ryder's face before finding his answer in the dark gleam of his eyes. "Because of that horn-dog look you got on your face. You googled her before you even picked my ass up, didn't you?"

Ryder's mouth twitched. "It was research...but yeah. And I gotta say, if my doctor looked like her, I'd actually get my annual physicals."

"Yeah, this is a job, not a dating service, and it's been far too long since you've gotten any. *I'll* take the doc."

"Says our resident monk."

The truth in Ryder's snarky comment pissed Roman off. Thanks to their Steele genes, he and his brothers had never struggled to find female companionship when they wanted it...even as knobby-kneed teens. The problem was that he *didn't* want it.

Not really. Sex didn't relieve stress any better than working out in the gym, and anything more than a quick romp with the fairer sex was off the table. Relationships required trust, and the only people he counted on to mean what they say were his family and his team.

Ryder's smirk widened. "Fine. Take the doctor, and I'll question the assistant."

Fuck. He gave in way too easy, which meant both women were no doubt gorgeous as hell. "You're an asshole."

Ryder shrugged. "I've been called worse. Just remember that the point of going in there is to see if we can coax information out of them they may not realize they know."

"Your point?"

"That it requires finesse. A delicate touch."

"I can be delicate," Roman lied.

Ryder snorted. "You're about as delicate as a sledgehammer, Ro."

So he wasn't a teddy bear, and he didn't beat around the bush. Tact was something people used when they wanted to dance around a subject instead of plow right through it, and Roman sure as hell didn't dance.

Roman shouldered his brother out of the way. "I'll take the doc... and I'll finesse the hell out of it."

Ignoring his brother's chuckles, he tugged on the door and stepped into the room.

Eyes closed and head tilted back against the wall, Isabel Santiago sat on a metal cot not unlike the ones he'd encountered in the Army. Her curtain of long dark hair framed her heart-shaped face and was a stark contrast to the white jumpsuit she wore.

She didn't look like any scientist he'd ever seen.

"Dr. Santiago?"

Her eyes opened and scanned the room before falling on him.

Large golden brown eyes inspected his presence, narrowing in unfocused concentration. He recognized that half-glazed look all too well. Hell, he'd seen it a million times out in the field. Anyone who'd been deployed into an active combat zone scenario wore that same face at one time or another.

Especially him.

But there wasn't a war happening outside this room, and they hadn't been dropped into a hot zone.

Roman shoved aside all his self-professed finesse and did the only thing he knew would work in pulling her out of the funk.

"Dr. Santiago, I'm Roman Steele. I'm with the private security firm your employer hired to find out what happened to—and to track down—your missing virus." Locking Isabel in his sights, he summoned every ounce of assholessness he possessed. "Care to tell me how the hell this happened?"

* * *

Isa wasn't as immune to the male form as Maddy thought, but even if she had been, there was no ignoring Roman Steele's. He stood well over six feet tall, his leather jacket–encased broad shoulders rivaled only by his wide chest and trim waist. And his eyes...dark to near black and framed by long, thick lashes, they studied her as if attempting to look through her, and the intensity stirred something she hadn't felt in a long time.

Interest.

At least until she pulled her thoughts away from the deep timbre of his voice and onto his words. "Did you just...?"

Isa blinked once. Then twice. His stare turned accusatory as he waited on the other side of the three-inch safety glass. Oh hell yeah, he did.

Ignoring her earlier exhaustion, she stiffened her shoulders and met him glare for glare. "I don't know how something like that happens, Mr. Steele. Maybe they had second jobs as magician's assistants."

Roman kept his blank mask in place as he leaned against the small table in the observation room. "There's no reason for the sarcasm, Doc."

"Yet it was the first thing you dished out the moment you stepped into the room."

"Because things don't add up, and I don't like it when there are big question marks hanging over my head."

"Then I suggest you wear a hard hat and go in search of the answers."

"That's what I'm doing here."

"No, you're trying to piss me off, and guess what? It's working. If you have a real question I may be able to answer, then ask. If not, you know where the door is."

"Your lab is practically impossible to breach without having appropriate clearance."

Isabel waited a beat. "*Practically* impossible, but

seeing as we're in this situation, it's obviously not out of the realm of possibility. What's your point?"

"My point is that nine times out of ten that impossible becomes possible because there was an inside man...or woman."

If she were superhuman, Isa would've sent her fist through the window and throttled the gorgeous jerkwad on the other side.

Isabel uncrossed her legs and stood, summoning her best icy tone. "I don't like what you're insinuating, Mr. Steele."

"That's not me insinuating, Doc. That's me making a factual statement."

"None of my colleagues had anything to do with what happened," Isabel said adamantly. "We do what we do to *rid* the world of dangerous diseases, not so we can unleash them on a vulnerable public."

"I'd like to believe that, but we have four armed men getting off an elevator with no visual proof that they'd gotten on it in the first place. And then they disappeared pretty much the same way. If they didn't have inside help, they really are magicians."

"You're the ridiculously priced security expert Carmichael hired. Isn't it your job to figure out how they pulled it off and locate the FC-5 virus? Because in case you haven't realized it from the fact that I'm in a glass fishbowl, it's not a simple flu strain."

"Oh, my team and I will track them down. It's just a matter of time."

Isa was already shaking her head. "That's something none of us have. FC-5 isn't *just* an Ebola-like strain. It's *the* strand. It's an end-of-days virus that could wipe out millions of the world's population before anyone has a chance to react."

"How is it different from Ebola?"

"Standard Ebola has an average incubation of fourteen days and then a fifty percent survival rate."

"And FC-5?"

Isabel's stomach rolled as she fought back rising bile. "A four-day average incubation…and a *five* percent survival rate. In case you're not keeping track of time or the math, it's already been a day since the virus was taken from the lab, and a five percent survival rate means that ninety-five out of one hundred people infected don't make it back to their families."

Roman's jaw clenched, the muscles in his cheeks flexing wildly.

Good. Fear, in her line of work, was a necessity. It kept you on your toes. It made you careful. And in this instance, it made her determined to keep FC-5 as far away from any civilization as humanly possible.

CHAPTER
THREE

"When you called and told me to bring climbing gear from headquarters, this isn't what I expected to be doing with it." Ryder hung suspended on the rope next to Roman as they slowly lowered themselves down the elevator shaft at Tru Tech Industries.

Isabel Santiago's adamancy that she'd watched the four thieves step back onto the elevator only fueled Roman's wild hunch, a hunch he prayed to God was wrong.

While with Special Forces, he'd worked with CIA teams in high-profile urban extractions, and it was the only way he could explain it. And if he was right, it threw a whole different kind of wrench into this brewing shit-storm, because it meant whoever was behind it wasn't a low-level fly-by-the-seat-of-the-pants crook. It took careful planning, expert knowledge, and a whole lot of balls.

Anyone with that kind of skill set was a loose cannon, and it was that unknown factor that made him damn uncomfortable.

"Did you look at that file Carmichael gave us on FC-5?" Ryder eased himself down another few inches, his head swiveling as he looked around them. "I looked at it right before calling it a night, and I couldn't fall asleep. I like all my orifices the way they are—blood-free and without liquid oozing out of them. I think this will be the first year Ma won't have to threaten bodily harm for me to get my flu shot."

Roman grunted in agreement. Hell, he'd be the first bastard in line, too.

After Isabel's parting warning yesterday, he'd also looked up the supervirus and had wished to hell that he hadn't. By the time he'd read the last page, he'd experienced nearly all the FC-5 symptoms—except bleeding orifices—and had climbed into the shower and scrubbed head to toe no less than two times and then again a third right before he turned in for the night.

He still didn't feel completely clean.

People thought his line of work was dangerous, but he'd take flying bullets over viruses any day of the week. You could visualize a gun aimed at your head, or a ticking bomb counting down in front of you. You couldn't see what microscopic shit came your way from a sneeze or, hell, touching a damn doorknob.

In his opinion, what Isabel Santiago and Maddy Calhoun did every single day took real guts—unless one of them was the reason he was sliding down this elevator shaft.

"Interesting." Ryder's voice pulled Roman from his thoughts.

"What's interesting?" Roman shifted his Maglite around the walls.

"You've never been a great conversationalist, but you've been quiet even for you...ever since you had your chat with Isabel Santiago. I'd think it was a coincidence, but I'm allergic to coincidences."

Roman retorted, "And I think you'd better pay attention to what you're doing, or you'll end up a greasy spot on the bottom of this elevator shaft."

As Ryder's laughter echoed in the tight quarters, Roman's mood worsened. The deadly FC-5 virus wasn't the only thing he'd had difficulty getting his mind off last night. Isabel Santiago had also followed him home.

Roman prided himself on being able to read people. It was a talent embedded into his genes. And his gut told him that what you saw with Isabel was what you got—a talented, dedicated woman who was as allergic to failure as Roman was. If she had something to do with this fiasco, he'd donate his left nut to science.

But he'd learned five years ago that his gut wasn't infallible.

As if reminding him, a sharp pain sliced through his left leg, right beneath his prosthesis straps. The shadow pain didn't come as often as it had even a year ago, but when it did, fucking A.

Roman clenched tight to his rappel line and breathed through the stinging pain. It took two counts of ten until it didn't feel like someone was hacking through his bone with a dull bow saw, and by the time it was over, Ryder's gaze settled on him like an anvil.

"You know it's not the end of the world, right?" Ryder's tone was suddenly serious.

"Pretty sure that's exactly what this virus could do in the wrong hands."

"You know that's not what I'm talking about. Feeling a connection to someone isn't a bad thing...especially when that person's a smart, successful woman like Isabel Santiago."

"There *is* no connection," Roman lied. "Other than the one I'll feel against my jaw when she's finally let out of her little glass bubble."

Ryder's gaze bored into the back of his head. "You were *that* much of an asshole?"

His lack of a response answered the question.

Ry muttered under his breath, questioning at what point in time Roman had become an ass. But hell if he knew.

Roman shined his flashlight over the walls, looking for any sign someone other than them had been down this way. "Maybe you should worry less about my female *connections* and more on your own. When will you stop fawning over a certain klutzy bartender long enough to ask the woman out? Or are you hoping she digs the creepy stalker vibe and extra hours you're clocking at Iron Bars?"

Ryder glared. "We were talking about you. Not me."

"All's fair in love and ass busting." Roman snuck a look at his brother's puckered expression and chuckled as his flashlight beam hit a vent. "I got something."

He swung his body out and landed on the far side of the shaft, where an HVAC vent grate dangled precariously from a lone corner bolt. The exposed hole gaped open, large enough for a broad set of shoulders.

Instant fucking tunnels.

"I'll be damned," Ryder murmured.

Roman snatched his walkie. "Jaz, you anywhere near the east end of the building?"

The speaker buzzed before the former Marine sniper's voice answered. "Turning the corner now, but I'm not seeing anything out here that's raising any alarms."

"Is there a venting system? It'll be grated, probably a tight three-by-three or somewhere close to it?"

"Hold on." A minute later, she came back. "Nope. Don't see—uh, wait a sec. Well, hell. There's one hidden behind a construction dumpster about halfway down the building."

"Feel like going on an adventure?" Roman asked.

It took less than three seconds for his meaning to sink in. "You're fucking with me. You expect me to crawl in there?"

Jaz's curses made both brothers chuckle. "Thanks for asking, Curva. Pretty great of you."

"I should've let Tank come and stayed back at Steele Ops."

Roman smirked. "That's what you get for always trying to one-up him."

Jaz cursed again, but a few seconds later, low, rolling thunder echoed through the vent as she crawled through the small space. The closer she got, the louder and more creative her curses became. Five minutes later, she glowered at him in person.

Sweat dotted her brow. "Next time someone needs to crawl in a hot, dark hole, I'm not it. Care to tell me what the point was behind this exercise?"

"This is how they did it." Roman's gut feeling from before roared back.

"This is how who did what?" Jaz's dark eyes widened. "You think this is how those assholes got in and out of the lab without detection? How the hell is that possible?"

It was more than possible. It was *probable*. During his stint with Special Ops and the Euro division of the CIA, he'd executed nearly the same type of operation, but that had been years ago and continents away. Seeing it here in his hometown—now—caused a bad taste to climb up from his throat.

This wasn't a hostage extraction. This was a bio-threat. People who went to these kinds of lengths didn't come with a whole lot of boundaries...or a very long list of things they wouldn't do to make sure they got their prize.

Ryder whistled. "So Isabel Santiago wasn't lying when she said they appeared and disappeared into thin air. They basically did."

"To play it safe, we still need eyes on everyone with any kind of access to the Legion, and that includes Carmichael, the guard, Maddy Calhoun...and Isabel Santiago." Roman volleyed his brother's questioning look with a determined one of his own. "What?"

"You want to keep an eye on the doc because you think she actually had something to do with it, or is it because you're concerned?"

Roman wanted to say it was the former reason, but he made it a rule not to lie. His gut told him that Isabel Santiago didn't have an evil bone in her body. Sarcastic?

Yeah. Short-tempered? Probably that, too. But just because she didn't emit an evil mastermind vibe didn't mean that someone within Tru Tech didn't have their hand in this mess.

Or their whole damn body.

CHAPTER
FOUR

"I can practically hear you grinding your teeth through the mike. It's distracting," Liam complained from the ear comm tucked into Roman's right ear.

"I wouldn't be grinding my teeth if you picked up a lead. A facial rec. Voice ID. Hell, I'd be happy with a half-assed image of a tattoo."

From his perch back at Steele headquarters, Liam sighed. "It's not like I haven't been trying, but like we thought, these guys are fucking smart. They don't show anything identifying on the video surveillance, and the bastards took out every security cam in a two-block radius of Tru Tech. They weren't taking any fucking chances."

Roman couldn't blame his brother. After casing the elevator shaft the previous day, he'd spent all night staring at the security feed himself only to come to the same conclusion. *They had jack shit.* It was a jagged pill to swallow that came precariously close to the one he had to down after he'd lost his leg.

Sitting on the sidelines and waiting for things to happen had been one of the toughest things about life post-amputation. He wasn't wired that way, and that hadn't changed because he was now one appendage short. With Liam working his magic on Tru Tech's security system and scouring the dark web for any sort of virus talk, that left only one other thing for Roman to do to stave off the formation of a bed sore on his ass.

Isabel Santiago.

He could've stationed himself outside of the security guard's hospital room, or across the street from Carmichael's fancy Georgetown townhouse or Maddy Calhoun's modest studio apartment, but instead, he'd taken responsibility for Isabel himself.

And hell if he knew why. At the idea of one of his brothers or Cade following her around the city, he'd quickly tagged Hunter "Tank" Dawson as his second and hadn't left room for negotiations.

Liam resumed whistling, the tune changing from the peppy sounds of the fifties to something that sounded like the Beatles.

"Are you going to be doing *that* much longer?" Roman demanded grumpily.

"When music dies so does a small piece of my heart…so yeah. Gotta make sure the entire muscle's intact for when I meet my special lady."

Roman snorted. "Thought you met her last week at O'Malley's."

"So did I, but the physical beauty far surpassed the library she had going on upstairs, and I love myself too damn much to compromise. Guess we can't all be as lucky as you."

"What the hell is that supposed to mean?"

It was Liam's turn to stop. "Dude. I may be the youngest, but I'm by far the smartest. Isabel Santiago is the legit thing—beauty and brains—and it's obvious she's gotten to you."

"She hasn't *gotten* to me."

"When you're done there you should hit up the ER at George Washington."

"Jaz is on guard duty."

"Yeah, not for babysitting detail...to have someone check out those third-degree burns on your ass, because your pants just went up in flames as if they'd been doused in gasoline."

Tank's low chuckle came over the comm. "You're going to have to put that ER visit on hold because we're headed toward you, Ro. Half block out."

"On it." Roman secured his sunglasses, thankful for the momentary reprieve.

He leaned against his motorcycle as if waiting for someone inside the small neighborhood coffee shop. Keeping tabs on Isabel since she'd been released from quarantine twenty-four hours ago, it had come to everyone's attention that Perk It Up was her go-to spot for caffeine boosts...and she required a lot of them. At the end of a late afternoon jog was no exception.

Roman sensed her before he saw her, his entire body nearly humming from the close proximity. No one would've guessed that Tank had already trailed her for a full five miles. Her stride was long and even, dark hair swaying with each pound of her sneakers. As she passed him, she didn't spare him so much as a second glance, and then she tugged the coffee shop door open and disappeared inside.

Roman's gaze dropped to the generous swell of her ass in her tight running pants.

Fuck Tank for having stared at that ass for the last five miles.

"Thank you for turning down the run," Tank's voice, full of humor, pulled Roman's attention across the street, where his friend smirked. "Gotta say, it was a nice view."

"Swipe that shit-eating grin off your face, or the next time the weapon cage needs to be cleaned out, you're doing it with Jaz."

Tank's smile fell. "Jaz in the cage? Surrounded by a shit ton of weapons?"

"And ammo…so do you really want to goad me right now, man?"

"Point taken."

On Roman's left, a white utility van turned toward M Street. It slowed as it approached, and then took off before making a right at the end of the next block. His gut stirred in warning. "Did you see the van?"

"Did it have a rusty patch over the front passenger wheel well?"

"Yeah."

"That's the third time it's past me and Isabel on this run."

Fuckin' A.

"Tighten the perimeter around Isabel." Roman pushed off his bike and headed toward Perk It Up. "Liam? Do you think you can find it on traffic feeds? I want to know if it's coming around again."

Liam's fingers clicked on his computer. "Give me one

sec...and...yeah. There it is. It looks like it made a second right. If it makes a third I think it's a pretty safe bet it's coming your way again...and there's the third. It's coming back around."

* * *

Isa paid for her extra-large caramel macchiato and stepped back into the gorgeous summer day. A lot of people had taken advantage of the nice weather, and she was no exception. It was either leave her Foggy Bottom townhouse in favor of a run to—and around— Constitution Gardens, or crawl out of her skin.

The second she'd gotten her clean bill of health, she'd visited Frank at George Washington University Hospital and was thankful to find that his outlook was hopeful. But seeing him on the mend hadn't gotten rid of the eerie shiver that had taken residence in her spinal column, one she'd hoped a little sun and physical exertion would help evaporate.

It was still there hours later. If a five-mile run wouldn't shake it off, she wasn't sure what would. Sleep hadn't helped, because every time she'd closed her eyes last night, her mind replayed the scene at the Legion over and over again. Maybe Roman Steele was right. Maybe she *did* know something. Maybe she saw something. And maybe she'd missed a chance to stop it from happening. But hell if she knew what that something was.

As the sun set, Isa slipped her phone from her armband and dialed the one person she hoped could put her mind at ease. It took five rings for her grandfather to pick up.

"What's wrong?" Carlos Santiago answered in lieu of a greeting.

Isa chuckled. "That's how you're answering the phone now, Abuelito? What if I had been a potential customer wanting to book a room at the ranch?"

"Caller ID is a miraculous thing, sweetheart. Now tell me what's wrong so I can help you fix it."

"How do you know something's wrong?"

"Because despite me telling you it's not needed, you still feel the need to check up on me every week like clockwork. You missed a check-in."

Isa couldn't help the smile that came to her face. There wasn't much her grandfather missed, or an obstacle he couldn't tackle. A former US Air Force pilot, he'd seen and done it all—including having been one of the first pilots involved in the Pedro Pan flights from Cuba to the US in the sixties.

That's how he'd met her grandmother.

At eighteen, Marisol Ortego had fled Cuba with her two younger siblings and was their solid rock during an uncertain time. She'd been strong and independent, and according to Isa's grandfather, it had been head buttings at first sight.

Tales of Romeo and Juliet, King Arthur and Lady Guinevere had nothing on Carlos and Marisol Santiago. They'd had a love story like no other, the kind Isa had always held up in comparison to her own relationships.

Even after losing her grandmother to a long arduous

battle with breast cancer, her grandfather still lived every day in hopes of making her happy by opening up their Texas horse sanctuary to the public.

"Nothing's wrong, Grandpa," Isa lied. "Work was a little chaotic yesterday, and by the time I had a free moment to call it was already late. I didn't want to wake you."

"Bah. You work too much, sweetheart."

"Says the man who refuses to listen to doctor's orders and hire a few more hands around the ranch. One of these days you need to tuck your superhero cape away and let others step up a bit."

Her grandfather scoffed, making her smile. "Don't be sassing an old man."

"I'm not sassing an old man. I'm sassing my grand-father."

He chuckled before sighing. "Ah, I miss you. When are you coming home for a visit? It's been far too long."

"Soon. I promise," Isa whispered.

There wasn't any place she wanted to be more than the ranch where she'd been raised. Growing up as an Army brat, she'd been shuttled all over the globe, but the only place she'd ever felt like home had been Texas. The day her parents let her choose to stay with her grandparents had been one of her happiest.

To this day, a million things could be happening and her life could be imploding in front of her eyes, but the moment she stepped onto Mari's Sanctuary, everything *calmed*. Breathing came easier. Things that seemed insurmountable suddenly didn't look so bad.

She needed that right about now.

"There's some stuff happening at work right now," Isa admitted vaguely, "but as soon as it's settled I'll be on the first plane out. I swear."

Her grandfather grumbled. "You know I love you to the sky and back, sí?"

"Te amo, too, Abuelito...and *please* hire a ranch manager like Dr. Oleson suggested. You're supposed to be doing less of the physical work as you get older, not more."

"I'll think about it. I promise. And when you decide to really tell me what's wrong, you know where I'll be."

After saying her goodbyes, Isa ended the call. Sometimes her grandfather was too perceptive for his own good—and sometimes her own. Knowing she'd caused him even an ounce of worry twisted her stomach into knots, but she couldn't deny feeling a bit better just hearing his voice.

As Isa tucked her phone back into her armband, a movement on her left caught her eye. The eerie tingle that had been with her since she left her apartment roared back, and with it a loud screech of tires. A white van jumped the curb in front of her. The door slid open, and before Isa could shout, two sets of hands yanked her off her feet and into the back.

"Let me go!" Isa ripped her left arm away and swung it back, her elbow slamming into something soft.

One of her attackers teetered backward from the unexpected blow, but his friend shoved her facedown onto the van floor as the van roared to life.

"Guess you haven't learned your lesson, Dr. Santiago." Her hands were yanked behind her and secured with what felt like hard plastic ties, nearly cutting off circulation as he cinched them tight. "I should probably say that I'm disappointed, but I'm actually kind of glad. Makes this more fun."

That voice...

Isa's heart clogged her throat as she registered its owner—the same masked man from the Legion. "What do you want? Haven't you done enough?"

"Not even remotely, sweetheart." The van jerked right, and the man on her back shifted his weight. "What the fuck? Be fucking careful!"

"Yeah, we got a problem," someone said from behind them. The driver. "Road's blocked up ahead from an accident, and I think we've been spotted."

Isa didn't know what that meant, or who would've spotted them, but she didn't care. Her hands may be tied, but her legs weren't. Using her kidnapper's distraction to her advantage, she tucked her knees close to her chin, and aimed straight for the back of the driver's headrest.

The man cursed and the van jerked right, jumping the curb before slamming into something that brought them to a complete stop.

"Fuck!" The driver spun in his seat and held his gun inches from her face. "I should shoot you right the fuck now."

"We need to split." One of the other men peered out the back window. "We have about fifteen seconds. What do we do with the woman?"

"Leave her." Yanking her up by the front of her shirt,

Blue Eyes hardened his gaze on her. "But don't think for one second that this is over, Isabel."

With a low growl, he slammed his fist into her face. Stars danced across Isa's vision as her would-be abductors spilled out of the van. Blue Eyes, standing in the middle of the road, aimed his Glock to the right and fired off a shot.

People screamed. Shouting echoed from down the sidewalk as all four captors sprinted off in opposite directions. Now alone, Isa breathed easier, one breath cutting off another until she was on the verge of hyperventilating.

The van's side door squealed open wider a second before a large figure stepped into view. Isa snapped her leg out and nailed the man in the jaw, whipping his head of dark hair to the side. But despite the blow, he stayed solid on his feet. Isa shifted to kick again, but this time, the man's hands caught her ankle.

"I know I'm not your favorite person, but I think one kick's enough, Doc. Don't you?" Roman Steele's dark eyes fell on her. The right side of his jaw was red where her sneaker had impacted his face. "Are you okay?"

She blinked, unable to hear him through the sudden train hurtling through her ears.

Roman climbed into the van with a faint grimace, and after producing a pocketknife from his back pocket, cut her ties. "Breathe for me, Doc. Slow it down. In for three, out for four."

"I can't..."

He cupped her face and held her gaze on his, his touch surprisingly gentle. "In...and out."

She couldn't help but obey, and by the time her ears cleared and her breathing became easier, she was all too aware of his face only inches from hers. Her gaze flickered down to his mouth.

"Are you okay?" He searched her face and slid his gaze down her body and back. "Doc? Did they hurt you?"

"Bastards split up and ran off in opposite directions. They're in the wind." A second man jogged over. Despite his casual T-shirt and basketball shorts, he held a gun in his hand, which he tucked into a holster at the small of his back. "I'm guessing you had something to do with them running into the evil bike rack?"

"I kicked the driver." Isabel winced at the sharp stab of pain that went through her jaw. She'd no sooner reached to test the damage than Roman's hand gently caught her chin and tilted her head closer for his inspection.

"One of those bastards did that?" His voice dropped.

"When I ruined their plans...whatever they'd been. They were the same guys from the Legion." She forced herself to pull away before she did something stupid like kiss him, and instead, she shot him a hard glare. "Or I guess you'd just call them my teammates or something, right? You probably think I orchestrated this, too."

"What makes you think these were the same bastards from the lab?"

Isa thought about Blue Eyes and the scrape of his mouth on her ear. She shivered. "Trust me. It was them. I don't think I'll forget that man's voice for as long as I live."

"What did they want with you?"

"Hell if I know. They weren't exactly in a chatty mood." Isa slid her gaze to the second man and back to Roman Steele, remembering the driver's words right before she'd kicked him. *They'd been tailed.* "If you hadn't been tracking the lab guys, then that means you were following me. For how long?"

He didn't need to answer for her to know. That eerie tingle she'd been having since being released from quarantine was all thanks to the infuriating man in front of her.

"Well, I hope you got a good peep show, Mr. Steele, because your entertainment ends right now."

"I'm not getting any enjoyment out of this. Trust me." He stepped back and let her ease herself out from the back of the van. Her knees buckled, and he was right there, supporting her elbow. "But I'm afraid this isn't as over as you'd like. It just won't be happening without your knowledge anymore."

She shot him a glare. "Is that supposed to make me feel better?"

"Not really, no. I don't give false assurances."

Upfront and without apologies. Isa wasn't sure if she liked that about him, or if she'd rather things be sugar-coated. One thing for certain was that the Legion theft tugged her out of her comfort zone, and this second attempt, whatever it was, ripped her so far away from that safe space that she wouldn't be able to see it with a map and a pair of heavy-duty binoculars.

CHAPTER
FIVE

Roman had seen his fair share of ticking time bombs, but this was definitely one for the record books—and it didn't even have anything to do with what happened a few hours ago. He'd had no choice but to bring Isabel to Iron Bars until they figured out what to do, and if the place had been empty, it would've been fine.

But the Steele Ops headquarters was far from secluded. It was damn near stifling with everyone in attendance except Jaz and Ryder, who were still on Frank and Maddy watch detail.

Knox leaned against the far wall, Zoey snuggled against his side, and Cade and Roman's cousin Grace shared the chair on the opposite side. But the fact that his two favorite women were on opposite ends of the room didn't settle Roman's unease at all. It just put them in position to attack that much more effectively.

Like velociraptors.

And judging by the gleam in their eyes, it was only a matter of time before the big pounce happened.

Sitting on the couch, Isa's gaze soaked up everything from Liam's tech toys to the weapons cage tucked in the back corner. Up until this point, they'd always been careful to keep the Steele Ops inner sanctum away from outside eyes, but the bastards from the lab hadn't given them much of a choice.

Roman got up from his chair and paced. "If these bastards already have the virus, why do they need you?"

Isa folded her arms across her chest as she glared. "I asked them, but they were a little too busy dishing out threatening ultimatums to bother giving me an answer."

"There's no reason to get snarky, Doc. I'm just trying to help here."

"You haven't even seen snark yet. And help? How can you stand there and say that with a straight face? You've been following me—judging by the itchy neck I've had for the last twenty-four hours—since I got out of quarantine. I'm not delusional enough to think that you've kept tabs on me for my safety."

"Things change."

Isabel scoffed, muttering, "So glad my almost-kidnapping finally convinced you that I'm not a bioterrorist."

Zoey and Grace shared a look before locking their sights on him and grinning.

Fuck. That was never a good sign.

Knox cleared his throat, interjecting. "What did these assholes say to you in that van? Anything?"

Isabel pulled her glare away from Roman. "The big one, the one who shot Frank, accused me of not learning my lesson, but I don't know what lesson I was supposed to learn."

Grace hmmed in thought. "They obviously see you as a threat to their overall plan, because it's not like they need you to make the virus more deadly, right? It's deadly all on its own."

Isabel nodded. "At this point, our only saving grace is that FC-5 isn't airborne, but that doesn't mean that it can't wipe out entire communities before anyone's had a chance to identify it. That's what makes it so deadly. Patients are most contagious when there are few to no symptoms, and when they finally do manifest, they're like a dozen other illnesses, the common cold included. By the time it presents itself as a hemorrhagic disorder, it's often too late to quarantine."

Roman grunted. "It's an ideal compound to use for bioterrorism. Not well known to the public. Not curable. Besides Tru Tech, what labs have access to FC-5 samples?"

"One. A GHO-sponsored lab in Switzerland somewhere, but as far as I know they're simply storing it, not actively testing. I hate to say it, but as far as viruses go, it's not one of the *sexy* ones to people at the GHO."

Zoey cocked up an eyebrow. "Viruses can be sexy?"

"Not in the Magic Mike way, no. But most of their funding—and their attention—go to the bigger, well-known viruses. Smallpox. Ebola. Things that make appearances in big ways. Because there's only been two documented outbreaks of FC-5, we barely get a spittle of funds sent our way."

"But it's deadlier?"

"Very much so." Isabel nodded. "Ebola has a fifty percent mortality rate. FC-5 hangs around ninety-five."

Everyone cursed, dwelling on the shit-storm hovering

over their heads, but there was one other thing nagging Roman that he couldn't quite shake. "You said the lab in Switzerland is only storing FC-5, which means you're the only one actively studying it."

Isabel said after thinking about it, "I guess you can say that."

"So we can safely assume that you're probably the reigning global expert. There probably isn't a strand of that viral code that you don't know. And you said it yourself, you've been making some big breakthroughs recently."

"I wouldn't call them breakthroughs, but it does look more hopeful than it did..." Isa's face paled. "They don't want me interfering with whatever they have planned. They don't *want* me finding a cure."

"Because if their intention is to sell it, or even if it's to use it themselves, they don't want someone around who can make it as harmless as a case of the sniffles." Roman turned to his brothers. "Until we nab these bastards, we keep her safe. We can do that in our sleep. Hell, we have a bunker right here."

Concern showed on every line of Isa's face until the mention of her temporary relocation.

"Wait, you expect me to stay *here*?" Lifting her pretty brown eyes, she locked Roman in a hard, unflinching stare. "I'll be damned if I hide away and do exactly what those bastards want me to do. They're threatened by my work on FC-5? Then that's exactly what I'm going to keep doing."

"You can't expect us to let you just walk out of here."

"You can keep me safe in your sleep, right? You guys

do what you do so that I can keep doing what I do. But one thing I won't do is hide."

"It's not hiding, Doc. It's surviving."

"It's giving them what they want, and it's not happening." Isabel stood and got within inches of Roman's face. "Did I not paint a clear enough picture of what could happen if these people decide to expose the public to FC-5? I don't exactly want to be stuffed in the back of another van—or worse—but I also don't want to see innocent people dying on the ten o'clock news."

Roman clenched his jaw until it ached.

Finally, Knox intervened. "No one's putting you into hiding, Isa. I actually think keeping you visible will work in our favor and possibly make these assholes climb out from under their rocks."

Roman snapped his attention to his brother. "You mean to use her as bait. No fucking way."

"Come on, man. You know me better than that. But you have to agree it would make them uneasy wondering why she's not more concerned with them. It'll make them nervous...and nervous people make mistakes."

"They also lash out," Roman pointed out.

"I'm willing to risk it," Isabel interjected.

Roman knew when he was beat. A quick glance around the room solidified that Isabel Santiago had already hauled his family and team firmly to her side of the line.

"Fine." He growled. "But you're not going topside until we've had time to make some kind of security arrangements...both for a personal detail and for Tru

Tech. That means you're staying here until we have both sufficiently in place."

"Fine." She folded her arms across her chest. "I hope you work fast because I have every intention of spending a full day at the Legion tomorrow."

Zoey jumped to her feet. "I'll go make up a room. You can pretty much have your pick of which one you want, but I'm warning you, they're all pretty much the same. Bland."

At the sight of Isabel turning to follow, Roman grabbed the abandoned ice pack on the table and, calling her name, tossed it her way. "Keep this on, or you'll wake up tomorrow with one hell of a swollen lip."

"Got punched a lot, did you?" She shot him a coy smirk. "Actually, you don't need to answer that, because I already know the answer. You have a very punchable face."

"So each of my brothers have told me on multiple occasions."

Next to him, Liam barely swallowed an amused chuckle. "Many, many occasions." At Roman's scowl, his youngest brother shrugged. "Just agreeing with you, dude."

"Well, stop."

Grace left the room with Isabel and Zoey, and Roman couldn't help but stare in the direction they'd gone.

"So how does it feel?" Knox asked, his mouth twitched into a smirk.

"How does what feel?"

"Getting your ass handed to you by a beautiful woman. Tickles a little bit, huh?"

"You tell me. Zoey's got you wrapped around her little finger."

Knox grinned wider, not falling for his bait. "Yeah, she does. And her lips. Her hips. Hell, her entire body."

Cade smacked his hands to his ears. "Stop! Fuck! Do not say anything else about my baby sister!"

Roman ignored his brothers and friend and stalked toward the gym, where he could whale on something without getting in trouble with his mom.

Isabel Santiago, if he wasn't careful, could most definitely hand him his ass and probably take great pleasure in doing so. That shouldn't intrigue him, but it did.

* * *

Isa startled awake, nearly jumping out of both her skin and the unfamiliar bed. With her heart in her throat, it took a few moments for her to collect her bearings, the events of the last twenty-four hours slowly easing their way back: being stalked, being tossed in the back of a moving van, and then being whisked away to a secret underground bunker beneath a distillery just off the Potomac River.

Somehow her mundane, unchanging routine had been knocked on its side and flipped around, and even though she couldn't directly pin it on Roman Steele, he served as a good target.

Isa reluctantly slipped out of bed, thankful to Zoey for the extra set of clothes, and padded barefoot into the hall. With no one around to guide her toward coffee, she used her questionable sense of direction to find the kitchen and once again was taken in by the industrial homeliness of the Steele Ops common area.

Polished cement floors and red brick walls complemented the warm tans and leather-accented furnishings, and colorful abstract artwork gave the sprawling underground space pops of color. It was the perfect blend of rustic home and modern industrial...and then you looked to the left and it was like stepping into one of the situation rooms you see on television.

Instead of artwork, computer screens took up nearly the entirety of the far wall, and a large cage nestled in the corner held weapons and unrecognizable high-tech toys. Steele Ops had a forward operating base smack in the heart of downtown Alexandria, and the people sipping on boutique whiskey sours above their heads hadn't the slightest clue.

Isa helped herself to the still warm pot of coffee and, clutching her mug, wandered the underground halls. Music drifted down the corridor. She followed the sound and the vibrating floor and found its source in a gym that made her own community center look puny.

On the left, a modified boxing ring took center stage, and a small army of treadmills and a rower commandeered the right. Isa stepped around a garden of suspended heavy bags and came to a dead stop.

Roman Steele, hair pulled back into a short ponytail clipped at the base of his neck, sat on a bench, sweat rolling down his bare chest. Faint red welts covered his knuckles as he unwrapped sparring tape from his hands and flexed his fingers.

Whatever he'd been doing down here, he'd been doing it for a while.

Isabel studied his hands. Large and calloused, they were obviously adept at taking and giving a beating, but she couldn't help but remember how gentle they'd been after her almost abduction. He'd shocked them both when he'd palmed her cheek, and then she'd shocked herself by hoping he'd lean in and kiss her.

Ever since she lost her fiancé, she'd turned off the need for male companionship. Oliver Park had been her ticket to a love like her grandparents had had, and he took that with him the day he died. Standing there wondering what Roman Steele's hands would feel like on parts of her body that aren't her face wasn't the right way to honor him.

Isabel chastised her raging libido just as Roman leaned over, stretching his legs out in front of him. Actually, his one leg and his prosthesis.

Roman's left below-the-knee amputation took her off guard, but not because she wasn't familiar with them. In the Army and stationed at Walter Reed's research facility, she'd seen her fair share of amputations. She just hadn't known Roman was an amputee.

He removed his prosthesis, a brand she couldn't pinpoint, and slipped off his sock. The thin piece of nylon fabric protected the sensitive skin from being rubbed raw, but Roman winced as he rubbed his stump. The compression stocking obviously wasn't working.

Roman's head snapped up. The second his dark eyes lasered in on her, he replaced his grimace with a determined mask of blankness. "Can I do something for you, Doc?"

"Can I do something for you?" As fast as she'd run away from bedside medicine, sometimes old habits were hard to kick.

Roman's face looked anything but pleased. "See a lot of BTKs working in the lab?"

"No. But I did in the Army." Smirking, she took a step closer. "I should probably be insulted at the surprised look on your face, but I'll let it slide. *This time.* Besides, it's not like you'd be the first." She nodded toward the intricate prosthetic in his hand. "You mind if I take a look? I haven't seen one exactly like this before, but I've handled my fair share."

He handed it over. "This is a prototype. A buddy of mine started designing them after coming home with his own amputation. He wanted me to try it out for a while and see how I like it."

"It's impressive." She studied the intricate system of gliding pistons and gears. "These joints allow for a lot of free movement. I bet your friend is big into extreme sports."

Roman's lips twitched. "Yeah. How'd you guess?"

"Shock absorbers." She pointed to the layered pads surrounding the contraption's heel and where the ball of the foot would be located. "So what's happening?"

"Nothing at first. It moved like silk, but the harder I pushed it, the more it lagged. Felt like it was catching on something every time I took a step."

Isa flexed the toes and bent the ankle, studying all the shifting parts. Roman's careful scrutiny didn't go without her notice, warming her cheeks until she finally found the issue. "It's that middle piston in the center. It looks like there's some gunk on it. Working it over with some oil or WD-40 might do the trick."

Roman studied her carefully. She didn't offer to help him, knowing the kind of answer she'd get. Judging by the look of his amputation, he'd had it for a while and knew more about prosthetics and limb massage than she did.

He took the prosthetic and set it aside to grab a blade device. "Guess I'll go old-school until I can get my hands on some."

Giving him privacy, she looked around the room. "So this is where you guys train?"

"Some of us. I think Knox and Tank use it the most out of everyone. I prefer to use the one at my place."

"But does yours have one of those," Isa teased, gesturing to the thermal tub tucked into the back corner.

"Actually, I have three."

"What do you mean?" She turned toward him as he got to his feet.

"I live on the second floor of a warehouse off the pier, and I'm converting the first floor into a gym for people like me."

"Veterans?"

"For anyone who needs a little extra head space to go along with their exercise regime. I know what it's like to be used to living one way and then get knocked down a few hundred pegs. Crawling your way back isn't always pretty, and it's easier to do what you need to do if you're not worried about being someone's entertainment."

"That's great, Roman."

He narrowed his eyes. "But...?"

"But nothing. I think that's an incredible idea."

Roman looped a towel around his neck and stepped closer. "It's still a work in progress. For now, I have my hands full with Steele Ops...and a certain mouthy doctor."

Isa rolled her eyes, and then their trajectory slid down the impressive view of Roman's torso. Damp with sweat, his six-pack abs glistened and just begged her to reach out and touch, to see if they were as rock hard as they looked.

Actually, an eight-pack. She recounted.

Isabel balled her fists at her sides and tried to shift her gaze from the impressive hip ridge that cut across his lower waist and dipped into his basketball shorts. Evidently Roman wasn't the only one who needed a cold shower.

Her body flushed, suddenly way too warm, and got warmer when Roman cocked an eyebrow up into his hairline. "When you're done mentally objectifying my body, do you want to tell me why you're up so early?"

"You were up earlier than me." Tempted to steal his towel and use it to fan her suddenly overheated body, Isa shifted on her feet. "And I was not objectifying your body."

"I don't sleep much...and yes you were." Roman leaned against the wall, giving her a model-worthy pose that put every muscle on display. His lips twitched as he tapped the corner of his mouth. "You still have a little drool right about there, Doc."

"What do you...?" It took a few seconds for her to register his meaning. "Oh, get over yourself, Mr. Secret Sexpert. Yes, you're attractive, but I'm old enough to know sometimes the pretty outside packages can be rotten to the core on the inside. Besides, I have a general rule to not get involved with guys who think I'm capable of biological terrorism. Call me fickle."

"I never said that I thought you were involved."

"You didn't need to. Your face may be a blank mask ninety percent of the time, but your pretty brown eyes are extremely telling."

"*Pretty?*" Roman's voice dropped a few octaves, its gravelly tone practically brushing against her skin as he pushed off against the wall and stepped closer. "I don't think anyone has ever used that adjective to describe me before."

"Let me guess what people have used: frustrating, irritating, mule-headed, and stubborn. Have I gotten any of them right so far?" Isabel matched his step with one of her own. She wasn't sure if it was her temper making her hot, or Roman's heated gaze. Either way, too much longer of this and her panties would leave scorch marks on her rear end. "Do you want me to keep listing? I could probably go on for days."

Roman stepped closer, putting them an arm's length away. "I may not have any fancy letters behind my name, but I'm pretty sure a few of those words are basically the same thing."

His body heat beckoned her, and she shivered as she stepped forward. *Two feet and counting.* "And yet using one doesn't seem like enough."

"Every single one of those adjectives can be turned around and used to describe you, too, Doc. Or did you forget your little edict before storming out of the room yesterday?"

Isa's mouth dropped, and she leaned closer until her shoes bumped Roman's. "I did not storm."

He challenged her with a faint lift of his brow. "But you did give an edict? Or a demand? How would you like to spin it?"

"I may be mule-headed, Roman Steele, but you're the whole damn donkey."

Isabel didn't know who moved first.

Their bodies clashed together in a tangle of limbs and tongues. Thrust and retreat, they devoured each other with every breath. Isa speared her fingers into his hair, fusing their mouths together as Roman, fingers biting into the flesh above her yoga pants, backed her against the wall.

A small moan escaped her throat as she swiveled her hips against the growing erection pushing against her stomach. Holy crap, the man was huge *everywhere*. Lifting one leg, she anchored it around his thigh and tilted to get closer, cursing the clothes that kept her from feeling every inch of his body.

Maybe it was lack of oxygen, or a freak rush of hormones, but by the time she forced her mouth away from Roman's her head spun like a carousel. He trailed his mouth down the curve of her neck and nipped and kissed until she was a whimpering ball of need.

"Roman," Isa groaned.

As if saying his name broke through the fog of lust,

they broke apart as suddenly as they'd come together. Isa's heartbeat thundered in her ears, the only thing she could hear other than her and Roman's heavy pants.

At least she wasn't the only one affected by whatever the hell had just happened.

Instead of telling her the kiss was a mistake, or that it couldn't happen again, Roman stalked out of the gym muttering a long string of curses. Isa leaned against the wall until she could lock her knees, and absentmindedly touched her mouth, her lips pleasantly swollen.

In her thirty-one years, she'd never been kissed with that kind of heat. That much need. It was a little bit scary and a whole lot of overwhelming...but not any more than admitting her body was already itching for it to happen again.

CHAPTER SIX

Jumping back into work was easier said than done, and this time it had nothing to do with Maddy's music choice and everything to do with Isabel's headspace. Particularly involving one infuriating Steele man.

At least Roman had made good on his promise of getting her into the lab, and today's babysitter of choice was Jaz Curva, former Marine sniper and genuine badass. The two of them had immediately hit it off. Both the operative's hysterical commentary and her descriptions of everyone involved with Steele Ops kept Isa's mind off why she was there at all—and why Maddy wasn't.

Isa didn't fault her friend one bit for not being ready to step back into the Legion, and while Isa's stand-in assistant, Mark, did his job, he wasn't quite as exuberant about it.

"I shouldn't be much longer. I just need to clean up the workspace and document the results in the computer system," Isabel said aloud, knowing Jaz heard her from her stool in the clean room. "Maybe you can get boredom pay from your bosses. I'd completely back you up on that."

Jaz leaned closer to the window, her chin propped up

by her hand. "Are you kidding me? This is a night on the red carpet compared to listening to Liam's tirade about shoddy backdoor tech and uploaded computer viruses."

Isabel chuckled. "I think that's the first time I ever heard someone choose real viruses over computer viruses."

"I like being unexpected."

Isabel put away the last of the samples and stepped into decontamination. By the time she changed into street clothes and entered the clean room, her temporary assistant already had his bag on his shoulder and his car keys in hand. "You're all good, Dr. Santiago? Do you need me to stick around for anything?"

"I'm all good, Mark. Thanks for standing in for Maddy."

"No prob. Take care." With a brisk wave, the doctoral student hustled over to the Legion elevator and pushed the button not once, but twice, as if it would make it come any faster.

Jaz chuckled. "I don't think Marines run that fast when it's New York pizza night in the mess hall. And let me tell you, when it comes to the meat lovers, it's like the beginning of a post-apocalyptic movie."

"Mark's nice, but he's not Maddy."

"Is she doing okay?"

"As well as can be expected. I told her to take all the time she needed, but I secretly hope it's sooner rather than later. Is that horrible of me?"

"Not in the least. Honestly, I'm surprised *you* were so eager to come back."

Isa plotted her results in the computer's tracking program and logged off. "With FC-5 in God only knows whose hands, I can't afford not to jump right in. I have a job to do."

Jaz playfully bumped her shoulder. "You almost sounded like a Marine."

"Nope. Army."

Jaz's eyes widened. "Wait. What? Seriously?"

Isa nodded. "Seriously. I was a major by the time I left."

"Were you ever deployed, or did you stay state-side? Your specialty isn't exactly conducive to combat medicine."

"I went to med school and passed all my boards, so theoretically, I could've worked in field hospitals, but when it came time for speciality selection, I chose virology. Most of my time was spent in stateside military-run research facilities, but I did do a few tours with Ranger units helping to build clinics in disease-ridden countries."

Isa held her breath and prayed Jaz didn't ask too many questions about her career track, because the truth was, she hadn't set out to study viruses. Like most people who want to become doctors, Isa had wanted to make a difference. She wanted to help people, and after serving her country, had wanted to put her skills to use by working with organizations like Doctors Without Borders.

But the reality and demands of med school had been way too much for her, and her emergency medicine rotation nearly pushed her to the breaking point. Every doctor had that one patient, the one who exposed their weakness and made them question everything they thought they ever knew about themselves or their capabilities.

For Isa, it hadn't been just *one*... it had been an entire family: a mother and her two young children, victims of unnecessary gun violence perpetrated by someone who was supposed to care about them. Isa never again wanted to be in the position to tell a young boy that his mother wouldn't be walking through the door.

"I'm sorry if that's a touchy subject," Jaz apologized, interpreting her silence.

"No. No, that's okay. I just don't talk about it much." *Or at all.*

"You know what we need?" Jaz hooked her arm through Isa's the second she shut down the computer. "Good company and stiff drinks—and a lot of them. So many I lose the desire to punch Tank in his smug face."

"Is that possible without getting alcohol poisoning?"

Jaz howled in laughter, making Isa chuckle. "We're going to be best friends. I can already see it."

"Do you think Roman's idea of lying low involves happy hour?"

Jaz snorted. "Screw happy hour. I'm aiming for happy evening...and you let me worry about Ro. I know his kryptonite."

"Which is what?"

"Not what. *Who.* And they're Grace and Zoey, who just so happen to be the good company I was talking about."

An hour later, tears rolled down Isa's cheeks as she laughed so hard she couldn't catch her breath. When she'd first realized Jaz's girls' night took them to Iron Bars, she'd been hesitant. But thanks to Jaz, Zoey Wright, and Grace Steele, she hadn't thought about Roman and his devastating lips all night.

Isa turned to Zoey, a petite blond dynamo who worked crime scene investigation for the DCPD. "So I just want to make sure I got this right. You and your brother, Cade, grew up across the street from the Steeles, and the guys all basically formed their own little fraternity."

"Sounds about right. I was the pesky little girl who always got in their way."

"But now you're with Knox?"

"The oldest Steele brother, and Cade's best friend." Zoey smirked from over her beer. "I'd crushed on him *forever*, but you know how it is with men. It takes them an annoyingly long time to see what's staring them right in the face."

"Please, she just finally lost her patience." Grace bumped into her best friend's shoulder. "Don't let this quiet demeanor fool you. Zo's as tenacious as a drug-sniffing dog who smells a kilo of heroin. Knox didn't know what hit him."

"I think the same could be said for my brother." Zoey smirked.

Grace rolled her eyes. "No, I know what hit him."

Jaz snorted. "Yeah, your .22-caliber Mag."

They all laughed, using the moment to clink their drinks together in solidarity.

Isa turned toward Jaz. "Zoey's with Knox. Grace is with Cade. Are you with someone from the team, too? Or have your eye on someone from the team?"

"Yes," Grace and Zoey exclaimed emphatically at the same time Jaz adamantly announced, "Fuck no."

Grace scoffed. "Oh, come on, Jaz. Who do you think you're fooling?"

"No one." Jaz folded her arms across her chest. "Because there's nothing for me to fool people about."

"Li-ar," Zoey sang with a smirk. "Grace and I have said that very same line—right before the love bug bit us on the ass."

"Then maybe you should've worn your bug repellent. I slather mine on daily. It's practically my moisturizer."

Isa laughed, trying to keep up. "Wait, wait, wait. Let me guess. *Tank*? He's the Special Forces guy with the sexy Cajun drawl, right?"

Jaz wrinkled her small nose. "Let's go easy on the 'sexy' adjectives, and absolutely nowhere around him, okay? His head's already so big, I'm surprised he's able to fit it through the door. I would much rather talk about Isa's bug bites."

Isa, in mid-swallow, choked on her water. "Me? I'm pretty biteless these days. Actually, for a lot of days. Weeks. Months. Honestly? *Years.*"

Zoey's eyes twinkled. "So you're not seeing anyone?"

"Unless you count the petri dishes in my lab? No." Even though Isa hadn't known these women long, it felt like they'd been friends forever, so she took a breath and admitted, "I was engaged once. To my childhood sweetheart. Olly."

The table quickly sobered.

"Was?" Grace asked carefully.

The women let her take her time to pull her thoughts together, and she appreciated it. Olly wasn't someone she discussed on a daily basis—or, if she was honest with herself, at all. It hurt too much.

That ache that came whenever she thought about him took center stage in her chest. "Oliver was literally the boy next door. He lived on the ranch next to my grandparents', and we grew up together, eventually becoming a clichéd small-town golden couple. Everyone always assumed that we'd head off to college together and come back to Golden Plains, but we didn't. Olly followed his dreams right into the Navy and onto the SEAL teams, and I let the US Army pay for my medical training. We spent more time apart after graduation than we did together but we said we'd made it work, and we did...for a while."

Until suddenly it hadn't.

Isa still wasn't sure where they'd gone wrong, or what ignited the fight all those years ago. All she recalled with perfect clarity was ending their video chat with angry words and then getting a phone call from Olly's best friend a week later.

He was gone, something having gone wrong on a simple escort assignment, something his SEAL team had done countless times before.

The girls must have read her face, because suddenly Zoey was grasping her hand, and Grace was squeezing Isa's arm.

Jaz, sitting next to her, patted her shoulder before

shifting awkwardly in her seat. "That really sucks, Isa. I'm sorry. It's hard losing someone you care about."

"It is." Isa nodded. "And I tried dating sporadically. I've just never met anyone who I'd rather spend time with more than my viruses... and hearing that aloud, I realize how pathetic that sounds. But I'm not about to compromise for anything less than what I deserve, which is love, lust, *and* sparkage."

Jaz muttered, "Pretty sure we've seen at least one out of three." Grace elbowed Jaz in the side, and the former Marine frowned at the brunette. "What? You've seen them. I've seen them. Hell, even the guys, who are oblivious to anything unless it's dancing naked two inches from their face, have seen them."

Isa looked from friend to friend. "Seen what? What are you talking about?"

Zoey fiddled with her drink while Grace appeared to weigh her words carefully.

Isa turned to Jaz, knowing she'd get a straight answer. "Seen what?"

"The fireworks."

"I don't know what you're talking about." Isa blinked innocently.

Jaz scoffed. "I'm talking about the fireworks show that goes off whenever you and Roman are in the same room. The explosions rival the ones they light off the Brooklyn Bridge every New Year's Eve."

Isa's face heated.

After what happened earlier that morning, she couldn't deny that Roman Steele lit something inside her she'd never before experienced, and not having felt it before, she couldn't attach a name to it. Lust was definitely involved, and so was a heady dose of desire. But there was something else she couldn't pin down.

Excitement maybe? Or danger?

After Olly, Isa had sworn off men with hero complexes, so maybe that was the draw? Roman Steele epitomized everything she'd convinced herself she didn't want in life.

"Roman's definitely... different. I'll admit to that." Knowing these three women were also his friends, Isa treaded carefully. "And there's no doubt that he's artfully skilled in the kissing department, but—"

Zoey spit her drink halfway across the table, and Grace patted her back while the blond tried clearing her airway.

Jaz's grin widened. "I *knew* it."

"Whoa. Whoa. Whoa." Grace held up her hands as if capable of pausing the conversation. "*Kissing?* There was *kissing?*"

"I told you, didn't I?" Jaz leaned back in her chair, looking smug. "One of these days you guys will learn to listen to me."

Isa bounced her attention between each of their shocked reactions. "Oh, come on. You act like this is something new. Are you telling me that Roman's never—"

"Nope."

Grace shook her head. "Never."

"But he's so..."

"Grumpy? Broody?"

"Virile."

Zoey's mouth dropped slightly. "I think I need to sit down."

"You are sitting down."

"Oh. Good. Then I'm ahead of the ball game."

Isa uneasily tucked a loose strand of hair behind her ear. "You guys really know how to make a girl self-conscious."

Grace patted her hand, grinning ear to ear. "We don't mean to, but you have to realize that Roman doesn't bring women around us when there's sparkage. He doesn't bring women around *period*. Family events? Solo. Parties? Alone."

"He's not *bringing me around*. He's keeping me close because of what happened at the Legion."

Jaz was already shaking her head. "Where did you sleep last night?"

Isa was almost afraid to answer. "Here. Well, down-stairs."

"And where did Roman sleep?" She paused but didn't let her answer. "He also slept here, which to you prob-ably doesn't sound like a big deal. Everyone in Steele Ops has their own quarters. But Roman's never actually *slept* in his—until now."

"I don't think you can—"

Zoey nodded. "We can. Ro could be exhausted and due to come back to Iron Bars in two hours, and yet he'll cross the river to his place rather than take a power nap here. I don't know why, but it's a thing."

When Roman admitted to not sleeping much earlier this morning, Isa wondered if that had been man code

for he didn't sleep at all. And then she wondered why
he'd stayed. Supposedly Cade and Grace had been
around, and Liam, too. She wouldn't have been alone,
and hello, fortified bunker. Definitely no one was getting inside.

Isa's adamant sparkage denial died on her lips as
a fluttery warmth slid down her spine and wrapped
around her stomach.

On cue, Jaz, Zoey, and Grace all looked over her
shoulder.

Jaz smirked. "Guess we'll be witnessing the sparkage
ourselves."

Isa twisted in her seat just as Roman stepped onto
the Iron Bar's back patio, and like he possessed an
internal homing beacon, his heated gaze landed directly
on her.

Even from yards away, her entire body lit up as if she
were sitting too close to a bonfire, her heart racing into
double time. No man before had ever taken her breath
away, but Roman Steele stole it and held it hostage, her
head going slightly dizzy the longer he stared.

Leaning casually against the patio's awning pillar, he
never took his eyes away from hers. His dark T-shirt
had been replaced by a white Henley, its sleeves pushed
up to reveal tanned arms corded with muscle...muscle
that had held her tight against his body and practically
weeping for more.

A heat wave hit Isabel full force, making her pick
up her cocktail napkin and fan herself before forcefully
ripping her gaze away from the other side of the patio.
The second she did, her eyes already ached to slide

back. And they would have if it weren't for her new friends' knowing smirks.

"You're right. Not a single spark," Jaz said dryly, sliding her water toward Isa. "Here. You need this more than I do . . . to put out the fire on your pants."

Oh, Isa was tempted to use Jaz's water, but not to douse the fire *on* her pants, but the one *in* them. It wasn't lost on her that just talking about the broody Steele made her antsy, but seeing him in the literal flesh? Feeling those dark eyes, filled with an intensity she'd never before encountered, directly on her?

She bypassed antsy and went straight to downright horny. If she wasn't careful, she'd burst into flames and not from her lying pants, but years' worth of pent-up sexual frustrations.

Ignoring the mischievous twinkle in the girls' eyes, Isa stood. "Didn't someone mention a cornhole tournament?"

* * *

On getting Jaz's text about bringing Isabel to Iron Bars, Roman had been furious. He'd cut short an interview with a potential new operator and hightailed it back from Quantico at breakneck speeds that definitely would've resulted in his license being taken away if he'd been stopped. Now that he saw Isabel for himself, an odd sense of relief went through him. And fuck if he knew what to do with that.

Jaz knew her way around kicking asses and was more than capable of working a protective detail. Hell, she was probably better suited than him, since he'd already proven he couldn't be close to Isabel and keep his hands—and mouth—off of her.

He shouldn't be near her. He couldn't stay away. Hell, he'd slept at Steele Ops, and he hadn't done that ever before. Well, *tried* to sleep—he hadn't actually closed his eyes. Mostly, he'd laid on his bed and stared at the ceiling and tried not to think about the dozens of feet of concrete above his head. Sometimes on the top floor of his studio, he still woke up in a puddle of his own sweat, expecting to be covered with a shit ton of debris and scrap metal.

But the fact was that Isabel Santiago had been introduced into his life only a few days ago and had already managed to shake up his normal routine. He felt it. He sensed it. And it was only a matter of time before one of his asshole brothers called him out on it.

On the grassy knoll to the right of the gazebo, Isa, Grace, Jaz, and Zoey set up the alcohol-themed cornhole Liam had purchased on the first warm spring day. They laughed and divvied themselves up into teams as Knox and Cade came up on his left.

His brother's eyes fastened on Zoey as she bent over to retrieve a pair of sacks. "That sight sure as hell never gets old."

Cade groaned. "Come on, man. We agreed on no sexy sister talk."

"If I have to listen to sexy cousin talk—who's basically my little sister—then you can deal with hearing how much I want to take Zoey to the boat right now and—"

"Stop!" Roman grimaced and shot them both a glare. "How about you both go take cold showers and leave your significant others alone for a night?"

His brother and friend shared a look.

Cade smirked from over the rim of his beer. "I don't think we're the only ones who should be taking a cold shower. You're looking at the doc like she's the main dish at an all-you-can-eat buffet."

"Did someone say buffet?" Tank chose that moment to join them. "Don't think there's much open right now." His gaze traveled over to the girls. "Ahhhh, now I get it."

"What the hell is it everyone seems to get that I don't?" Roman growled.

Knox smacked him on the back. "What would be the fun in telling you? In the meantime, I think we should go up the stakes on that game of cornhole."

Roman swallowed a curse and slowly followed his brother, Cade, and Tank as they joined the girls. Zoey immediately jumped into Knox's arms, and Grace drew Cade into a slow kiss that left him glassy-eyed and grinning like a fool.

They'd all fought against painful personal pasts, conquered demons, and leaped over obstacles to get their happy endings, both figurative and literal. Coupledom worked for them.

For him, not so much.

Yet as Knox whispered into Zoey's ear, eliciting a rosy glow in her cheeks, Roman briefly pictured himself having that kind of connection with someone, of feeling more comfortable in someone's presence than he was in seclusion.

And then he skated his eyes toward Isabel as she watched the doe-eyed couples, too.

A wistful smile curled her top lip and crinkled her eyes right until a smirking Jaz dropped a set of bean bags in her hands.

"You're first up. Don't choke." The Marine chuckled evilly as she walked toward the other end of the game zone.

"What do I do?"

"Throw it . . . and get it in the hole."

Jaz, always the smart-ass.

Biting her lip, Isabel nervously estimated her throwing distance until she let the first bag fly. It went rogue, nearly taking an observing Tank's head off in the process.

"What the hell?" Tank ducked, throwing Jaz a hard scowl when she doubled over in laughter.

"Oh my God." Tears slid down Jaz's face. "*Please* do that again. I'll *pay* you to do that again but to hit him this time."

"Maybe I'm just not cut out for this." Isa grimaced.

"The trick is to follow through with the arm like in golf," Roman chimed in with his own advice. Forgetting his earlier plan to keep his distance, he came up behind her. "Don't adjust the size of your swing. Change the amount of energy you apply to it."

Isa teased, "Are you a reigning cornhole champion or something?"

"Two tournaments running. Remind me to show you the trophy later," Roman said dryly.

Isa gasped with a mock clutch of her chest. "Was that a *joke*? Did Roman Steele just crack a funny?"

"I don't joke about cornhole, Dr. Santiago." This time, Roman's lips betrayed him, inching up at the corners.

Isabel's gaze dropped to his mouth, her own bottom lip trapped between her teeth in a sexy-as-hell nibble that he wanted to free with a small bite of his own.

Fucking hell.

Roman swallowed a groan and reminded himself where they were, but his dick didn't seem to care. It twitched in his pants, recalling with perfect clarity how her mouth had felt fused to his...and how much it wanted to fuse with other parts of her body.

Roman yanked his thoughts from his cock and onto the second hole across the grass. "Want a lesson from a cornhole god?"

Isa chuckled. "Why not? Teach away."

He gently turned her so she stood in front of him. Keeping one hand on her shoulder, he slowly slid his other to her elbow. "First, test the weight of the bag. Bounce it in your hand. Let your muscles figure out how much oomph you need to put behind your swing."

Isa did as he said and leaned closer to the opposite board.

"Nope." Roman dropped his hand to her hip. "Posture straight. Leaning closer only messes up your trajectory."

Roman bit his tongue as she straightened. Her dark hair brushed against his nose, and damn she smelled good, a mixture of sweet vanilla and cinnamon... definitely an edible combination if he'd ever smelled one.

"Test the weight. Measure the oomph factor. And throw," Roman instructed. She listened, concentrating hard, and this time, half the bag dropped into the board's opening. "Closer. Now start the process again."

With determined focus, Isa kept her eyes on her target, and threw. Her last bag dropped straight through the hole.

"Oh my god! I did it!" Spinning around, she flung her arms around his neck in a tight hug and jumped excitedly. "I really did it!"

Wrapping his arm around her waist to prevent them both from toppling over, he chuckled at her enthusiasm—right until they both realized that every hard plane of his body was now pressed flush against every soft curve of hers. His hardened cock pushed into her stomach, not making a secret of how much it liked her closeness.

"Shit. Sorry." Isa pulled both her body and her gaze away. "I think I'll end my cornhole career on a high note, and maybe turn in for the night."

"You're mine tonight." The words left Roman's mouth before he could think about how they sounded.

Isabel's dark eyes widened. "What?"

Fuck. Roman cleared his throat and shoved his hands in his pockets. "I meant that I'm on doctor duty tonight. Which is going to happen at my place...if you don't mind. In case you're wondering, it's just as secure as here. No one gets in or out unless I say so."

"Okay. Well, then, I guess I'll just go grab the things Jaz picked up for me."

Jaz shouldered her way between them, not bothering

to hide the shit-eating grin on her face. "I'll go down-stairs with you."

Roman nodded. "I'll get my keys and meet you back out here in five."

He watched Isa and Jaz disappear into the distillery before jogging to the back room behind the bar to grab his keys.

Five minutes later, he still hadn't talked his dick back to half-mast. "What the fuck is your problem, Steele?"

"Would you like me to text you the list?" Liam stepped into the storeroom and grabbed two bottles of their newest whiskey brews. "On the other hand, my fingers might get tired. How about I do a verbal rundown?"

"What the fuck do you want, Liam?"

"A bottle of the vodka you're standing in front of."

Roman grabbed one from the crate and tossed it to his brother, making him juggle it with the two others. "There. You got what you came for. Feel free to go."

"I should. If I were smart, I would..." Liam paused. "Oh, hell, I'm a freakin' genius, and yet I'm not going anywhere until you tell me why you're hiding in the back room."

"I'm not hiding," Roman growled.

He hoped to warn his baby brother away with a glare, but no such luck. Liam leaned against the shelving unit, his hazel eyes narrowed in concentration as he studied him as if he were a circuit board.

"There's nothing to figure out, Liam. Don't bother wasting your brainpower," Roman warned.

"It's my brainpower, and I'll waste it on whatever I want. Besides, it's not like I have to use much to figure out why you're in here and she's not—and don't insult my intelligence by denying you're keeping your distance from Isabel."

Roman hated the fact that Liam could read him so well. "Distance is what's best right now. Trust me."

Liam tucked his glasses higher on his nose. "I trust you on a lot of things, my brother, but matters of the heart and the fairer sex are not two of them."

"Don't let Jaz hear you call women the fairer sex."

"And don't try and change the damn subject."

"She's involved in a current assignment, which means it's hands-fucking-off. What's a better reason than that?"

"Because none of that matters when you meet the right person. Look at Knox and Zoey. At Cade and Grace."

He had...which was why he currently stood in the back room. In the short period he'd known Isabel Santiago, Roman had already questioned his moratorium on close relationships at least a dozen times. If he let himself get any closer, that number would only go up.

He wasn't about to let that happen.

Relationships meant trust. Trust meant vulnerability. And no way would he take someone's trust in him and throw it in the trash when he inevitably fucked things up.

"Fine. You want to keep your distance?" Liam said. "Then why don't you take over at the bar and I'll take doc duty tonight. Again."

"Like fucking hell," Roman growled.

At his brother's smirk, he knew he'd played right into Liam's hand. "Looks like you're not as distant as you claim. I just want to go on the record as saying that if you walk away from something without even giving it a good ol' college try, then you're an asshole. Actually, worse. A *cowardly* asshole."

Without another word, Liam left. Hell, Roman couldn't even be pissed at his brother's lecture because it was the same one he'd given Cade himself not that long ago when he'd contemplated letting Grace walk away for the second time.

With Liam's words still tumbling around in his head, Roman returned to the back patio and Isabel. They said their goodbyes and a quiet car ride later, reached the warehouse. Roman tossed his keys on the entryway table, more than ready to take an ice-cold shower.

With the exception of his family, no one had set foot inside his warehouse apartment before. It was his safe haven. His escape. And not only did Isabel Santiago make herself comfortable by kicking off her shoes, but he damn near fidgeted, wondering what she thought about it.

He'd spent a long time and a lot of elbow grease converting the abandoned riverside warehouse to suit his needs, and he was more than happy with it. The downstairs gym was practically finished, waiting for him to get enough time to spread the word, and his upstairs apartment was every inch the New York studio apartment, jumbo-size, that he'd wanted.

Roman didn't like walls or confinement, and the

open floor plan, bisected only by stylish privacy screens
that Zoey and Grace had been adamant he needed,
worked for him.

Isa padded barefoot over toward his wall-length
bookshelf and thumbed through his eclectic selection.
"Did you actually read all these, or are they just for
decoration?"

"I don't do decoration, so yeah, I read them."

Her lips twitched as she slid one out. "Even Jane
Austen?"

Roman shrugged. "Not much else to do when you're
laid up in a hospital bed."

She slipped *Pride and Prejudice* back into its slot and
shifted toward the pictures. He had a lot of them, most
of them gifted to him by his mother. There were pics of
him and his brothers growing up, of celebrations and
parties. Milestones. There were even a few from his time
in the Army, before he'd been selected for the special
assignment.

"I like your friends and family." Isa finally broke the
silence as she stopped in front of a group picture that had
been taken at Zoey's welcome home party after her last
heart surgery. In it, no one was looking at the camera,
and Ryder and Liam were in a heated argument.

"They're all family . . . even my friends."

"That's nice." Her gaze slid from his framed pictures
to him, the tension that had been in the truck filling the
larger room even more. "I don't have much of either.
I'm an only child, and I see my parents maybe a weekend a year. I try to visit my grandfather more often, but
sometimes life gets in the way."

"It does have the habit of doing that."

"And I have the bad habit of letting it." Isabel's big brown eyes darkened, more expressive than a five-thousand-word essay. Desire and a healthy dose of need swam in their depths and pushed Roman right back to the ledge he'd been teetering on in that back room.

One small jolt was all his body needed to light up like a live wire—but he'd be damned if he'd make the first move without knowing with one hundred percent certainty that she was completely on board with whatever happened next.

He could see her heartbeat pulsing at the base of her throat as she turned toward him. "Who's the real Roman Steele? The man who voluntarily reads Jane Austen and has a dozen family pictures on his bookshelf? Or the broody, arrogant Special Forces operator who dishes out orders like candy to trick-or-treaters?"

Roman leaned against the end of the large shelving unit. "Honestly? Both. But I'm not real big on letting the first Roman roam free too often."

"That's a shame, because the latter Roman epitomizes everything I've told myself I don't want in a man. No offense."

Roman cocked an eyebrow. "And what is it that you're looking for, Dr. Santiago?"

"What my grandparents had before my grandmother died—comfortable moments of silence and sweet gestures of thoughtfulness." Her gaze locked on his. "Something cozy and long-lasting."

"Are you describing a man or a damn couch?"

Roman quipped. "But you're right. None of that's me. I'm more into hot, quick, and dirty. Anything else?"

"I want slow walks and long talks." Isabel took a small step closer.

"My motto is run, don't walk. And I'm sure as hell not a big talker—especially about my feelings."

Isabel stepped again, stopping as her bare feet bumped against his boots. She tilted her head back, maintaining eye contact, and her dark hair cascaded down her back like a silken wave. Roman fisted his hands at his sides to avoid reaching out and testing the softness himself.

Isabel's attention briefly flickered down to his mouth. "And I want someone to look at me as if they'd steal the moon for me if I asked."

"You want an awful lot."

"I do." Isa slid her hands up his chest. "But it just so happens that I also want *you*."

Roman gently captured her wrists before she slid her fingers into his hair. "You should know that everything you just mentioned? You're not getting it from me, Doc." Roman's voice rumbled from his chest like a low growl. "I don't do sweet. And I don't do *feelings* unless you count the orgasms I'll give you with a good hard fucking."

"I know, and I'm okay with that. I just need...*this*."

Roman eased his grip off her wrists and trailed his fingers up her bare arms. "I want you to spell this out for me, Doc. What are you asking for?"

She shivered, eyes closing on a small sigh before locking on him. "I'm asking for you to fuck me."

Hearing her say the words aloud snapped Roman's frail control. He dove his fingers into her hair and dragged her mouth to his in a hot, hard kiss that nearly knocked him on his ass. For the last twenty-four hours, he did his damned best to maintain his distance, and now he couldn't pull her close enough.

CHAPTER
SEVEN

An all-consuming need for Roman Steele tossed every ounce of good sense right out of Isa's head. The man was everything she wasn't looking for—broody and closed off—and not to mention the owner of a hero complex a few miles wide.

But she couldn't deny he made her *feel* things she hadn't in a long time. It wasn't one emotion, but *all* of them. One minute she'd envision throttling him with her bare hands, and in the next, hugging his hurts away. Thirty seconds later, an egotistical comment would send her right back to plotting his demise... or kissing him mute.

There was absolutely no rhyme or reason for the draw she felt toward the infuriating man, and the more she tried figuring it out, the more confused she got. The only thing she'd deduced with one hundred percent certainty was that emotions were damn addictive... and she didn't want it to stop anytime soon.

She'd gotten way too good at living her life on autopilot, never detouring from the normal route. She'd plateaued, fearful of all the pitfalls that came with risk taking, but if the last few days had taught her anything it was that following the straight path also meant never soaring high above.

That's what Isa wanted right now. She wanted to soar . . . even if it was temporary.

Shifting her hands beneath Roman's T-shirt, she trailed her palms up his rock-hard abs and across his chest, her nails catching on his hardening nipples.

A growl rolled from Roman's chest. "You're playing with fire, Doc."

"Good." She pushed his shirt up, and as it hit his shoulders, he took over, ripping it over his head before tossing it aside. Once clear, he dove right back into their kiss as if he hadn't been able to physically stay away.

Roman cupped her ass, grinding his hard cock against her stomach. "Legs around my waist."

Eager to be closer, she slid a leg up the outside of his thigh and felt the edge of his prosthesis beneath his jeans. "No. Don't."

Roman froze. "Don't?"

"Don't pick me up. Your—"

"You think I can't pick you up?" Roman's dark eyes transformed to near black as he registered her concern. "Is that the only reason you told me to stop, Doc?"

She nodded, not trusting her words.

"Good," Roman growled. "Wrap your legs around my waist. *Now*."

She didn't need to be told twice. With the support of his large hands on her ass, Isa locked her legs around his waist. The second her feet left the ground, he pinned her against the wall, trailing his mouth down her neck.

"Please tell me you're not drunk." Roman kissed the sensitive patch of skin just below her earlobe, making her groan.

"I had one beer hours ago, and then nothing but sparkling water since." Unable to help herself, she leaned forward and nipped his bottom lip. "Most guys wouldn't take the time to get a drink tally when they had a woman's legs wrapped around their waist."

"I'm not like a lot of other guys," Roman grumbled.

Wasn't that the truth...

"That's why I'm exactly where I am right now." Isa tugged his hair free of its band, and it fell around his shoulders like chocolate silk. She brushed her mouth against his once, then twice as she slowly rotated her hips against the large bulge pressing against her mound. "I'm not under the influence, Roman. And I'd very much like you to take me to your bed and fuck me senseless now, if you don't mind."

With a low, sexy growl, Roman walked toward the bed and dropped them onto the mattress, where they worked together to take off her shirt.

"Pink lace?" Through the sheer fabric, Roman fastened his greedy mouth to a hardening nipple.

She arched her back, already sensing her body prepping to ignite. "Wait till you see the matching underwear."

"I don't think I can...wait, I mean."

She really hoped that was the case.

With a quick flick of his fingers, Roman unclasped her bra, his mouth ready and eager as her breasts spilled out. Alternating between slow, firm sucks and gentle glides of his tongue, he feasted on every inch of exposed skin.

She reached for his pants, but his hand stopped her

from lowering the zipper. "If they come off now this will be over in a flash."

"Then we'll have time to do this all over again. It's been an embarrassingly long time since I've had sex, Roman. I don't want slow and easy. I want you inside me fifteen minutes ago."

He waited a beat.

"Fifteen minutes and ten seconds."

"And you accuse me of being bossy." Roman chuckled as he trailed his mouth from her breast down the center of her torso. They worked in tandem to ease her jeans—and lace panties—down her legs...and then there wasn't an inch of her body that he didn't let his eyes feast on. "That is one hell of a gorgeous sight."

He ran his nose along the inside of her leg. "Beautiful."

Isa's knees would've buckled if she'd been standing.

He flicked his tongue against her already swollen folds. "Fucking delicious."

Isa whimpered. "Roman, please."

"No need to beg, Doc," Roman murmured less than an inch from her mound. "It's my pleasure...and soon it'll be yours."

As his tongue came into contact with her mound, Isa's body bowed off the mattress. Her fingers dug into his hair as she held him closer. Not that she needed to. Pleasure rippled through her as his tongue rolled over her aching clit in soft, slow circles, again and again, with no sign of stopping.

"Whoa boy." Her eyes drifted closed before she

wrestled them open to watch the greedy man between her legs.

And Roman *was* greedy. He licked and nibbled, and as she panted to keep from losing consciousness, she registered the slow rub of his fingers...never entering, only caressing.

Teasing.

"Let go." Reaching one large hand up to her breast, Roman brushed his thumb over her already deliciously aching nipple and continued to feast. "Come on my tongue, Doc. I want to taste everything you have to give me."

And that's just what she did. The pleasure coiled low in her abdomen crested in one huge wave, rolling its way through her entire body. Roman stayed with her through it all, his mouth caressing her until her orgasm dimmed to a warm, dull throb.

Roman crawled his way back up her body, a smug look of satisfaction on his face. "Enjoy that, did you?"

"Most definitely." Smirking, she reached for the button of his jeans. "And now that you took the edge off, these jeans need to disappear."

* * *

No matter how bad he wanted to be inside Isa, Roman needed a breather or this would end before it even got started. As she dealt with his zipper, he reached into his bedside table for the unopened box of condoms and inconspicuously checked out the expiration date. *Still good.*

Isabel wasn't the only one who'd had a long sexual hiatus.

Her small hand wrapped around his aching cock and squeezed.

"Fuck." He fumbled with the condoms, dropping a strand of rubbers on the bed.

Isa chuckled. "Was it something I did?"

"You didn't strike me as a tease, Doc."

"It's only teasing if I don't plan on following through—which I do." She pushed him onto his back. Her bare body hovered over him as she worked his jeans down his legs.

His prosthetic came into view. "Leave the jeans on."

Isa's eyes shifted up to him. "Why?"

Because the number of sexual partners—post-amputation—could be counted on one hand, and none of them had been particularly comfortable experiences, never mind sexually satisfying.

"Makes it easier to believe it's still there," Roman answered gruffly. "Some women get a little freaked out when they realize there's not as many appendages in the bed as there should be."

Keeping her eyes locked on his, Isabel's hand deftly worked the straps of his prosthetic. "Just like you're not like most guys, Roman Steele, I'm not like most women."

She sure as hell wasn't.

Isabel's long hair brushed against his already tingling skin. Having her on top of him, naked, hadn't diminished his desire one damn bit, but as he eased his stump sock off and set his prosthetic on the floor, he watched her for any sign she'd changed her mind.

But Isabel didn't bat a single dark eyelash as she shifted over his legs, her fingertips brushing over his scars and up his thighs. Roman sucked in a breath and her hooded brown eyes drifted up to him.

"Is this okay?" she asked.

His gaze flickered down to his growing erection. "Does it look like it's okay?"

Isabel's little pink tongue flicked out, wetting her bottom lip as she plucked a condom from his fingers. "Let me."

Roman flexed his grip on her hips and prayed he didn't embarrass himself as she rolled it onto his shaft. The second it was rolled right up to his base, he tugged her on top of him and took her mouth with his.

"Oh, *now* you're Mr. Eager," Isabel teased, her tongue playing with his.

"I've never *not* been eager to get inside you."

"Good. Then we're on the same page." She rubbed her wet slit over his cock twice before he couldn't take it anymore. Gripping her waist, he flipped her to her back, and then he sunk into her in one hard thrust.

They groaned simultaneously.

"Yes. More." Isabel's hands dug into his back, urging him on, and that's what he did.

Hiking her left leg high over his hip and palming her ass, he thrust again.

"Don't stop." Isabel panted. "Harder, Roman."

He groaned. "You're killing me here, sweetheart."

But he obeyed, dropping his mouth onto hers as they

worked themselves into a hard, quick rhythm that had sweat dripping off their bodies. His cocked throbbed, and his balls, begging for release, tightened against his body... but no way was he coming without her.

Slipping a hand between them, he brushed his thumb against her clit. Once. Twice.

Isabel screamed his name, her pussy squeezing his cock. The pulse of her body fueled his own climax and Roman erupted. Wave after wave of pleasure crashed over them both until he dropped next to her, sweaty and out of breath.

"Now *that's* how every sexual hiatus should be shattered." Isabel sighed.

He half expected her to give him her back, or hell, kick him out of his own bed. Instead, she hooked her thigh over his right leg and nestled into the crook of his arm.

Roman froze.

He *never* snuggled—not once in his thirty-two years. Just the idea of it had always sent him running for the hills or, at the very least, out for a jog. But that wasn't the case now. Unwilling to move to even hit the bathroom, he dealt with the condom one-handed and curled his other arm around Isabel's shoulders.

Her sleepy sigh wrapped around him, as did a warm feeling of contentment.

Dropping his chin to the top of her head, Roman was too damn exhausted—and physically satisfied—to worry about how right it felt.

CHAPTER EIGHT

Isabel's brain slowly woke up, as did the rest of her body. Lifting her arms above her head, she savored the warm stretch of muscles that had been well used. This time it wasn't because she'd run a few laps around Constitution Gardens.

She'd done a few rounds with Roman.

No one could regret sex like that. She'd shut off her overactive mind and just *reacted*, each decision made based on the heat of the moment. Figuratively and literally. Her only concern was what happened next, because the second they found her virus and the people responsible, Roman Steele would be out of her life.

She could enjoy his sexual prowess until then. As a matter of fact, she really hoped that's what he had planned, too. If last night showed her anything—other than multiple orgasms—it was that she'd closed herself off to people for way too long.

It was what came next that concerned her, because that feeling of freedom was addictive, and Roman still wasn't the type of man she envisioned herself with for more than anything than he did last night.

He was camo when she saw a suit. He was an Uzi when she saw a briefcase. Roman Steele was an unpredictable, wild, carefree spirit when all she hoped for was steadfast, safe, and dependable. There wasn't a doubt in her mind he wasn't the perfect guy for someone...but she wasn't an FBI profiler like Grace, or a crime scene investigator like Zoey.

She was just *her*. Yeah, she'd served her country in the Army, but she'd spent more time behind the microscope than she did a battlefield. Roman needed his own Grace, or Zoey, or even Jaz.

Scents of coffee and frying bacon permeated the air and coaxed Isa from bed and back into her panties. She tugged Roman's discarded T-shirt over her head and padded barefoot toward the mouthwatering smell. Instead, she found a mouthwatering sight.

Shirtless in front of the stove, Roman turned bacon with one hand while flipping pancakes with the other. Drawstring shorts hung low on his hips, showcasing the abs she'd spent a lot of time tasting last night.

This was the first time he'd had his prosthetic on display other than that first morning in the gym, and she wondered if that had been accidental or on purpose. Her belief that nothing could rattle the former Special Forces soldier had been proven wrong last night.

He hadn't wanted her to see his amputation. Maybe because he'd dreaded *her* reaction to it, or maybe the apprehension was all on his own. Either way, it was obvious that the steel-spined Roman Steele wasn't as hard as he wanted people around him to believe...and damn it if that didn't make her like him all the more.

"It'll be kinda hard to eat all this food from all the way over there." Roman slid a crispy mound of bacon from the pan and onto a plate.

As his appreciative gaze slid down his oversized shirt and her bare legs, a lock of loose hair fell over his eye. Her fingers itched to brush it away, but instead, she helped herself to a piece of bacon and the waiting glass of juice.

She grinned. "You play cornhole with the big guys, own a collection of classic romances, and kick asses. I shouldn't be surprised that you can cook, and yet here I am."

He snorted. "If I don't cook I don't eat."

"There's always takeout, and that new-fangled app where you can order yourself a breakfast burrito and someone brings it right to your door." At his look of abject horror, she chuckled. "Not that I know anything about it."

Roman's lips twitched, making her stomach drop. *A smile.* An *almost* smile. Its fleeting presence made her want to see another one, and as she debated on the best way to make it happen, he propped his spatula on the pan and tugged her flush against his chest.

The same heated look he'd worn before each of last night's sexual romps was back. Her body shivered reflexively as if it remembered what came next.

"I'm not real big on people invading my personal space." Roman's gaze dropped to her mouth. "Unless they're tall, sexy brunettes with a penchant for telling me off."

"I haven't done that for at least an hour." Isa nibbled

his bottom lip, chuckling when he groaned. "How easy is it to warm up breakfast?"

"I think we should find out." He turned off the burner and backed her up against the counter, taking her mouth in a hot kiss before pulling back and doing it all over again. He had her panting in need in a matter of seconds, her fingers diving into his hair to prevent him from moving away.

Seconds from sliding her hands beneath the waistband of Roman's pants, the *Who's the Boss* theme song echoed from somewhere in the apartment. It stopped and started again a few seconds later.

"Is Tony Danza about to walk into my apartment or something?" Roman murmured against her lips.

"My cell." *Who's the Boss*? "Crap. I can't ignore that call. Hold that thought."

They both groaned as she pulled away and hustled into the other room, where her phone vibrated with each ring. Isa frowned down at the screen. A half dozen missed calls, even more texts, and a few emails—all from the Global Health Organization.

Her phone rang again, and this time, she answered. "Hello?"

"Isa? Bloody hell." Anthony Winter, her one-time mentor cursed. "Why haven't you returned any of my calls?"

"Because I was sleeping." Isa dished out the half lie easily. The sixty-three-year-old epidemiologist didn't need to know about her marathon night of crazy sex. "Do you want to harp on me for being human—unlike some people who shall not remain nameless—or do you want to tell me why you're filling up my inbox?"

"If you're not near a computer, get near one and check your email. I'll wait."

"How is it you always make orders sound like polite suggestions? Is it the English accent?" Isa teased.

"Isabel . . . *now*."

The smile melted off her face. Tony *never* used her full name.

Roman half watched from the kitchen as she sat on the couch and booted up her laptop. "What exactly am I looking for?"

"You'll know it the second you see it," Tony said, voice grim.

Isa counted eight emails from him in the last seven hours. "Am I supposed to open up anything particular first?"

"Start with the oldest one and go right down the line. And Isa?"

"Yeah?"

"I hope you haven't eaten breakfast yet."

Isa's post-sex glow immediately evaporated. "I hate it when you say cryptic shit like that."

At the click of the first attached photo file, Isa's stomach rolled. The single strip of bacon she'd had curdled in her stomach, threatening to make a reappearance.

In each email, Tony sent four or more pictures, each one more disturbing than the next. Zoomed images physically documented open sores and enflamed petechiae—reddened dots—that indicated bleeding at the capillary level. The last few showcased broken blood vessels in the white of eyes and, in the last photograph, nail beds.

"What the fuck is that?" Roman cursed from over her shoulder.

She'd been so busy mentally registering what she saw that she hadn't heard him approach. "That's what I'm about to find out." She put Tony on speaker phone and shifted one more time through the pictures. "Is this Marburg, Lassa fever, or Ebola?"

"None of the above."

"You know I think you're nothing short of a genius, but are you sure?" Isa hated second-guessing her old friend. "These images—"

"Are from here, Isa." Tony paused, and she could practically see him tugging on his scraggly white beard as he often did when stressed.

"What do you mean *here*?"

"Those pictures were taken from a handful of patients in Beaver Ridge, Alaska. It's definitely a hemorrhagic disease, but it's not Marburg, Lassa, or Ebola. It's something a hell of a lot worse."

Isa was already shaking her head. Dread balled up in her stomach like a rock. "*Please* tell me it's not."

"I wish I could rule it out, kid. I need your confirmation, but I'm about eighty percent certain I found your missing FC-5 virus."

Isa closed her eyes on a sigh. "That's not what I wanted to hear, Tony."

"Then you'll *really* hate this…but I need you, Isa. This town's not capable of handling something like this. They're remote and closed off from the world. Hell, they don't even have a functioning hospital. If this isn't contained—and soon—it'll rip through this town before we can even blink."

"The GHO—"

"Will take their sweet ass time sending out *anyone*, much less a full investigative team. At the rate of transmission, Beaver Ridge will be wiped out before the first plane touches down. You know I wouldn't ask you if I didn't need help, Isa. I need *you*."

Tony was one of few people who knew why she'd abandoned bedside medicine and switched to research, and for him to ask this of her, or to ask for help *at all*, was a big deal.

The man strutted into pandemic areas like Superman with a cape. He scoffed at things that would give most people nightmares for life, and he never admitted needing help because there wasn't anything that he couldn't handle.

Except *this*.

"Isa?" Tony asked when she'd gone silent.

"Yeah. No. Okay." Isabel took a breath and tried to rein in all her thoughts at once. "I'll see what supplies I can wrestle away from Carmichael. Email me as much information as you can about what you're seeing, and I'll try to get caught up while I'm in the air."

"Thank you."

"Why are you thanking me? This is why we do what we do. I'll let you know when I'll be arriving." Isa hung up and turned to Roman, her next words dying on her lips.

The easygoing, horny man who'd almost smiled had

been completely replaced with the stubborn former Special Forces soldier she first met in the Legion lab.

* * *

Funny how a damn good morning could go all to shit in a snap—or a phone call. Roman should've been prepared for the other shoe to drop, and now that it had, he wouldn't be caught off guard again. At least now he had backup.

And an enemy—one pissed off and determined Isabel Santiago.

At Steele Ops command, everyone sat around the table, and the haggling hadn't stopped for the last thirty minutes. Opinions and thoughts were hurtled back and forth, but none on which anyone could agree.

Knox pinched the bridge of his nose, looking as shitty as Roman felt, and Ryder tried—and failed—to settle a tiff between Jaz and Tank. Liam was the only one who looked relatively calm, but only because he was probably plotting something in that crazy smart brain of his.

"I get this isn't ideal, for anyone," Isa announced to the group, "but it *is* necessary."

"Says you," Roman muttered under his breath, but not quietly enough.

Isa shot him a glare. "That's right, *me*, the only one who's qualified to say what's necessary in this scenario...unless one of you has a medical or biology background I'm not aware of." She looked around the room. "No? No one? Then yep, I'm the only one."

Knox leaned back in his chair and leveled her with a heavy stare. "You said your friend already has boots on the ground, right?"

"Tony, yes. He was on vacation on some ice fishing adventure when he got wind of something happening in Beaver Ridge. As per typical Tony fashion, he went right into work mode."

"What makes him think this is FC-5?"

"Everything." Isa pulled out some of the pages she'd printed off that morning from the files Tony had emailed her but left the pictures in the folder. "There isn't a doubt it's some kind of VHF—viral hemorrhagic fever."

"*Some* kind of VHF? How many are there?"

"I can list eighteen off the top of my head, but there's quite a few more."

Ryder took the paper and read through the list. "I've never heard of more than half of these."

"A lot of people haven't, and some of them have been all but eradicated off the face of the planet. And before any of you ask, I know it's none of the ones on that list. Although their basics are the same, there's significant markers that identify them. Lassa fever is airborne, and Marburg has a very distinct papular rash. And then you compare incubation periods and onset of symptoms." Isa took a deep breath. "Tony's right to think this could be FC-5. There are way too many similarities for my liking."

Roman couldn't stay quiet anymore. "Then I'll go and meet your friend, get samples from him or whatever you need to verify, and hop on the next plane home."

She was already shaking her head. "Won't work."

"Why the hell not?"

"Because the sample Tony gives you won't be the same sample I get when you come back. Time, heat, handling...they all change viral properties. By the time you get back to DC, those samples will be worthless. I need to go *there*. I need to lay eyes on the patients myself, and I need to examine samples at the exact moment they're collected."

Roman folded his arms over his chest and met her glare for glare. "If this is FC-5, what's the likelihood that its popping up in Nowhere, Alaska, is natural selection? Is it fond of cold temps? Does it burrow in glaciers or something?"

For the first time, Isa's glare wavered. She looked away as he waited for her to answer.

And waited.

"No," she finally admitted. "If this is FC-5, then it had help getting there."

"So this missing virus, taken by armed commandoes who've already tried nabbing you off the streets in broad daylight *once* already, pops up somewhere it shouldn't be, and you're packing your bags and taking the first flight out?"

"Yes, I am." Isa, her jaw clenched, reached into the file and tossed the photos on the table.

Muttered curses and gaspes sounded around the room.

"Fucking hell," Ryder muttered.

Grace winced. "Whoa. That's...horrible."

"*That's* just the beginning. If this is FC-5, it won't

be long before the people in those pictures are begging for death. *People*, Roman. Elderly. Children. Entire families. If I prevent even one of them from dying, then that's what I'll do. If you don't like it, then stay the hell here."

He didn't like it. One damn bit. But he'd be damned if he'd let her go off on her own.

Knox's attention bounced from Roman to Isa, who glared at him as if daring him to argue. "If you need to go, then we have to make it work."

"Then I'll take her myself," Roman announced. "There's no reason to put anyone else at risk."

"That's fucking stupid, man." Tank shook his head. "You go at it alone and you're putting both of you at risk. This Beaver Ridge is the epitome of seclusion, right?"

Liam nodded toward where he'd brought up the area map. "Only way in or out is by seaplane."

"Exactly my point. Best-case scenario is if this *is* our super virus, those lab assholes aren't far away. Worst case is that they fucking chose this town to lure you the hell out there, counting on the fact that you're mice trapped in a cage."

Jaz nodded. "Tank's right—and you know how much I love admitting that. You need more than one set of eyes."

Jaz and Tank weren't telling him anything that he hadn't told himself multiple times over since Isabel ended her phone call with Tony. Whether these bastards had accidently infected the town by choosing it as a place to lie low or they did it on purpose, they'd have to know Isabel would make an appearance. Roman and anyone who came with them needed to be prepared when they made their move...and in the event Steele Ops needed to go on the offensive, he also needed a tracker.

And he knew just the man. "I'm cashing in a favor that I have with a guy I know, but I'm not telling any of you that you need to come. Between these lab assholes and whatever's happening in that town, it's not a low-risk assignment."

Isa agreed. "We need to minimize the risk of exposure and go with the bare minimum you guys consider *safe*."

"Well, you can count me in." Jaz spoke up first.

"Me too." Ryder nodded, face grim. "Plus I have a medic background, so I'll be able to be a little more hands-on with the patients if it comes to that. Sounds like Beaver Ridge doesn't exactly have its own level-three trauma center."

"It's not," Isa admitted. "They have a small clinic that's good for minor aches and pains and preventative care, but that's about it. They're totally overwhelmed by all this."

"Then that's it." Roman glanced around the room. "It'll be me, Jaz, and Ryder, and I'll talk to my guy. That'll make four of us and Doc." He slid his gaze over to Isa. "That okay with you?"

The look she gave him told him no. "Do I have any other choice?"

"No."

"Then yeah, I'm okay with that."

CHAPTER
NINE

Roman pulled his truck onto the lane, knowing with every rotation of his tires that this encounter was doomed to go as well as his attempt to get Isabel alone this morning. Since the meeting the night before, she'd been on the phone, first with Carmichael, and then with her former mentor from the GHO.

He'd hoped to talk her out of this ridiculous idea, appeal to her common sense or, hell, her survival instincts, because after studying Beaver Ridge's topography for a few hours, Roman identified it for what it was—a clusterfuck waiting to happen.

And that was before factoring in the sick patients.

Nestled between a massive mountain range and a lake, the small town's only access point was by air—seaplane to be exact. Roads in and around town proper were micro-sized, big enough for side-by-side four-by-fours or a pair of snowmobiles, and anything farther than a few miles outside the perimeter was considered off-roading.

No roads to civilization. No easy extraction.

If those lab assholes were behind this, they'd be fish in a barrel waiting to be picked off one by one. Roman hoped the sucky odds would cater to his old buddy's love of a challenge.

"A regular Mr. Social Butterfly," Roman muttered as he brought his truck to a stop at the end of the lane.

Parked cars lined the front and side fields surrounding Ethan King's cabin. Music echoed through the West Virginia mountains, rivaled only by the loud cheers coming from the backyard. Roman stepped through the back gate and right into the thick of Backyard Brawls.

Barefooted and sporting gloves, two men circled each other in the makeshift boxing ring, each looking like he was out for blood. The crowd around them lapped it up with a spoon, cheering when their guy got in a good hit. Judging by the state of both men, they'd been at it for at least a few rounds.

Roman pocketed his keys and spotted Garrett Porter, King's unofficial bouncer, leaning against the wall.

"Look what the cat dragged in." Garrett took a long pull on his cigarette. "I'd say it was good to see you, but it's not. You look like shit, man."

"Always with the sweet talk. King around?"

Garrett grunted with a nod. "He had to unwind himself from tonight's side piece to deal with some asswipe trying to place money on matches, so he's in a mood."

"Nothing worse than Ethan King getting cock-blocked. The asswipe still have full function of his appendages?"

"Most of them."

"Then he's damn lucky."

Backyard Brawls may look like a free-for-all fight-fest to the casual observer, but Ethan King prided himself on keeping it aboveboard and in line with West Virginia law. That meant no betting or exchange of money of any kind on his property. Anyone who broke that rule was dealt with accordingly, which usually meant getting their ass kicked by King himself.

Garrett's eyes narrowed. "Well, fuck. I know that face. You're gonna put the boss man in an even worse mood than he's already in, aren't you?"

Roman shrugged but didn't deny it.

"Don't get compensated enough for this shit." Garrett dropped his quickly disappearing cigarette onto the ground and stepped on it with his boot. "Let's go. Last time I laid eyes on him he was letting some pretty blonde sit on his lap. If you're lucky, she'll have improved his mood some."

When they tracked down King, not only was there not a blonde on his lap, but he had a wire-thin guy pinned against the side of the house. King leaned close, never raising his voice, but judging by the loss of color in the guy's face, he didn't need to. Whatever message he was in the middle of delivering was received loud and clear.

"Careful there, King, or you may break a nail," Roman quipped dryly.

"I'd like to break something." His old service buddy glanced his way before releasing the guy in his grip. "Today's your lucky day. Get gone. And if I see you back here again, you'll be betting on your life."

"No problem, man. I'm outta here."

"Porter? Make sure he gets off the property."

"Not a problem, boss." Garrett followed the wiry guy around the side of the house.

Anyone who didn't know Ethan King would've shit a brick when the six-foot-four and nearly 220-pound former Special Forces soldier drilled him with a hard look. Not Roman. He'd witnessed him trying to fold his bulky frame in a damn Humvee and had been the prime suspect in a prank that had King shitting his brains out for forty-eight hours straight. He knew the bastard as if he were one of his brothers...and he knew the man loved danger.

He loved the thrill.

He loved not just beating the odds, but crushing them into a fine powder.

And he also happened to be one of the best trackers he knew...short of the four-legged furry kind.

"The answer's no." With a growl, King turned on his heel and headed toward his cabin.

Roman followed. By the time he stepped into the small kitchen, King had already poured himself a generous helping of tequila. "I didn't even ask you anything."

"Yet." He pointed an accusing finger at him. "But I know all your dumb faces, and that one right there tells me I not only need to say no, but no-to-the-fucking-*hell*-no. So this is me officially telling you to bug off."

Roman shook his head. "Can't do it. There's too much on the line."

King knocked back his drink and immediately filled the glass with another. He put up a good front, but deep down under King's rough exterior beat the heart of duty-driven softy. Roman just needed to chisel his way through granite to get there.

"You know I wouldn't be here if it wasn't necessary," Roman added.

King folded his huge arms across his chest and leaned against the counter. "Let *me* determine if it's necessary."

Step one—*complete*.

"Wipe that fucking smirk off your face before I punch it off, brother," King warned. "I agreed to hear you out. That doesn't mean I'm packing my bags."

Roman told him about the lab theft, the virus, and about the possible outbreak in Beaver Ridge. With each new bunch of facts, his buddy's frown deepened more, and so did Roman's. Hearing it out loud made this assignment sound more and more like a one-way trip.

"Let me get this straight," King interjected. "You want me go to Bumblefuck, Alaska, where the town's most likely infected with some kind of *Walking Dead* virus *and* surrounded by armed assholes who spend their spare time breaking into maximum-security labs?"

"About sums it up. Pretty sweet deal, right?"

"There's something you're leaving out."

"I literally told you everything."

King narrowed his eyes, studying him as if trying to find hidden answers somewhere on Roman's face. He fought to keep his face a blank slate, but leave it to his buddy to find that microscopic crack.

Ethan grinned, chuckling. "This doctor you mentioned...you have a hard-on for her. Well, I'll be damned. I thought I'd never live to see the day."

"Keep it up and you won't."

King lifted his hands in mock surrender. "If I agree

to this crazy-ass assignment—and I'm not saying I am—but when would we be wheels up?"

And step two—*complete*. "Tomorrow morning. Seven sharp. Manassas Regional."

"You're asking for a lot, man."

"I know."

King grunted. "I'll *think* about it...but don't do anything stupid like go counting on me. I'm not exactly the self-sacrificing type."

Roman battled a threatening smirk and instead nodded in feigned agreement. King would be there—dragging, probably hungover, and a whole lot of grumpy, but he'd show ready to kick some ass.

* * *

Despite her day wrangling the supplies they'd need to handle a possible FC-5 exposure, Isa still didn't believe that in twenty-four hours she'd be on a plane to Alaska. The work they did at the Legion was meant to avoid these kind of scenarios, not bring them into fruition, and she couldn't help but feel responsible.

If she'd only fought against the intruders a little harder. If she'd only managed to hit the alarm. If she'd been inside the lab at the time they'd breached, she could've tossed all the damn FC-5 samples into the freaking incinerator.

They couldn't use FC-5 as a bioweapon without the virus itself.

But they *did* have it, and an entire town may have paid the price for Isa's mistake. If jumping into field medicine was what was needed of her, she'd do it, and she'd do it without complaint. Her discomfort meant nothing compared to what the people in Beaver Ridge faced.

A burst of laughter pulled Isa's attention from the laptop, where she was checking for an update from Tony. Holed up in what the Steele Ops gang considered their family room, the team was unwinding after a long day. Beer and specialty cocktails brewed from Iron Bars' own boutique alcohol had been flowing freely for the last two hours.

To anyone looking in, they appeared like family and friends relaxing and enjoying each other's company, but it hadn't been that way a few short hours ago. They'd inventoried weapons, strategized exit routes, and fine-tuned security measures to be taken once they reached Alaska. A lot of it had gone over her head, but what she had grasped was that beneath the intense planning—and now rampant joking—was a hell of a lot of worry.

Isa included.

With everyone temporarily teasing Ryder about his lack of pick-up skills, Isabel slinked away to the back room she'd call home for the night and made the phone call she'd delayed long enough.

"Isabel," her grandfather answered. "I wasn't expecting a phone call from you tonight."

"I wanted to check in because I'm going out of town tomorrow, and I'm not sure when I'll be able to call next."

"Is everything okay?"

Yes. *No.* Isa longed to spill everything, but she

couldn't bring herself to make him worry more than he already did. "I have to go into the field. There's a lot of sick people in Alaska that need help."

"Then they're in good hands."

Isa sat on the bed and sighed. If only she believed that. "This has the potential to be really, really bad, Abuelito. If it's not handled the right way..."

She didn't need to say more.

After she lost Olly, her grandfather had let her work through her grief at her own pace. He'd listened to her angry rants and held her as she'd cried. There wasn't anything he wouldn't do for her...except let her question her own abilities. That's where Carlos Santiago drew the line, and it was one he'd never let either one of them cross.

"Isabel Marisol Santiago, you're exactly what those people in Alaska need, just like you were what that little boy in the hospital needed."

Tears welled in her eyes because of course he knew what went through her head. "What that little boy needed was someone to save his mother. Instead, he got me."

"Sweetheart, what happened is a sad reality of the world we live in today. You're a doctor, Isabel, not a miracle worker. You can't do what's out of the realm of possibility." Her grandfather's voice softened. "As much as it pains me to say this, you weren't meant to save that young mother."

"What if I'm not meant to save the people in Beaver Ridge, Alaska, either?" Isa's voice trembled. She took a breath and held it until her chest ached. "What if I'm not enough? Again?"

"If there is a way, sweetheart, you will find it. I have complete faith in you...more than you have in yourself."

Isa couldn't help but smile sadly, because it was true. "I love you, do you know that?"

"I do...and I love you, cariño."

Hearing a noise in the hall, Isa glanced up. Roman stood in the open doorway, shoulder pushed against the jamb as he watched her. She didn't know how long he'd stood there or how much he'd heard.

"Grandpa, I have to go. One of my colleagues is here, and we have a few more things to go over before tomorrow. I'll try to check in when I can."

"Be safe, sweetheart."

"Always am." Isa said goodbye and took a moment before meeting Roman's gaze. She couldn't read his facial expression, and for a moment she thought he was gearing up for another argument about why she needed to stay in DC. "Is everything okay?"

"Guess I should be asking you that."

"I don't know what you mean," Isa lied and stood, suddenly anxious to repack her bag and make sure she had everything she needed. "Carmichael promised that the supplies I asked for will be at the airport first thing in the morning, and Tony emailed that he's set up a makeshift hospital in Beaver Ridge. I should be able to hit the ground running the second we get to Alaska."

"You didn't answer my question."

"Technically, you didn't ask a question." Isa dumped her clothes on the bed and busied herself with refolding and packing.

"Fine. You want a question?" He caught her elbow and eased her away from her duffel. "Do you really think you're not capable of getting in front of this?"

"Eavesdropping on private conversations doesn't become you."

"Neither does that nervous doubt I heard in your voice a few minutes ago. What's changed since yesterday? Or the day before that? What happened to the woman who nearly castrated me while in quarantine? She sure as hell wasn't full of doubts."

"That women wasn't faced with having to pick up her stethoscope for the first time in years," Isa snapped. "Don't worry about it, Roman. I'm sure it's just like riding a bike. And in case it's not, that's why you'll be keeping your distance. Distance in Alaska...and distance *here*."

Something flashed in Roman's dark eyes, there and gone before she could identify it, or take back her words. "Distance."

Staying away from Roman Steele was actually the last thing she wanted to do, but when she let herself get close to him, everything else seemed to melt away. "With Beaver Ridge hanging over our heads on top of the missing FC-5, I can't afford to get wrapped up in this thing with you, no matter how exciting and freeing it feels. I can't let myself get distracted."

"Knock-knock. There you guys are." Jaz and Liam stood by the open door. "We need the two of you to break a tie. And FYI, if you choose drunk charades, you'll be dead to me."

Liam's gaze bounced from Isa to Roman. "We can come back..."

"Like hell! This needs to be settled right now."

Isa forced a smile and casually stepped away from Roman. "Actually, there's no time like the present...and I'm sorry, Jaz, but drunk charades sounds like a lot of fun."

"Isabel," Roman growled.

Isa tucked her arm through Jaz's and let the other woman direct their way through the labyrinth that was Steele Ops. Avoiding Roman—practically running away—wasn't one of her finer moments, but it was one that needed to happen, because if she was all that stood in the way of a possible outbreak unlike anything the world had yet seen, then she needed to have her head on straight.

Not on Roman Steele.

CHAPTER
TEN

Leaning against his truck's front bumper, Roman cast a glance at his watch. The Steele Ops jet had been packed and fueled, nearly ready to depart from Manassas Regional Airport except for one small hiccup.

Still no King.

Roman wasn't worried yet. He'd show, if for no other reason than to be able to use the humanitarian mission as a way to impress his next big-hearted and probably big-breasted conquest. As if the guy needed additional help getting laid.

Ryder popped his head out of the plane. "Pilot's ready to go."

"Five more minutes."

"Whoever you're waiting for obviously isn't showing. We'll be fine—unless we make Isa wait too much longer. She's already walking up and down the aisle like a caged tiger. I never saw anyone so eager to walk *toward* a death virus."

Roman pushed off the truck, nearly ready to give in, when a bright yellow VW convertible screeched to a stop in front of the hangar.

A hair-tangled redhead sat behind the wheel, King on the passenger side. He leaned across the gearshift and dragged the woman into a heavy, tongue-filled kiss before grabbing an old Army rucksack from the back seat and hopping out from the cramped space.

"Still cutting things close, I see." Roman's lips twitched as he grasped King's forearm in a friendly grip. "And still making sure you get a proper send-off."

"There's no other way to do it, brother. Especially when you're taking me somewhere where I might die from a hemorrhage in my ass."

Hearing King's arrival, Ryder and the others approached. He needed to make this next part quick. "Look, about our time in Burundi...no one knows. Even my family. And I'd like to keep it that way."

King's smile evaporated. "Fuck, man. Seriously?"

Roman's hackles rose. "You telling me you give everyone you come across the pros and cons of working on a CIA black site for nearly two years?"

"No, but I also don't have a close-knit family like yours." King's gaze flickered down to his left leg. "Or that to explain. It's been five years. You seriously haven't told them a damn thing?"

He hadn't. At first because his time on the Burundi black site was classified, and then because he wasn't eager to put his naïveté on full display. Admitting he'd trusted the wrong person and paid for it with his leg wasn't a conversation he really wanted to have with people who expected him to have their back. Despite not wanting to, his family still treated him differently since his amputation.

Roman hardened his gaze to make sure King knew

he was serious. "No Burundi. No Kat. No explosion. Tell me you can handle that, or walk away now."

"Yeah. Okay." King hoisted his rucksack higher on his shoulder. "But you're climbing a slippery slope, brother. You know me. I'm not exactly an open book, but keeping that kind of shit on the inside—especially when you have people around you that give a rat's ass—is like a damn cancer. It eats you from the inside out."

"Not a damn word."

"Got it."

Ryder and Jaz joined them, Isa on their heels. Her hair pulled away from her face in a ponytail and dressed in khaki cargo pants and a plain white T-shirt, she looked the epitome of functional and sexy as hell.

True to what she claimed the previous night at Steele Ops HQ, she'd avoided him all morning. At first, it pissed him off. While everyone had played games in the commons, he'd knocked around the heavy bag for a while, but when he was done, when it was just him and his bruised knuckles, he understood—if just a little bit—what she'd meant about being distracted.

When he'd been buried balls-deep inside of her, he hadn't been able to see anything but her. The entire world had disappeared. There'd been no threat. No virus. No nagging past hounding his every step. There'd just been the two of them, and it had felt fucking *incredible*.

And it could also be fucking dangerous, considering where they were going and what they had to do. But just because he reluctantly understood didn't mean he hadn't contemplated making the distance between them disappear about a dozen times since then.

Ryder stuck his hand out to King. "You must be the mysterious friend we've heard nothing about. Ryder Steele."

"One of the infamous brothers. I can't say I didn't hear anything about you guys." King turned to Jaz and Isa, his voice dropping to a low purr. "But *you* two beauties I definitely would've remembered. Ethan King at your service."

"And at the service of the redhead who practically sucked off your face a few minutes ago." Jaz took his hand, not the least bit fazed by his flirtation.

He smirked. "Saw that, did you? Sweet girl. Kindergarten teacher. But don't worry, I'm still very much a free agent."

Jaz snorted and turned back toward the plane. "Oh, I wasn't worried."

Ryder laughed and clapped King on the back. "Word to the wise: Don't piss off a world-class sniper."

"Thanks for the heads-up." King chuckled nervously and extended a hand toward Isa. "Are you a sniper, too?"

"Doctor. Isabel Santiago."

King held her hand a little too long for Roman's liking. "So you're the reason we're walking into a scene of *Outbreak*." He slid a coy look at Roman. "I get it now, my friend. Totally get it."

Isa glanced to Roman and back. "I'm glad one of us does, because I'm obviously out of the loop."

"Nope, you're right smack in the middle, sweetheart."

Roman wanted to punch the grin off his friend's face. "We're wasting time standing here gabbing. We have a ten-hour flight to Anchorage and then at least another hour by puddle-jumper until we get to Beaver Ridge."

On the plane, Jaz commandeered one of the two couches, her feet kicked up as she flipped through a magazine, and Isa took a seat at the small conference table, her laptop and papers spread out around her.

"I'll tell the pilot we're ready to take off," Ryder announced before heading toward the front of the plane.

Roman's gaze drifted toward Isabel, but not before catching King's shit-eating smirk. He flipped him off and took the seat next to her. Almost immediately, she tensed, a far cry from the physical reaction she'd had to him back at his place.

"You don't think you've looked at all this information enough?" Roman risked asking. "I'd think you'd have it all memorized by now."

"I do, but there's always the chance that I missed something."

There was that second-guessing herself again. Roman didn't know what happened to feed into her self-doubt, but he could honestly say he wasn't sure he'd met anyone more capable of anything than her. Not that she'd believe him if he told her.

"There's something we need to talk about before we get to Beaver Ridge."

Isa pulled her brown eyes away from her computer. "I'm pretty sure we talked about everything we needed to talk about."

Roman shook his head. "Not this. Tony said things are escalating there, right?"

"More people are showing symptoms, which we expected to happen."

"Exactly, and as more people get sick, the fear factor rises. When people get scared, they do stupid shit."

"Spoken like a man who's seen that firsthand."

"I have. It's one of those things you can always count on happening."

Isa studied him through narrowed eyes. "That's a little pessimistic, don't you think?

"Maybe, but it's also reality. I'm bringing it up because we'll be hit with a lot of possible worst-case scenarios once we're wheels down—the patients, the community, and the possible assholes waiting in the wings."

Isa subtly bit the bottom corner of her lip. "That's a lot of worst-case scenarios."

"Which means you should use a few flight hours to catch some Z's . . . rest up for whichever scenario lies ahead."

"Do me a favor, Roman."

"Anything." And he meant it.

"Never coach a little league team. Your pep talks leave a little something to be desired." Her mouth twitched with the threat of a grin.

The sight of it conjured one of his own. "Noted."

They sat in awkward silence until Roman forced himself to his feet. "Work. Then rest."

She waved him off, ignoring him completely. By the time he made his way to where King sat sprawled in a chair, she'd already gotten lost in her computer.

King rested a hat over his face to make it look like he was sleeping, but Roman knew better. He kicked his boot with his own so he could take the seat across from him.

King chuckled. "That was fucking excruciating to watch. Did you completely lose your mojo with the opposite sex or what? It was worse than a teenage boy angling for his first hook-up."

"And if I were angling for another hook-up that could be a problem."

"Another?" King waggled his eyebrows. "Hot damn, you sly bastard. Banging the smart chick. You always were a ballsy son of a bitch."

On his way to prop his ankle on his knee, Roman swung his leg wide and nailed King in the shin.

He howled, laughing. "Fuck, man. You put steel tips on those boots?"

"Talk about Isabel like that again, and I'll kick you in the ass so you can find out."

Yeah, they'd fucked. Fast and hard. And he practically ached to be able to do it again, but he didn't want her just to get his rocks off, or even because it had been the best sex he'd ever had—which it was.

It had been great sex that didn't make him second-guess shit. He'd let himself enjoy being with her and didn't think about the usual crap that followed him around like the shadow from a bad horror movie.

Hell, he'd *snuggled* and gotten so comfortable he'd slept for nearly eight solid hours. That shit hadn't happened ever...even before Burundi.

"You know your lab friends are only one of a handful

of issues we could run into in this little town, right?" King stated. "Isolated borders. Possible quarantine if this virus thing gets out of hand. Fear—"

"Makes people go stupid. I just had this conversation with Isabel."

"You'll be okay with hauling her over your shoulder and dragging her ass out of there if we have to? Because she doesn't strike me as the type to just call it quits and walk away when there's people's lives on the line."

Roman had asked himself that same question, and he'd like to think he'd cart her away in a heartbeat. Hell, prior to walking into Tru Tech that first time, that's just what he would've done. Now he wasn't so sure.

After hearing her talk to her grandfather the other night, he knew how important it was for her not to fail the people of Beaver Ridge. If that meant keeping her in Alaska for as long as possible, he'd do whatever he had to do to make it happen.

* * *

The small puddle-jumper they got on in Anchorage shook with turbulence, jostling both the cargo in the back and the occupants up front. Isa's shoulder bumped into Roman's, and she sent him an apologetic smile, albeit a strained one. On the other side of her, Jaz groaned.

"Looking a little green there, Curva," Ryder quipped from the seat next to the pilot. He jiggled a bag of onion rings. "You sure you don't want something to put in your stomach?"

Jaz's unease had been the target for teasing for the last hour, and the only reason the Marine hadn't throttled him was because her hands were too busy white-knuckling the seat beneath her. "Get those damn things away from me, or you'll look black and blue."

King, sprawled out in the last row of seats, chuckled. "Don't know what your problem is. It's just a little plane ride."

"This isn't a plane. It's a folded-up piece of notebook paper. No offense, Roger," Jaz said to their local pilot just as they were hit with another big bump, this one emitting a faint groan of steel.

"None taken." Roger waved off Jaz's sentiment. "But you won't find a sturdier paper airplane this side of the mountain. I make sure this baby is tuned up and ready to go at all times. You picked good when you chose to use Sky's Ahoy."

Isa leaned forward in her seat, her arm brushing against Roman's. "Do you fly to Beaver Ridge often?"

"Depends on what you call often. There's a handful of us that make routine supply runs out here. Almost nothing from town isn't flown in. I would say one of us is making a trek out this way at least once a week, sometimes twice. This past week we've already made three trips with a fourth scheduled in two days. A hell of a lot of medication, by the looks of it."

Tony had already told her about the supplies he'd demanded from the GHO—IV kits and bagged fluids as well as meds like ibuprofen and acetaminophen to control the fevers that went with FC-5 infection. More than likely, they'd need to be replenished multiple times over before everything was said and done.

"Looks like we're just about there." Roger nodded toward the edge of the skyline and picked up his radio in preparation of their final approach.

As the plane crested the nearest mountaintop, Isa looked out the window. A vivid orange and pink sunset backdropped the snow-capped peaks. One rolling mountain staggered into another in an almost endless view of Alaskan wilderness, and right in the middle of it, nestled between a mountain base and a large crystalline lake, was Beaver Ridge.

Boats lined a small dock, and buildings, with varying shades of gray and brown roofs, looked like small, ant-sized structures.

Ryder peered out the window and whistled. "Doesn't that look cozy?"

"Nothing we didn't prepare for." Roman handed Isa her pack. His fingers brushed hers, sending a warm electrical zap up her arm that had nothing on the zing of his stare. "You're always to stay within two feet of either me, Jaz, or Ryder. No exceptions."

Behind them, King scoffed. "What am I? Chopped liver?"

Roman ignored his friend. "Me. Jaz. Or Ryder."

"That'll be difficult to do when I'm treating patients or working in the lab." Isa lifted her brow and dared him to argue.

"Doc—"

"It's not negotiable, Roman. None of you are trained to handle patients, and donning personal protective gear in this kind of setting isn't something you can *wing*. When each and every step isn't followed to the letter, accidents happen. Are you willing to risk the well-being of anyone here? Because I'm not."

It was a low blow, but she needed it to make her point, and judging by Roman's scowl, she'd achieved her goal.

By the time Roger landed, Isa was more than ready to get off the plane and get to work. Only so much planning could be done without seeing the town—and Tony—for herself, which meant everything else would have to be adapted on the fly.

A triage area. A clinic for the ill. A system for minimizing exposure risk to those who were still healthy. None of it could be determined until they knew for sure what they were dealing with, and as much as Isa hoped it wasn't FC-5, she also prayed it wasn't something new and equally as scary.

"Get me the hell out of here." Jaz stumbled over their legs to be the first one to deplane. By the time the rest of them followed, her color had returned to normal and she looked up and down the lake's rocky shoreline and into the mountains. "Wow. It's . . . gorgeous. Kinda hard to believe something as terrible as that virus is here."

"In my experiences so far, the places often hit by the worst things are often the most beautiful," Isa admitted. *And the most ill-prepared to deal with it.*

From what she understood from Tony, Beaver Ridge had what equaled an urgent care run by one doctor and nurse. No way would they be able to handle something like this alone.

In the distance, two golf carts zoomed down the shoreline, weaving around large rocks and washed-ashore branches.

"Everyone look alive." Roman stepped in front of her in an instant, his hand flying to the gun tucked under his shirt as the carts stopped on the other end of the dock. "Stay behind me, Doc."

Isabel recognized the hideous tan hunting jacket of the first driver, and quickly grabbed Roman's arm. "Easy, cowboy. It's Tony."

Her old mentor climbed off the first cart, his shock of white hair sticking out from his knit cap, and oversized parka adding a few additional inches to his slender frame. As Jaz and Isa approached, he tugged his sunglasses off his face and offered her a weary smile through his well-kempt beard.

"And I didn't think it possible you could get any more beautiful." Tony opened his arm and pulled her into a tight hug.

"I wish I could say the same to you." Isa noted the dark circles framing his blue eyes, and frowned. "Have you slept at all since you got here?"

"A little here and there."

"How many times have you told me that you need to take care of yourself in order to take care of others?"

"I knew the day would come where you'd eventually use my lessons against me." Tony squeezed her again before finally releasing his hold. "I'm sorry about this, Isa. If I thought anyone else could handle it I would've—"

She touched his arm. "No. You were right to call me.

Even if this isn't FC-5, it's dangerous enough it needs to be addressed. How long until the GHO gets here?"

"Truthfully? Your guess is as good as mine. As is their MO, they're dragging their feet to see what happens in the next few days." Tony's gaze strayed to Jaz and the now approaching Roman, King, and Ryder. "I'll be damned. You really did bring an entourage."

Isa made introductions, and it wasn't long before they piled their gear, supplies, and themselves into the two golf carts. Roman rode shotgun next to Tony with Jaz and Isa in the rear and Ryder and King in the second vehicle with the bulk of their stuff.

"As you can see, everything here is on a smaller scale." Tony navigated the micro roads of Beaver Ridge, giving an occasional friendly wave to curious onlookers walking the quaint streets. "Tight quarters. Close relationships. Everyone knows everyone else, and if someone sneezes, the person a few houses down can tell them bless you."

"This place is a virtual breeding ground for cross contamination," Isa replied, knowing he wasn't just giving them a rundown of Beaver Ridge life.

"Exactly." Tony slid her a quick look as he turned off the main street. "And it hasn't been easy getting these people to understand why they simply can't go about life as normal. Hell, until about an hour ago, the mayor still had them all prepping for the tourist season— which evidently makes this small idyllic Alaskan town come to life."

"*Tourists?*" Isa's thoughts immediately went to the nightmare that posed. "The last thing we need are visitors coming in and out of town and taking whatever this is home with them to the rest of their family and neighbors."

"I'm in complete agreement, which is why I beached myself on the mayor's front stoop at the crack of dawn and refused to budge until he agreed to push it back a week."

Jaz asked, "A week? Do you think this can be contained that fast?"

"No, I don't," Tony answered, grim-faced. "But as it turns out, the mayor is up for reelection, and he's afraid to upset the masses. Beaver Ridge residents rely on the money tourism brings in to get them through the rest of the year. If Old Joe doesn't take out hunting parties, or Kyle can't give ski lessons to college coeds, they don't eat a meal one day in June."

"Better to skip the meal than skipping the rest of your life," Jaz muttered.

Inciting panic wasn't something Isa wanted to do. It wasn't good for anyone and often created more problems than it solved, but no one ever died from instilling a healthy dose of urgency. "We'll keep trying to get through to them. We don't have much of a choice."

People walked in and out of small shops, some alone, and others in groups of twos and threes. More than one person wore a surgical mask, much like some people do in high-smog cities, but unfortunately, masks wouldn't do a damn thing against FC-5.

Even in the golf carts, they crossed town quickly, Tony driving them up a little farther up the mountain to where a small chain of cabins overlooked the town proper.

"Here's your home away from home." He stopped in front of largest one. A wraparound porch hugged the front, and big, arching windows reflected the last of the day's light. "It being the off-season means there were a lot of cabins to choose from. I nabbed this one for you because I figured you'd want to be closer to the clinic, which is literally about a hundred yards away down that hill. Plus it could accommodate the five of you pretty decently."

"This is great, Tony, thank you."

As they piled out of the carts, Roman's gaze fixed on the wooded area behind them. He'd been quiet all day, even for him, and had been since their not-quite-an-argument argument back at Steele Ops headquarters. Isa told herself it was silly to feel responsible for it, but she did.

Roman himself admitted that they wouldn't—and couldn't—happen. A relationship wasn't on his radar, and one with someone like him definitely wasn't on Isa's. And yet ever since she told him that she needed distance, he'd been broodier than normal.

It was probably a coincidence...but the part of her that had regretted saying it the moment the words left her mouth really hoped it wasn't.

"What's wrong?" Isa broke the moratorium on their silence and scanned the tree line looking for whatever he did.

"Just don't like how the cabin's out in the open like this."

"Isn't this better than being completely engulfed in the woods? It means we can see anyone coming from a long way off."

King grunted as he walked past them toward the cabin, a stack of boxes in his hands. "Also means they have a clear view of us, too. I'll pull out the perimeter alarms and start setting them up."

"Take Ryder with you." Roman nodded. "Jaz, I want you on the cabin. Make sure nothing and no one can sneak up without us having one hell of an advance warning."

Ryder hoisted an oversized bag onto his shoulder. "And what about the rest of the town? And the clinic?"

"We'll have to save that for tomorrow, when we have more daylight, and then kick our asses into gear."

Tony nervously glanced around as everyone immediately spread out to perform their designated tasks. "You really think the group that took the virus is here in Beaver Ridge?"

Roman didn't bat an eye as he answered, "If FC-5 is here, then I think it's probably a safe bet."

"And speaking of the virus." Isa turned to her mentor. "I'd like that tour of the clinic, and a look at any samples that you've taken from patients to date. If I get—"

"No," Roman growled at the same time Tony said, "I don't think that's a good idea."

"What? Why?" Isa bounced her ire between the two men in front of her. "The sooner I get started, the sooner—"

"No." Roman stared her dead in the eye, and with the

exception of the close quarters in the puddle-jumper, got the closest he'd been to her in hours. One deep breath and her chest would touch his.

It was all Isa could do to prevent herself from leaning closer, but then she focused on the fact that the man standing close wasn't the one who'd fucked her senseless and then held her afterward. The man glaring down at her was a growling Special Forces soldier prepping to dish out orders.

"Do you mind telling me why *no*?" Isa dared him.

"Because you were up all night preparing for today and had nearly twelve hours of flight time without so much as a five-minute rest. Now you want to walk into what you call a medical hot zone after not having slept a wink in the last thirty-six hours? Somehow I don't think that's a good idea."

Isa ground her teeth. "Is that your expert opinion?"

Without looking away from Isa, Roman asked, "Tony, can you tell me if that sounds like a solid idea to you . . . in your *expert* opinion?"

"Definitely not." Tony, the traitor, agreed with Roman. He lifted his shoulders in a shrug of apology when she shot him a look. "I'm sorry, Isa, but he's right. The clinic will be there tomorrow. I'll be able to hold down the fort with the volunteers, and I'll come to get you first thing in the morning."

Isa's annoyance bounced back and forth between the two men.

Despite the thirty-some-year age gap, they each wore the same determined expression. They wouldn't back down anytime soon, and she was just too damn exhausted to put up much more of a fight. "I don't like this joining forces thing you have going on."

Tony chuckled. "And I like the fact that I'm not alone in watching out for you while you look out for everyone else."

CHAPTER ELEVEN

7 years ago
Walter Reed Hospital
Bethesda, Maryland

"Did you turn in the last of your residency applications? I'm still debating whether or not I want to put surgery or obstetrics as my second choices." Lt. Samantha Barnes stepped into emergency room doctors' lounge and dropped heavily onto the couch. "Yoo-hoo. Barnes to Santiago. Do you come in, Santiago?"

"Sorry, what?" Isa blinked, suddenly realizing that her quiet reprieve from the steady flow of patients had ended with her friend's presence. She stuffed her phone into a pocket, telling herself that a watched screen never made someone call any faster. "No, I haven't. I still have time, so I'm going to see if I have a sudden epiphany as to which direction to go."

"You think Colonel Hardass, I mean, Harding, will let you pick anything except emergency medicine?" Sam cocked up a blond eyebrow.

"I think I want to make sure I pick the best fit and I'm not going to let him dictate the rest of my life." Isa pulled her cell phone out to check the screen again.

Nothing.

"Hey, are you okay?" Sam's smirk was replaced with a concerned frown. "You've seemed a little distracted the last week. What's up?"

"Nothing."

Her friend obviously didn't believe her. "Righhht."

"It's Olly. We had a fight the last time we spoke, and it's just been on my mind."

"Let me guess, he wants Navy blue linens on the wedding table and you want Army green?" Sam joked.

The fact that Isa and her fiancé served different military branches was often the source of good-natured ribbing among their medical class. The fact that he was a SEAL made it even worse. But she wished the argument had been tablecloths and color schemes. Instead, he'd accused her of not being invested in their relationship to the depth that she should be, which was completely ridiculous.

Except that it wasn't.

Not entirely.

They'd been high school sweethearts, and best friends before that. Everyone in their hometown joked that where one popped up, the other wasn't more than a step behind. Oliver Park was her path to an epic love story like that of her grandparents...or she'd always thought. After their engagement, things had suddenly changed.

Not much at first. Hugs felt a little awkward. Conversations took a bit more effort. Silences that had once been comfortable moments of reflection had turned to tension-filled concern. At first she blamed it on his deployments, his being sent overseas while she stayed behind finishing up her medical degree at the Uniformed Services University of the Health Sciences. She'd blamed it on the distance. The stress of school.

She'd blamed it on everything except where the fault should really be placed.

Herself.

And she hadn't heard from him in a week. Not a video chat, call, or email. Sam read her worry.

"So it's been a while since you've heard from Mr. Gorgeous," Sam said carefully. "But you've gone a while without hearing from him before. How often do they send his team out into the field?"

"No, you're right. Sometimes I don't hear from him in months. This time just feels different."

Sam squeezed her hand. "*That's* the stress of looming applications getting to you. Like you said, relax and wait for your epiphany. I'm sure it'll happen before you know it."

A sharp wail blared from the alert system, putting them both on their feet. In the hall, medical staff scattered, many dropping whatever they'd been doing. Isa and Sam jumped into the hall and looked around for their instructor. Isa found him barking orders to one of the few civilian nurses in the emergency room.

"Colonel Harding, sir?"

"Barnes, meet Tyson over at trauma door three. Santiago, with me. We were just notified that there's been a shooting at the festival a few blocks away. We have at least a dozen victims heading our way. When I say jump, jump. Don't ask questions. Just do it."

"Yes, sir." Samantha gave Isa nod of support before taking off toward the trauma bay.

Isa stayed hot on Harding's heels, her heart pumping loudly in her ears as they donned personal protective gear in preparation for receiving the first patient, but when the first ambulance pulled up, a grim-faced medic jumped out, shaking her head.

"We lost him en route. He's been down fifteen," the medic said.

Harding nodded, seemingly unfazed. Having worked in frontline field medicine, there probably wasn't a whole lot that the doctor hadn't seen. "Unload him and get the ambo out of here. We need to make room for the next patient."

The EMT quickly hustled to do just that, and as the second the ambulance pulled away, another took its place. The back doors burst open.

"Santiago," Harding barked. They jumped into action, helping the EMT unload the young woman, an Air Force lieutenant, judging by the emblem on her uniform.

"I counted four shots, only two with exit points," the EMT quickly rattled off. "Blood pressure eighty over forty-three and quickly dropping. Heart rate one forty-two and rising."

"She's losing blood and fast." Harding directed them into the first hybrid trauma bay, where a nurse immediately began cutting away the patient's uniform. "We need O-negative hung, and let's get some pressers on board. Santiago, grab the surg kit. We need to clamp off whatever arteries have been hit, and we need to do it now."

"We're not taking her to the OR?" Isa's hands reflexively did as asked.

"She'll die in the elevator if we do. Hell, I'm surprised she's not already gone. Locate and clamp first, *then* we'll transfer."

"Her son's the reason she's still with us," the EMT said, hanging back and letting the X-ray tech into the room.

"Son?" Isa asked.

The paramedic nodded. "He's in another ambo with a little brother."

"Is he okay?"

"Mostly scratches, and maybe a dislocated shoulder from getting jostled in the panicked crowd. Still, even with all hell breaking lose, the kid had the presence of mind to rip off his and his brother's jackets and stanch the worst of the wounds. *Ten years old.*"

Isa wanted to be sick, but there wasn't time.

"Scan's done." The X-ray tech stepped back, the image immediately blinking to life on the screen.

"Yep," Harding nodded, already ripping open a surgical kit and handing it to her before opening one for himself. "Four wounds. Shoulder, chest, abdomen, and leg. Two bullets still inside and a whole lot of blood. We're tag-teaming this one, Santiago. Where do you think the bleeders are?"

"Abdomen and leg," Isa said, quickly scanning the woman's body. "The abdomen's probably the lower aorta and the leg...femoral artery."

"Correct. You get the leg. Locate the issue. Clamp it. All done until we get her upstairs. Got it?" The attending looked at her from the other side of their patient.

"Got it." And she did.

Her hands didn't shake once as she laid her scalpel to the lieutenant's upper thigh. Harding worked on piecing together the aorta and walked her step-by-step through her own task. For a minute, the nurse eyeing the vitals called out an improving blood pressure, and Isa felt hopeful...right until Harding cursed.

"Aorta's shredded." He cursed again seconds before the monitor alarms blared again. "How's that leg coming, Santiago?"

"Done, sir. Clamped and ready."

"Good, now get your hands in here."

Isa and Harding worked to repair the damage. Blood poured out from the aorta, making their task to clamp off the holes that much harder. By the time it slowed, the sound of the screaming monitors ice-picked their way through Isa's head.

She'd barely registered Harding's words and the reason for the slowing blood flow until a nearby nurse gently rested her hand on her shoulder. The blood flow stopped because the patient didn't have any more flowing through her veins.

"Time of death," Harding growled, "eight-oh-two."

Isa blinked through the shock, struggling to make sense of everything that just happened.

"Colonel Harding, sir." A civilian nurse stuck her head into the room and grimaced seeing the tech flip off the now silent monitors. "Her sons are here in room three. The father's on his way, but he's not here yet."

"I'll—"

"I'll go sit with them," Isa heard herself volunteer

before turning toward her CO. "If you don't mind, sir, I'll clean up and go sit with the kids until their father gets here."

He paused, seeming to think about it before nodding. "Have someone come and get me when he does. We'll tell them together."

"Yes, sir."

An hour later, with a four-year-old on her lap and a brave ten-year-old tucked into her side, Isa knew that her epiphany had come to her at the expense of a young Air Force lieutenant. No way could she handle that kind of loss again. Her heart broke in half as she watched the father pull his children into his arms, all three of them sobbing.

As she slowly trudged back to the lounge, more than ready to finally submit the paperwork that would hopefully send her into research medicine instead of bedside, one of the nurses came up to her.

"Isabel. You left your phone. Someone's been trying to get hold of you." Nicki handed Isa her own phone, which she'd left sitting on the lounge table.

"Thank you." Isa hurried into the empty room just as it alerted with an incoming Facetime. Tears pouring down her face, Isa swiped to open the call and apologize to Olly for everything she'd done and the way that she'd acted. "Olly, I'm—"

"Isa."

Pausing, she looked at the face that was definitely not Olly's.

Isaac Peters, his unit's team leader and Olly's best friend, stared back at her, his face dirtied and bruised...and not the least bit happy. "Isabel, I...I don't know how to say this, but..."

"No..." Isabel shook her head, both unwilling and unable to hear the words. Her knees buckled, dropping her onto the couch. "No."

"Isa, I'm sorry. He's gone. Olly's...gone."

* * *

Soul-wrenching sobs dragged Isa from her sleep.

She strained to hear where the noise had come from and flipped over, shoving her hair away from her face when her fingers came back wet. It had been her, and as brief snippets of her dream slipped back into her consciousness, she realized it hadn't been a dream, or a nightmare.

It had been a memory—the worst day of her life, and the last day of Oliver's.

It wasn't that long ago that she'd mentally replay that day every time she sat still for longer than a few minutes. Then, it visited only when she slept. The last time had been on the anniversary of Olly's death. The fact that it returned on the eve she dove back into bedside medicine made sense.

Unfortunately.

Isa sat up and blew out a heavy breath when someone knocked on the door.

"Doc? You good in there?" Roman asked from the other side.

"Yeah. No." Crap. *How loud had she been?* Padding barefoot across the room, she patted her cheeks dry, and then opened the door to a fully dressed Roman. "You weren't sleeping?"

"I told King to get some shut-eye while I took the late watch." He studied her with his intense, critical gaze. "Sounded like you were having a nightmare."

"I wish it was just a nightmare," Isa muttered under her breath.

She left the door open in an invitation to come inside. Roman did, although reluctantly, closing the door behind him. This was the first time in days they'd been alone without the threat of someone eavesdropping on the conversation, and as much as Isa knew it wasn't a good idea, she couldn't tell him to leave.

She didn't *want* him to leave. The only problem was that she didn't know what she *did* want.

Being near Roman somehow calmed her emotions and hurtled them in all directions at the same time.

"If you want to talk, I'm here." Roman leaned against the small dresser tucked against the far wall, directly across from where she sat on the bed. "If you want me gone, I'll go."

She couldn't bring herself to say anything, and after a while, he shifted to leave.

"No, stay. I . . ." Isa dropped her head onto her hands with a heavy sigh. "I don't know anything anymore. Have you ever got caught in that sticky in-between where you want two things, on far ends of the spectrum, and you don't know which way to lean?"

"All the damn time."

She believed it. As much as opening a part of herself to Roman would do the exact opposite of keeping him at arm's length, she also longed for the understanding that she knew he'd give her. Or maybe he'd give her a swift kick in the ass. She'd benefit from either, and whichever reaction she got from him, she'd know it was honest.

Roman didn't talk. He didn't push. He simply stood there and waited...and Isa appreciated it.

"You asked once before back at headquarters why I second-guess myself, and the answer is because I'd once had every intention of being a bedside doctor. I'd been days away from declaring my residency when I lost a patient." Isa took a deep breath and tugged her eyes away from her hands to brave a look at Roman "A young mom. An Air Force lieutenant. She wasn't the first person I'd lost in the course of my career, but everything about it had felt different. She literally died with her blood on my hands."

"But you're not the one who put her there."

She played with the edge of the blanket to distract her shaking fingers. "No. But I'm the one who couldn't bring her back to her family. And after I'd finished telling two little boys and a devastated husband that she wasn't coming home, I got the news that neither was my fiancé. So yeah. I'm more than a little nervous about tomorrow. They say history has a way of repeating itself for a reason."

The rustle of clothing had her looking up just as Roman crouched in front of her. His hand slid over hers, gently stilling her fidgeting fingers. "I'm not telling you this will be a cakewalk. There isn't a doubt in my mind that you wouldn't call me out on that lie if I tried.

But you're not on this walk alone. You have everyone here in Alaska. You have everyone back home. You have your family. Your friends. Your smarts and your determination...and me."

Isa tried not reading into his words. It didn't take a genius to tell she was a hairbreadth away from dropping some serious tears, and Roman being Roman, he was probably allergic to the sight. He'd do or say anything to ensure they didn't make an appearance.

Except when she looked into his eyes, she had a difficult time not falling into their depths. A mixture of sincerity and concern stared back at her, and it took down nearly all her defenses.

Her hand beneath his flexed, fingers reflexively entwining with his. "Will you stay here tonight? I'm not asking for anything. I just...want to be near someone."

Near *him*.

She knew that if it had been Jaz or Ryder in front of her right now, she wouldn't be making the same request...but she couldn't bring herself to think about that right then.

Roman didn't say yes or no. He stood, shrugging out of his weapons holster, and as Isa slid beneath the covers and finished settling into her pillow, Roman tucked the blanket around her body and climbed in next to her.

Isa couldn't help but chuckle. "You need a physical barrier to lie in bed with me?"

He grunted against the top of her head as he pulled her close. "Doc, I need a six foot-thick cement fucking wall—and a miracle—to lie in a bed with you and keep it G-rated."

But he did. In minutes, his rhythmic breathing brushed against her hair. He'd fallen asleep, but Isa's mind, still running through tomorrow's events, had her burrowing her cheek against his chest.

His scent of spice and musk soothed her rampant thoughts. Tomorrow, there wouldn't be time to think about much less take advantage of moments like these so she soaked in her fill now and eventually fell asleep to the steady, strong pound of Roman's heartbeat beneath her ear.

* * *

Roman needed a fucking vat of coffee despite having slept like a damn rock—once again with his arms wrapped around Isabel. He didn't even have intense, marathon sex to blame for it. All their clothes had remained on, the only skin-on-skin contact having been his hand on the curve of her hip thanks to her kicking the covers aside at some point in the night... and he still wished he was in that same position.

He'd reluctantly slipped away at the crack of dawn, walking the town's perimeter with Ryder to suss out the most vulnerable areas, and as expected, there were a lot of them. Mounting cameras along the Beaver Ridge border would only get them so far.

In no mood for any more obstacles before having another gallon of coffee, Roman nearly growled as he approached the cabin. King stood on the front porch, arms folded as he glared into the woods much like he had the previous day.

"I don't fucking like this," King said in lieu of a greeting. "As small as this place is, it's more exposed than we anticipated. This is even more of a gamble than *I* usually like."

"Do you have anything optimistic to say?"

"Dishing out optimism is your MO, my friend. Wouldn't want to encroach on your territory," King said sarcastically, and turned to him expectantly. "But seriously. You storing any brilliant ideas in that head of yours you haven't told me about?"

"Other than making sure Isabel's safe and no one gets shot in the process? No. Not really." Bracing his hands on the railing, Roman shifted his gaze from the woods to the back of the clinic doors a few hundred feet away. "There's nothing we can do to change the status quo right now. Isabel will find out if we're actually dealing with FC-5—and our asshole friends—and then we'll go from there. Redistribute and regroup."

Behind them, the cabin door opened. Jaz and Isa stepped onto the porch.

"Clinic time already?" Roman asked.

Isabel nodded. "Tony's meeting me there. We'll take a quick look at today's incoming patients, and then we'll head over to the school. Er, hospital. School-turned-hospital."

They'd already been hit with that info a few hours ago. An increasing number of patients had meant relocating the sick to a larger venue, and without a local hospital, the next largest building able to handle the load—and the need for infection control—was the school.

"Jaz takes the clinic's front entrance. Ryder has the rear. King and I will go ahead to the school and make sure it's secure prior to your arrival. If you see something you don't like, say something." Roman locked Isa in a stern glare. "And all plans get halted until we're in the clear again."

Isa folded her arms across her chest. "Why do I get the distinct feeling you're trying to tell me something?"

"Because I am. Your being here hinges on us being able to keep you safe. If that safety becomes compromised, and we tell you to hide in the bathroom for six hours with only your stethoscope for company, then that's what you'll do. You drop what you're doing. You run. And you hide."

"And what will you be doing?"

"Kicking someone's ass."

Roman's comment earned him three hell yeahs from the rest of the team, but Isa didn't look the least bit impressed, compressing her mouth into a tight line.

"Jaz. Ryder. Go ahead and secure the clinic. King, I'll catch up with you after I grab some coffee." Roman urged them all to go...except for Isabel.

Chuckling, King picked up his gear bag and tossed it over his shoulder. "Looks like we've been dismissed, boys and gir—uh, deadly sniper. Let's get to it."

"Nice save there, King." Jaz pushed by the larger man with a roll of her eyes. "Guess you're smarter than you look."

Roman waited until everyone was out of earshot before turning back to Isa.

"Is this where you dish out your warnings? *Again?*"

Isa waited expectedly. "If you recite them so frequently, you should think about recording them. If not, invest in some throat lozenges."

"Depends. Is any of it sinking in?"

"Stay alert. Report suspicious activity. Don't wander. Rest. Hydrate. And—"

"Breathe," Roman finished her sentence. Stepping close, his boots bumped into hers as he cupped her cheek and angled her gaze toward his. "And remember you're not walking into this alone."

Isabel's hands, resting on his hips, slid up his torso and around his back. He tried convincing himself to step away, but she had other plans, her fingers caressing the back of his shirt. Her gaze dropped to his mouth, her little pink tongue flicking out to wet her bottom lip.

Their determination to keep their hands to themselves shattered.

Isa's tongue slipped alongside his. On contact, she emitted a breathy groan. Wanting to hear it again, he walked them back against the porch railing and used it as an anchor, crushing his body against hers.

The days since he'd last had her suddenly felt like forever. It felt like too much and yet not enough. It overwhelmed his senses until he forgot they stood out in the open where anyone with eyes—or a rifle scope— could see them.

With a reluctant groan, he dragged his mouth away and reveled in the sound of Isabel's displeased growl. "And we were doing so well with that distance thing."

"But were we really? Because I don't know about

you, Doc, but it didn't keep me from picturing you naked and under me a million times a fucking day."

With a resigned chuckle, Isabel dropped her head onto his chest. "And here I thought it was just me."

"Not just you, babe."

Her big brown eyes looked up into his, and he immediately wanted to kiss her again.

"So what does that mean?" Isabel asked, her voice unsure.

Hell if he knew, but they didn't have time to read too much into it now. "It means we're screwed. Metaphorically and literally."

Isabel laughed, the melodic sound pulling a chuckle from his throat. And once he released it, it was followed by another. And another. The chuckles kept coming from them both until they both stood on the porch of the cabin, tears slipping down their cheeks.

Roman couldn't remember the last time he'd laughed, and he had a sneaking, underlying suspicion if it wasn't for the woman in front of him, it would've been even longer.

CHAPTER TWELVE

Bedside medicine challenged Isa right down to her very core, and not just physically. It was emotionally draining. They'd started at the clinic where parents, worried over their little one's sniffle or cough, flocked to the neighborhood doctor's office. The staff there triaged the huge influx of patients as best they could, making sure they were either sent to the makeshift hospital for closer examination or sent home to rest and recuperate.

In the few hours Isa and Tony had been at the school, the clinic had sent over four more potential cases...and yet it could've been so much worse if this virus were airborne. Isa was glad that wasn't the case, but also was more fearful that it meant they could be dealing with FC-5.

Once they figured out what this was, education would have to be a priority. People needed to know tried and true methods to protect themselves and their families, because even though surgical masks were a good idea with flu outbreaks and the containment of RSV, they didn't do a damn thing against hemorrhagic diseases.

"Isa." Tony, gowned head to toe in a suit not unlike those worn by healthcare workers in the 2014 Ebola outbreak, nodded toward the second staged ward of sick patients.

In the short time he'd been in Beaver Ridge, he'd done an amazing job setting up the school to suit their needs, triaging patients into separate rooms based on the severity of their symptoms. They'd been through the first two rooms—with about five patients each—for the better part of the morning, assisting the care volunteers and taking new batches of blood samples. Now it was time to do the same to zone 3—the sicker of the Beaver Ridge residents, and Isa knew from reading Tony's reports that it was also the largest group.

It made sense medically speaking because FC-5— unlike Ebola—was contagious even when the patient showed no physical symptoms. That's what made it so deadly. With no obvious illness, people go about their normal daily routine.

Lovers have sex without protection. Mothers and fathers change diapers without gloves. Children share snacks out of each other's lunch boxes, which were made with love—and possible germs—of an infected parent or caregiver. In close communities like Beaver Ridge, it didn't take long for entire families to fall ill, quickly, and one right after the other.

"You ready?" From behind his hood, Tony's blue eyes studied her so as to make sure she wasn't about to lie to him.

"Let's go." Isa braced herself to leave the locker room, which was being used as a clean holding room.

His gloved hand dropped on her arm. "I can make rounds by myself if you want to go take a rest. We have more volunteers manning zone three than we do the other units, so I'll be fine."

Always out to protect her. She shook her head. "There's more volunteers in there because there's more patients. I'm fine. It'll go quicker with the two of us."

And not to mention that the sooner they collected all of the samples, the sooner she could leave the patient care area and get those samples under a slide.

Tony looked like he wanted to argue, but he didn't. Nodding, he opened the door, and the scene in front of Isa took her breath away.

What was once a gymnasium had been transformed into an emergency shelter with medical equipment. At least sixteen cots filled the room, twelve of which were occupied. Intravenous lines hung from IV poles and, in some cases, coat racks, which made administering medications and fluids a lot easier.

In most hemorrhagic diseases, the deadly culprit wasn't the actual virus itself; it was what the virus did to the body. It damaged vital organs and disrupted the body's routine response and coping mechanisms for dealing with a foreign invasion. This meant fevers spiking to dangerous, seizure-inducing levels. It meant blood serums that didn't clot, or that clotted in organs unable to handle the increased load.

In dealing with hemorrhagic diseases, the goal was to keep the patient alive long enough for the virus to eventually wear out its welcome, and that outcome was a lot harder to achieve in the elderly, the young, and the immunocompromised.

"Tag team or splinter off?" Tony asked.

Isa took a deep breath and temporarily fogged her hood. "We can help more people if we splinter apart. Let's start at the far end and work our way inside."

"Sounds like a plan. And hey." He flashed her a wink. "Easy does it."

For the next four hours, Isa worked directly with one of the volunteers. Hopping from patient to patient, she performed and documented assessments. She drew blood. And with each person she spoke to, it got harder and harder to remain emotionally detached.

Maybe it was the exhaustion.

Maybe it was the people.

Maybe it was her.

By the time she reached her second-to-last cot, Isa was a half conversation away from bursting into tears.

"You okay, Dr. Santiago?" Marie, her assistant, stayed close. A first-year college student who had just happened to be visiting her family while on break, Marie handed her the audible stethoscope that would allow her to hear her patient's heart and lung sounds.

"I'm good." She smiled at the mother and small toddler sitting on the cot in front of her, worry and exhaustion on both their faces. Kneeling down to the child's level, Isa kept her voice light. "And who do we have here?"

"I'm Beth." The mother rubbed her daughter's back. "And this is Abby. She's two."

"Hello there, Abby-who's-two. I'm Isa-who's-a-lot-older-than-that." She gently brushed her gloved finger along the little girl's foot and immediately got a cringe in return. "I know this big ol' suit probably looks scary to you, but I promise I'm not that scary under here. Do you like balloons? Do you want to hold one for me while I take a listen to your heart?"

Abby nibbled her bottom lip, deep in reflection, before she finally nodded.

"Marie, can you hand me one of the purple gloves?"

The young girl handed her a purple nitrile glove. Using the spare portable oxygen tank on her hip, Isa blew it up until all five fingers wiggled. She drew a silly face on it before dancing it toward a curious Abby. "You'll have to think up a name for him, okay? And if you're a good girl for me, we'll make him a dance partner when we're all done. Would you like that?"

Abby stole a quick glance at her mom before tentatively reaching out for the wiggling glove, and as Isa hoped, it distracted the little girl long enough for her to slide the audible stethoscope around her back.

"How has she been doing?" Isa asked Beth as she turned off the machine and handed it back to Marie.

"She's not eating much, and she's slowed down on her drinking... even the juice."

Isa nodded and reached out to rub the small girl's back. "That's understandable. Your throat's pretty sore, huh, sweetie?"

Hugging her new friend, Abby nodded.

Isa kept wave of tears at bay as she stood, addressing both Marie and Abby's mom. "I'll have someone bring some electrolyte popsicles. It'll help restore lost fluids and also ease her throat."

"This isn't just the flu, is it?" Beth's voice was thick with tears.

"No, it's not. But we're doing everything in our power to figure out exactly what it is, and how we can help you. Okay?"

It wasn't enough—by a long shot. But Beth nodded, looking the smallest bit relieved.

With her mom's encouraging words, Abby was a brave little trooper through her blood draw, which was an expected challenge due to slight dehydration.

"If those popsicles don't come in ten minutes, ask one of the volunteers, okay?" Isa stood up, already mentally preparing herself for the next patient.

Beth's hand snaked out, squeezing Isa's fingers... hard. "Thank you, doctor," she sniffled. "Thank you so much."

Isa nodded, unable to form words. Thankfully, while she'd been handling Abby, Tony had seen to the last patient and waited for her near the rear exit. Even with his gear on, he looked as tired as she felt.

"You okay, kiddo?" he asked.

"Nothing about this is okay...even if this isn't FC-5. No one should worry if the kiss they gave their children the day before will be the last."

An hour and a hazmat suit change later, it was confirmed.

They *all* needed to worry...because FC-5 found its way to Beaver Ridge, Alaska, and unlike the men who'd already tried to nab Isa once, it would make sure it didn't leave any prisoners behind.

* * *

After being up since before the crack of dawn and setting up game cameras along the town's perimeter, Roman was more than ready for a shower, food, and some shut-eye. Not necessarily in that order. Sinking onto the couch, he groaned. The four hours he had before relieving Ryder at his post on the lakefront would come way too fucking fast.

He was dead on his feet, his stump protesting the excessive use of his prosthesis. He'd no sooner leaned over to tug off his shoes than Isa and Jaz, who'd been on clinic duty, came through the door with a grim-faced Tony on their heels.

"You're just getting in?" Roman tossed an annoyed glare at Jaz before sliding it to Isabel. "You've been up and moving just as long as I have. What the hell happened to taking care of yourself first?"

"Hello to you, too, dear. My day was just *great*. How was yours?" Isa's edgy tone contrasted with her look of physical exhaustion.

There wasn't a single sign of the nervous but hopeful woman who'd left the cabin that morning. Instead, Isa sunk into the chair across from him as if the weight of the world had dropped onto her shoulders.

"What's wrong?" he asked.

"What *isn't* wrong would probably be the shorter list. It's FC-5. Here. In Beaver Ridge."

Fuckin' A.

Even though they knew this was a possibility, it took an extra moment for Roman to wrap his head around the news. "How many?"

"Twenty-four at last count, but more come into the

clinic every day. And they range from two years old to eighty-one." Isa's lips quivered seconds before she steeled her jaw. "*Two years old*, Roman. Those bastards unleashed this virus knowing innocent people would get hurt."

Jaz leaned against the back of the couch. "I know we talked about this before, but what are the chances FC-5 showed up here on its own?"

Tony was already shaking his head. "Nil. The handful of FC-5 outbreaks that have happened since its discovery have always been locations with a significantly higher median temperature. If it's in Alaska, it had help."

"So how did it get here?" Roman thought aloud.

"Isa's practically the only person on this hemisphere who's properly trained on what to do with this virus, right?" Jaz tossed out. "Maybe one of the bastards got infected in the lab theft...or in however they've handled it since. That would definitely be karma coming back to bite them on the ass."

Isa rubbed her temples as if staving off a brewing headache. "It would, but it's not that, either. Blood and body fluids are the main modes of transmission from person to person. Even if one of the guys from the lab calls Beaver Ridge home, we wouldn't see *this* kind of a spread in a short period of time. There are people in the hospital who have no real connection other than they live in the same town."

Roman nodded. It made sense. "So how did FC-5 pop up those other times?"

"Like most other hemorrhagic diseases...a transmission from animal to human. Usually when people digest contaminated..." Isa jumped to her feet, all her earlier exhaustion gone. "It's the meat. Tony, call Mayor Rutledge. We've got to get everyone in Beaver Ridge to toss out any beef products that they may have in their fridge *right now*."

With a curse, Tony yanked his phone out of his pocket and rushed into the other room, his fingers immediately dialing.

"What the fuck am I missing here?" Roman asked.

Isa's face went ashen. "Ebola. Marburg. An outbreak nearly always starts from a tainted food source. Beaver Ridge gets food *flown* in—according to Roger the pilot—at least twice a week. It makes sense. Everyone in that hospital *does* have one thing in common. They rely on supplies that are brought into town. It's why there's so many sick in such a short period of time. They became infected roughly around the same time. Hell, they were infected while they ate their damn dinner!"

"These bastards really did do this on purpose." White hot fury burned through Roman's veins.

"Why here?" Jaz asked. "If it's to terrorize people, why not do it in a bigger city? More bang. More of a show."

"Because this is the pregame," Roman admitted. "This is either the precursor to a bigger venue, or someone's idea of a deadly show-and-tell. Either way, it means that this isn't stopping at Beaver Ridge. These guys will either do the deed themselves, or they'll sell FC-5 to someone who will."

Tony returned, stuffing his cell back into his pocket. "Rutledge wasn't happy about this to say the least, but he's calling a town meeting."

"When?" Isa asked.

"Tonight."

It was Roman's turn to get on the phone. "I'm bringing in Ryder and King from their posts because we'll need all hands on deck at that meeting."

"I'm not arguing, but why?"

"Because frightened people tend to do stupid things...and we're about to throw fuel onto their worst nightmares."

CHAPTER
THIRTEEN

It was the ground beef. Isa confirmed the transmission route with an hour to spare before the town hall. And as a testament to everyone's concerns, nearly the whole town, other than those in quarantine, were in attendance.

It was standing room only at the Beaver Ridge Community Center. Education and information would be everyone's friend and hopefully stave off panic-induced reactions—or moments of violence. Just in case, Roman, Jaz, King, and Ryder were all present, the last two hovering in the rear of the room.

Jaz stayed relatively close to Tony, which left Roman as Isa's living shadow.

His face a blank mask, it was hard to guess what he was thinking as he scanned the crowd.

"Do you think you could stop glaring like you expect one of them to pull a gun out on you or something?" Isa mumbled under her breath, but loud enough for him to hear. "The point of this town hall is to put people at *ease*. Everything about you right now screams 'Make my day.'"

"Better to be standoffish and alive than at ease and dead."

Isa shot him a glare. "You're not making this any better."

This time, Roman gave her his full attention. He stepped close. Only inches separated them as his gaze lasered into hers. "My job right now is to make this *safe*...for you, for them, for everyone. If that means I have to employ a few intimidation tactics to keep people in line, then that's what I'll do. While Tony is up there talking, I want you to unobtrusively scan the room."

"Scan the room? Why?"

"In case our assholes decided to get their kicks by coming out and watching the panic they've caused firsthand."

A sick feeling settled in Isa's stomach, and she couldn't help but shoot a quick glance at the growing crowd. "I wouldn't be able to identify any of them in a lineup. Not unless I got uncomfortably close, stared into their eyes, and had them talk. And only then, maybe."

"Don't tempt me to try it, Doc, because I will."

Mayor Rutledge took the podium and called for everyone's attention. Amazingly enough, the rumbles of conversations died down.

"I thank everyone for being here," Rutledge said to the room. "I know you all have questions and concerns, and I promise you we'll give you the answers you need. Doctors Isabel Santiago and Tony Winter assure me we're not leaving here tonight until every single one of them is answered. I do request that you be respectful and allow them to speak with as few interruptions as possible."

Tony nodded at the mayor and took his place. The first order of business was to make sure everyone handed over their beef products, and Tony was able to affirm that finding the source of the outbreak was the biggest hurdle. It didn't seem to appease the majority in the room.

Dozens of people called out medical questions about the virus itself, and Tony glanced to Isa in a silent plea for assistance. She took his place at the podium and fought to keep her voice calm in the rising tension.

"I've already met some of you, and for those I haven't, I'm Isabel Santiago, and I'm a virologist who has experience with FC-5... which is the virus responsible for making your neighbors ill."

"Is it like the flu?" someone called out.

"Or that other thing? The one people get on cruise ships?" someone else shouted.

"No. FC-5 is nothing like influenza, or any other virus that's ever shown up here in the United States." Isa's voice wavered, forcing her to take a deep breath. "At no point during this meeting will I, or Tony, ever lie to you. Knowledge—and cooperation—are the only ways we're beating this thing."

"We were told to turn over our meat and fresh produce," a man standing in the back interjected. "Why?"

"Because we believe the instigating source came in the form of your fresh beef product."

People roared, some standing, while others whispered to their neighbors in panic. Isa came out from behind the podium, her hands raised in an attempt to calm them down. From the corner of her eye, she could

see Roman shifting, his hand moving toward his hip—
and his gun.

She shook her head at him and addressed the people.
"I want to stress that *not all* beef product was tainted!
But, in an abundance of caution, we want everyone to
turn over whatever grocery items you have that did not
come to you in a sealed canister or tin can. We know
how FC-5 got here, so now it's up to us to contain it."

"And how do we do that?" someone bellowed.

"Are we even safe being here?" another shouted. "I
mean, how the hell did it get into our food in the
first place?"

Question after question fired from around the room
as fear grabbed hold. The situation was quickly spiral-
ing out of control, and in the left back corner, Ryder
jumped in between two men who looked seconds from
coming to blows.

A loud whistle ripped through the room.

Roman stepped forward, his stern glare in full force
and aimed out at the crowd. "You all don't know anything about FC-5." He pointed to Isa. "And this woman
knows *everything*. If you have questions, then pipe down
and wait for her to give you the damn answers."

Amazingly, the people quieted. When the last whisper echoed, Roman turned to Isa with a slight nod.
"Doc. Continue."

"To answer those first questions...FC-5 isn't trans-
mitted like the flu. You can't get it by a cough, or a sneeze,
or simply giving your child a hug at night. The virus
remains in body fluid—blood, urine, feces, sperm. For
us, this is a good thing. This is a *controllable* thing."

"People have been careful when we thought it was a flu outbreak," an older woman, somewhere in her mid-seventies, said. "And then when your doctor friend got here, he made all these changes, shut down the school and turned it into a hospital, and yet people are still getting sick. Why?"

Unwilling to keep a barrier between her and the people they were there trying to help, Isa stepped off the raised platform. "Because unfortunately, an infected person can be contagious without showing any outward physical signs."

"So people in this room may have this FC thing and not even know it?"

"Truthfully? Yes. *But*"—Isa raised her hands when voices started to rise—"I need you to remember there is *no risk* to you from casual contact. We're passing out flyers right now that highlight everything you need to know about FC-5 and how we're dealing with it, including what to do if you feel you or someone in your household has exhibited symptoms."

"How do you cure it?" an older man from the front corner row asked.

Isa reminded herself she promised them she wouldn't lie. "There isn't a cure as of right now, but it's something myself and my lab have been in search of for the last few years. Like other viruses, our best course of action is to treat the symptoms. Hydration. Fever reduction. In some rare cases, blood transfusions."

"And how can we handle something like that? We don't have the medical personnel here in town for that."

Tony interjected, "Fair question, and you're right.

Beaver Ridge isn't equipped to handle an outbreak like this, but the Global Health Organization is, and I've already been in touch with them. They're mobilizing a team as we speak. Soon, the town will have all the resources—people and medicine—that we need."

"You didn't answer the other question, Dr. Santiago," one of the first hecklers interjected. "How and why did this virus end up with our meat products?"

"We believe it was put there on purpose," Isa stated truthfully. "We think Beaver Ridge's seclusion, and the fact that it relies heavily on outside resources, made it the perfect target for people who stole the FC-5 virus from my lab."

A hum went through the crowd as they talked among themselves.

Roman came up next to her and whistled, gaining their attention once again. "This brings up another matter that everyone here needs to be aware of and that involves the people responsible for this outbreak. We have every reason to believe that they're going to want to stick close by so that they can view the fruit of their handiwork. You're a close-knit community. You know each other. Isabel, Tony, and my team need your help in identifying anyone who may not belong...but I cannot stress this enough...*you do not act*. You do *not* play hero or intervene in any way. These men didn't hesitate in poisoning your town. They won't hesitate to do more if given the chance. If you see something out of the norm, you contact that number on the flyer Dr. Santiago mentioned. And then you keep yourself and your family safe."

The more information the people of Beaver Ridge were given, the calmer the crowd became. Isa didn't know if it was increased knowledge or from shock, but by the time they opened up the floor to questions, she and Tony had no problems answering them.

After two hours, Isa was physically, emotionally, and mentally drained.

"Dr. Santiago?" The older woman who had asked one of the first questions came up to her while everyone filed out of the community center. "I just want to thank you . . . for being here and for what you did at the hospital."

Guilt washed over Isa at the older woman's words. "Please don't thank me."

Her expertise wouldn't be needed if she'd stopped those men from stealing the virus in the first place.

"Well, I am. If it hadn't been for you and Dr. Winter caring enough about Beaver Ridge to come here and investigate, there's no telling what would happen to our community by the time health officials rolled into town." The older woman flashed a watery smile. "And my granddaughter, Beth, tells me that because of you and your miracle popsicles, my great-granddaughter's getting a little stronger each hour."

A ghost of a smile slipped onto Isa's face as she thought about the little toddler. "I think her hereditary strength is more likely the reason she's getting a little better."

"Whatever the reason, thank you." The woman squeezed Isa's hand and filed out with the rest of the Beaver Ridge residents.

Isa stood and watched them go, more than a little amazed at how well they faced the news. More than a handful, including the two men who Ryder prevented from punching each other, volunteered their time and services in patrolling the town. Off to the left, Roman and King spoke with a few more, getting their contact information and already devising a plan.

Jaz saddled up next to her. "I think that went pretty well, all things considered."

Isa nodded. "It definitely could've been worse."

"So what's next?"

"First? Sleep. And then we do everything we did today all over again and hope something works."

* * *

King stomped into the cabin, only his eyes visible through the layers of clothing. "It's colder than a witch's tit out there, man. When all this is over, remind me to spend a week in Florida. Or the Bahamas."

"Anything out of the norm out there?" Roman leaned closer to the laptop, inspecting each of the feeds from the hunting cams. "I noticed camera six shifted a few inches to the east."

"Yeah, I moved it back. The tree was marked, judging from the tracks, by a damn big bear. Probably got bored and decided to use it as a paddle or something. But other than now having frostbite on my dick? There's nothing out of the norm out there. Jaz and Ryder took my post and are running through a few things with three of tonight's volunteers. Gotta say, I didn't expect people to step up like that. I think we have a pretty solid security rotation for the next three days."

"Sometimes people surprise you."

"Sometimes they do." King tossed his gear onto the table with a heavy *thunk* and dropped ass-first onto the couch. "I forgot how it feels working with a team...relying on others."

"Feels good and scary at the same time," Roman muttered.

"Exactly. I can see why you and your brothers decided to build Steele Ops. Instant trust. Known variables. If one of you steps out of the line, the other brothers kick his ass."

Roman dragged his gaze back to King. "All reasons why we did what we did, but we do hire outside of our immediate gene pool, you know. Jaz and Tank are good people."

"Not denying it. What's Jaz's story anyway? A Marine like her is usually in it until the walker on wheels has to come out."

"You really expect me to answer that?"

King snorted. "No, just checking to see if you turned into a gossiper in your retirement."

Like all of them, Jaz had her own past and her own reasons for leaving the military. Some of it he knew. Some of it he didn't. As long as it didn't affect her job with Steele Ops, he didn't need to be brought into the loop, and his brothers felt the same way.

"You know who else is a good person?" Roman veered the subject away from Jaz. "*You.* I mean, you're an asshole, but you're a good asshole. If you ever get an itch to be part of something bigger, let me know. We can always use another asshole on the team."

King's face split into a grin. "First, I wouldn't fling the term *good* around too much. I got a reputation to keep, man. And second, don't hold your breath. I'm a free spirit. Nothing and no one can contain me."

Something heavy dropped on the second floor, and a string of muffled curses immediately followed. Considering Ryder and Jaz were in the field, that left only one person...who was supposed to be sleeping but obviously wasn't.

King kicked his feet onto the coffee table and leaned back. "I'll keep watch on things down here if you want to head upstairs. You look like shit, probably could use a bit of rest."

"Not tired," Roman said truthfully.

His friend smirked. "I said rest, not sleep. For some people that means meditation or working out. Horizontal activities of the mattress variety always work best to turn off *my* brain, but since Jaz scares the hell out of me and Dr. Sexy is taken, I'm shit out of luck."

Even the suggestion of King making a play for Isa rose his blood pressure. "Yeah you are."

King grinned. "Go up and check on your woman. We both know you want to."

He did, but he also knew she wouldn't like what he had to say, which was why he'd kept his distance. *Knowing* the men from the Legion were behind this outbreak changed their next steps—steps that should now take them to Steele Ops, where he had a cement bunker, security systems out the ass, and an entire armory to keep Isabel safe.

He also knew she wouldn't go for it.

"Call me if there are any issues." Roman ignored his former teammate's chuckles and headed upstairs.

Isabel's door stood ajar. He heard her voice and, through the crack, saw her pace the length of her room while on the phone. He turned, about to leave her alone, when she'd said her good nights to the person on the other end.

What the hell... Roman rapped on the door jamb.

She glanced up and, at the first lock of their gazes, stole his breath. Dressed head to toe in black and red flannel PJs, there wasn't an inch of skin showing. Strands of silky dark hair escaped her messy half bun, visually begging him to free the rest from its confines, but he held back, concerned over the exhaustion dimming her usually vibrant eyes.

"Thought you'd already turned in for the night, but I heard you talking. Did you call your grandfather?" Roman asked.

"Maddy." She gestured for him to come inside. "She's rightfully still shaken up with everything that happened at the lab, but now that Frank is about to be discharged from the hospital, she's feeling a bit better. She agreed to continue my work at the Legion until I get back to DC."

Damn... *and here he'd hoped to ease into it.* "About that..."

"About what?"

"DC."

"No." She turned her back on him and busied herself with her laptop bag.

"I didn't even suggest anything yet."

She whirled around on him. "You don't suggest, Roman, you *order*. And save your breath, because I'm staying here in Beaver Ridge until the GHO sends in an action team that can take over, and not a second before."

"It's not safe here."

Her cheeks reddened as she flung her hands up in the air. "In case you haven't been following along these last few days, it's not safe *anywhere*! I'm not leaving these people to suffer alone while I go hide in a damn bunker. I'm staying here, where I can attempt to clean up my mess."

"This isn't on you, Doc."

"Your saying that doesn't make it true."

Trapping her chin between his fingers, he veered her gaze to his and held it hostage. "I'm saying it because it *is* true. You didn't create FC-5, and you sure as hell didn't infect these people."

"It was taken on *my* watch." Pain flooded her pretty eyes until Roman nearly felt it as his own. "There's a two-year-old girl inside that school who's fighting for her life right now because I didn't do anything to stop those bastards."

"It was taken by *force*, babe. You didn't giftwrap it and present it to those assholes on a silver fucking platter." Anxious for her to really hear him, Roman gentled his hands and made sure she couldn't look away. "First rule of any Special Forces operation is to keep *yourself* alive. Because if you're compromised, then everyone counting on you follows right behind. You hear what I'm saying?"

"You mean to tell me you haven't risked your own life to save someone else's?" Isa asked knowingly, but she wasn't upset or angry. She sounded resigned as her gaze dropped to his leg. "How did *that* happen, Roman? Because I know it wasn't while you were taking out the garbage. You risked your life for others every time you put on your uniform. Olly did, too. And hell, you're *still* doing it."

She wasn't wrong. And if he stood on that same minefield tomorrow and was given the same decision to make, he'd activate that IED all over again. He'd sacrifice his right leg, too, if it meant those kids got to go home to their parents.

"My weapon of choice is a gun, Doc. Yours is that beautiful brain of yours. If something happened to you, how long do you think it would take Tony, or even Maddy, to get anywhere near the knowledge you have of FC-5? And how many people would die in the process of them getting there?"

"I get what you're saying, but I can't leave, Roman. I won't."

And he couldn't force her.

Just like he'd risk his right leg if given the option, Isabel would risk everything, too. "Then you need to *rest*. No more calls that can be put off until tomorrow. No more unnecessary packing. You need to close your eyes and turn off your mind."

"I don't think I can without seeing the faces of

everyone in that hospital," Isa admitted in a soft whisper. "Of seeing little Abby..."

"What can I do to help make it happen, Doc?"

Her gaze dropped to his mouth, making him swallow a groan. She deserved a little peace. Hell, they both did.

Giving her ample time to pull away, he trailed his hand from her ear, down the curve of her neck. "Tell me how I can help you. Tell me what you need."

She shivered against him as she peered up through her thick, dark lashes. "Right now all I need is you."

Roman's heart thundered in his ears as he cupped the back of her head and guided her mouth to his. He'd wanted to take his time...be gentle...savor. But Isabel had other ideas. As her tongue plundered his mouth, her hands sought out every inch of skin that they could. His shirt was the first to go, then hers. In a matter of seconds, his pants hung around his knees and the only thing left between them was her thin, lacy red panties.

He hoisted her legs around his hips and deposited her on the dresser. "How much do you like these?"

"Enough to buy another pair if I need to." Isa murmured against his lips. "Condom?"

"Left pocket. Wallet."

"Hoping for something, Mr. Steele?" She dove her hand into his pants, grinning.

"With you around, I always seem to be hoping." Roman sucked down a groan as she cupped his balls with one hand and slid the condom on with the other. By the time the rim hit the base of his cock, he was ready to explode. "Hope these weren't your favorite."

He tugged on her panties and they snapped, instantly giving way. "Let's see how wet and ready you are, Doc."

"More than." Isabel tilted her hips, accepting the fingers he slid through her wetness with a roll of her hips. "No foreplay needed, Roman. Please. You. Now."

He wasn't arguing.

The second he removed his fingers, he tugged her to the edge of the dresser and sunk into her body in one hard thrust. They groaned in unison, Isabel's fingers digging into his shoulders.

"Roman." She panted, tilting her body up so he dove in that much deeper. Sweat dripped off their bodies as they worked into a frenzied rhythm. "Roman, please. More."

"Come for me." Gripping her upper thighs, he pounded into her harder. Faster. "Come for me, baby. I want to feel you wrap tight around me, Isabel."

He wanted to watch her come apart at the seams and know he was the one responsible. He wanted to sink into her and never come out. By the time her body squeezed his throbbing cock in a vise grip, bringing along his own release moments after hers, Roman realized that he just wanted *her*...over and over...for as long as she'd have him.

As he dropped his forehead to Isabel's, Roman realized that Isabel Santiago could very well be the one and only person who could bring him back to the land of the living.

And that scared the shit out of him.

CHAPTER FOURTEEN

Great sex didn't cure all, but it sure as hell didn't hurt. Ever since waking up wrapped around Roman after a night of intense marathon sex and sporadic cat naps, Isa had felt energized.

The effects of the magical peen.

But after ten hours in a hazmat suit, twenty intravenous line restarts, and more than thirty medication administrations, Roman's penis magic was fading fast. She jotted down a reminder note to herself to make sure more IV kits were on the next supply shipment when Marie, the college student volunteer, hustled over, the inside of her mask foggy.

"Isa! It's Abby! Quick!"

Isa's heart stumbled as she dropped the clipboard and ran as fast as her bulky suit would let her to the other side of the gym. She tripped once, thanks to the too-big rubber boots, and then forced herself into a brisk pace that would put any professional power-walker to shame.

"Excuse me. Pardon me." Isa gently inserted herself into the crowd that had gathered around Abby's cot, preventing her from seeing the young toddler or her mother. "Let me through. Come on, guys. I can't do anything if you don't…"

A childish giggle sounded just as Isa fought her way through the mob.

Abby, bright-eyed and grinning, sitting on her mother's lap, tossed another glove-balloon into the air before snatching it away moments before her mother pretended to make a grab for it. The balloon squeaked as the little girl clutched it tight to her chest, and then did it again.

Beth looked up, tears streaming down her cheeks as she smiled. "She woke up like this...playful for the first time in days. Is she...is she better?"

"Marie?"

The young student was already handing Isabel the audible stethoscope and thermometer, and this time, Abby curiously listened to her heart and lungs without needing any kind of bribery.

Despite the number of people in the gymnasium, a dropped pin could've been heard as everyone waited for Isa to say something...say anything. Satisfied with the little one's heart and lung sounds, she swiped the thermometer across the little one's forehead and held her breath while the numbers popped up on the display.

99.1.

Isa swiped Abby twice for good measure and got the same result.

"She's afebrile." Isa couldn't contain her relieved smile. "Her fever broke."

Beth bounced her daughter on her lap. "That's good news, right?"

"That's *great* news, but I have to draw blood and verify and her viral loads and—"

"Do it. Please."

By the time Isabel had two vials of Abby's blood in her hands, news of the toddler's improvement had spread throughout the room. Quarantined neighbors came by to add to the excitement, Tony one of them.

"Did I hear correctly?" Her mentor peered through the growing crowd, on his face a look of shock and awe. "Her fever broke?"

"For the first time in days she's below one hundred degrees Fahrenheit." Isa couldn't contain a small bark of laughter. "Tony, her lungs sound clear. Her heart's strong. What bruising she had looks aged, as if her body's healing itself instead of deteriorating. I won't know until I count the viral load myself, but I think that little angel just told us this isn't as unbeatable as we feared."

"Go." Tony took her stethoscope from her and flicked his hands. "Get to the lab and test it. I'll hold down the fort here."

Isa couldn't keep the smile off her face no matter how many times she mentally scolded herself for being prematurely hopeful. She went into decon, and then half-walked, half-ran with single-minded focus toward the school trailer they had turned into a lab.

Isa rounded the corner and collided with a tall, auburn-haired woman. They both bounced back, Isa landing flat on her ass.

"Oh, crap. I am *so* sorry. I was rushing to the hospital…uh, the school." The woman stretched a hand out to help Isa back to her feet.

"Hold that thought." Isa carefully opened up the bio

carrier she'd luckily tucked into her body like a football and breathed easier seeing Abby's samples safely nestled into their foam slots. "That could've been very, very bad. And thank you."

Isa accepted her hand and brushed the rocks and dirt off her butt.

The other woman shifted her gaze from the school back to her, her eyes widening. "You're Dr. Santiago. I recognize you from the town hall meeting. I'm Connie, Mayor Rutledge's niece."

"Did you say you were going to the hospital? Is everything okay?"

"No, it's not." Tears pooled in Connie's eyes. "My son Leo was feeling fine this morning, but all of a sudden he's so hot to the touch and yet keeps begging for more blankets. I tried alternating acetaminophen and ibuprofen like our pediatrician always suggested, but his temperature just seems to keep rising. Can you come take a look at him?"

"It sounds like he needs a complete work-up. It would be best if you brought him to the clinic."

"He won't get up, and he's too big for me to carry. *Please.* I can't let anything happen to him. His father passed away two years ago, and he's the only thing I have left."

Isa's heart ached for the other woman. Vials in hand, she glanced toward the lab and back to the frightened woman, already knowing she couldn't say no. "Show me."

"*Thank you.* This way." Connie grabbed her hand and hustled her down Main Street. They bypassed a few evening walkers, who paused slightly before giving them polite nods. She turned left after two blocks and walked farther away from the center of town.

Isa's steps slowed as she realized how far away from the school they'd actually gone. "Maybe I can have one of the volunteers come out and bring your son into the clinic. If his temperature is as high as you say, I don't want to waste time in all the back and forth."

"But we're already here." Connie gestured to a small cabin set apart from the others, its weathered siding and sagging windows screaming for some kind of aesthetic help. She unlocked the door and held it open. "He's right there on the couch. I couldn't even get him to his room, he was feeling so weak."

Isa glimpsed the blanketed figure lying on the threadbare couch, and stepped into the cabin. Her eyes slowly adjusted to the dim lighting, turning vague shapes into outlines. Connie's son groaned and shifted, and just as Isa reached his side and prepped to pull back the blankets, the person beneath flipped them down.

It wasn't a child beneath the covers.

"Having a good time in Beaver Ridge, Dr. Santiago?" Blue Eyes smirked, sitting upright, and sans mask. But it was *definitely* the man from the Legion...and from the van. If she'd seen him on the street, she probably wouldn't have given him a second look, but there was no mistaking that cold look...or that voice. "I told you that we'd be seeing each other again. You should probably take me at my word."

Isa spun around toward the door and nearly came into contact with the muzzle of a gun.

Connie's tears were nowhere to be found now. Grinning ear to ear, the woman, who was definitely not related to Mayor Rutledge and probably wasn't named Connie, looked at ease aiming a weapon in her face. "You're harder to get alone than the pope himself, Izzy."

"What do you want?" Isa steeled her voice to prevent it from wavering.

Blue Eyes got up from the couch, the old frame protesting with a groan. "Wrong question. What do *you* want? If it's to make sure your boyfriend, his friends, and this entire town keeps breathing, then I suggest you come with me like a good little doctor and keep your fucking mouth shut."

Pain slammed into the back of Isa's head, shooting through her skull and down her neck as her vision dimmed. Her world spun in a flurry of shadows until it—and her feet—finally gave way.

* * *

In his thirty-two years on earth, Roman had established two hard-core rules: Listen to his gut...and his mother. If he ignored either one, trouble almost always followed, which was why he'd taken two additional passes around Beaver Ridge's perimeter in the last hour.

Emptyhanded, with his internal warning system still blaring, he rounded the corner of the school to see Tony stepping out from the lab.

The older man's head snapped left and right until his gaze landed on Roman. "Have you seen Isa? She left the hospital to run some samples over to the lab, but she's not there, and I haven't seen her since."

Roman's gut alarm went off. "How long ago was that?"

Tony checked his watch. "An hour? Give or take a few minutes."

Fuck. Roman ripped the radio off his hip. "I need a location on Isabel. Now."

"Not here," Jaz called in from the dock.

Ryder chimed next via the clinic, "Not here, either."

One by one, both Roman's team and their volunteers checked in, and no one had eyes on her. With a curse, Roman bolted toward the cabin, Tony huffing breathlessly behind him, and prayed exhaustion had just sent her to bed for a quick recharge.

"Doc!" Roman burst through the door and immediately scanned the first level. Finding it empty, he immediately jogged up the stairs and into each of the bedrooms. "Doc! Are you here? Isabel?"

There was no sign of her. Anywhere.

He'd stepped onto the porch just as King appeared around the corner, breathless. "Anything?"

"Not a damn thing."

"Ryder's checking the hospital with one of the vols to see if she went back there after hitting up the lab."

As if saying his name aloud conjured him, Ryder's voice crackled on the radio. "Need you guys down on Main Street. ASAP."

King and Roman took off, Roman's leg—at first—protesting the burst of speed. Thanks to Isa's suggestion to oil the gears, his prosthetic moved easily, and in a matter of a minutes they reached Main Street. Ryder stood with an older couple just outside the local barber shop.

"You see her?" Roman asked his brother.

Ryder shook his head. "But Edith and Henry said they saw her an hour ago walking away from the lab, and she wasn't alone."

"Who the hell was she with?"

Henry answered, "A woman. Maybe in her thirties. I thought I've seen her around town once or twice before, but I didn't say anything earlier, because I thought she may be with you."

"She wasn't." Roman locked eyes with his brother and saw the same realization in Ryder's eyes he knew was in his own. Those bastards had her.

"Where were they headed?"

Henry pointed left, away from the general town hub. "North. But there's nothing up that way except for some empty cabins Rutledge keeps trying to tear down."

"King," Roman growled.

"On it." Part human and part bloodhound, King led the way up the northern face of the hill, where, just like Henry said, there was nothing except a half-dozen log cabins. Jaz met them halfway, her gun clenched in her hand. Roman and the others spread out as they headed up the hill, working the wide field in a line-search format without having to give directions.

One third of the way to the nearest cabin, King barked, "Got a trail!" He pointed at the disturbed grass. "Two sets of prints headed straight toward that middle building."

"They're side by side," Roman noted. Crouching with a grimace, he eyed the path left behind in the fresh mud. "That means at this point, Isabel wasn't taken under duress, or one would be closely trailing the other."

"You think she went willingly?"

"No, I think they played her until they got her where they wanted her." Roman nodded toward the middle cabin. "Guns out and at the ready. Jaz and Ryder, take the rear. King and I are on the front...and be fucking careful."

"You, too, brother." Ryder squeezed his shoulder as he passed. "Head on a swivel."

King led the way up the front of the cabin. The steps groaned in protest beneath his weight, but he didn't pay it any mind, plastering his body against the front of the cabin. "After you, my friend. On three."

At zero, King kicked the door open and immediately took a knee while Roman breached the entryway. Ryder and Jaz did the same at the rear door. With one room and a small hall, it didn't take long to clear—and to realize Isabel wasn't there.

"Fucking hell." Roman punched the wall. Rotting wood cracked under the impact.

"Check this out." Jaz bent down in front of the couch, where a small cooler was half-hidden by a discarded blanket. She peeked inside. "Two vials of blood. Isa was definitely here."

"But she's not now." Roman's fingers popped as he balled his hands into fists. "Get that cooler to Tony, and then collect the volunteers and anyone else who knows this area like the back of their hand."

"Please tell me we're going after the slimy fuckers," Jaz asked eagerly.

"Hell yeah we are. If any of them so much as touched a hair on Isabel's head, they're going to be the ones requiring medical attention when I'm through with them."

"Or a coroner," Jaz muttered under her breath.

Until he laid eyes on Isabel and saw for himself that she was unharmed, he wasn't about to rule that out, either.

CHAPTER
FIFTEEN

Isa's head throbbed, the flow and ebb crashing into her like huge storm waves as she forced her eyes open. She squinted through the cobwebs distorting her memory, but slowly, they cleared up, one coming after another.

Abby at the hospital. The excitement. The rush to the lab. The woman waiting around the corner...Connie.

No, *not* Connie, a voice whispered in the recesses of Isa's mind. *A trap.*

Remembering the gun aimed at her face, Isa yanked her arms. Twin bolts of pain shot through her wrist and up her arm as plastic ties bit into her skin, anchoring her hands and legs to a hard wood chair. "What the hell?"

Four bare log walls surrounded her, and one window, its panes boarded up, allowed the barest hint of moonlight through its slats. She was alone, that much was a given, but the low murmur of voices from somewhere else in the cabin told her it probably wouldn't be for long.

Behind her, a door opened, its hinges squeaking.

"Look who's finally awake." Footsteps approached, and the woman who called herself Connie leaned over her shoulder, brushing her mouth against her ear. "It's so nice of you to finally join us, Dr. Santiago. Guess the party can officially start now, huh?"

"Why don't you untie me so I can show you how festive I can be."

The woman's low chuckle grated on Isa's nerves, making her wish she had the power to make these ties disintegrate. "I like you, Isa. That's what most people call you, right? You seem like a pretty stand-up woman, which is why I hope you can be a good girl and cooperate."

"Well I *don't* like you, so you can go to hell."

Her captor jerked her head back, ripping hair from her head in the process. "I would mind your mouth if I were you, because in case you couldn't tell, you're not in a position to get snippy."

The door opened.

"Babe, take a walk," a low, familiar voice suggested. *Blue Eyes.*

"I'm fine. The nice doctor and I are setting a few things straight."

"Take. A walk. *Now.*" He didn't raise his voice, but it was definitely an order.

The woman obeyed, but not without another sharp yank before releasing her hold. "Behave, *bitch.*"

This time, Isa sucked down a whimper as pain sliced along her scalp. That one definitely cost her a few clumps of hair.

Blue Eyes waited until they were alone before dragging a chair from the corner and setting it three feet away. He sat casually, one leg crossed over the other.

Like their meeting in the cabin, he didn't bother hiding his face and this time Isa could see him better. Blond hair, cut in a short buzz close to his head, revealed a palm-sized birthmark just over his ear, and his tank top showcased well-defined arms and what looked to be a tattoo on his left shoulder.

"Sorry about... *Connie*," Blue Eyes apologized. "She sometimes gets a little excitable."

Isa snorted. "Just the kind of person you want to call *babe*... or let near a deadly virus."

A crooked smile slithered onto his face. "In a different world, Isabel, I could see us becoming friends."

"I don't think so. I have a general rule about not befriending homicidal maniacs who treat human lives as if they're disposable trash."

"You would see it that way, wouldn't you?"

"How else would I see it? I mean, you *did* intentionally poison Beaver Ridge's food supply, didn't you?"

"Figured that already? Wow. Beautiful and smart. No wonder you're so popular."

"What do you get out of this?" Isa thought about little Abby and her mother, and about their grandmother, who worried each day that *that* day was the one she would lose her entire family. "And how the hell do you sleep at night knowing you dished out a death sentence to an entire town? You've condemned innocent men, women, and children... and why?"

Tears threatened to fall, but Isa held them at bay, focusing on her anger. She couldn't fathom this man's lack of remorse.

"Actually, I sleep quite well with a feather pillow."

"You shouldn't be. It won't be long before my friends realize I'm gone. They'll come...and there won't be anywhere for you to hide. Even here in Alaska."

"Honey, I'm counting on your little boy toy forming a cute little search party." Blue Eyes smiled. "I'll try not to take offense, since we don't know each other very well yet, but one thing you should know about me is that I'm a man of action. I *do*. I *plan*, and then I execute. This sitting around and waiting shit isn't me. I guess you could say I get bored easily, which is why I'm not averse to livening things up a bit."

The door opened, and Blue Eyes' attention slid over Isa's shoulder. "What *now*?"

"Phone call."

"I'm busy."

"Told him that, but he doesn't seem to care. He's not happy...in the least."

"Like I fucking give a damn, but fine." He got to his feet and whispered in Isa's ear. "We'll finish up our little girl talk when I get back. Don't go anywhere now, you hear?"

Isa's jaw ached from keeping her mouth clamped shut as Blue Eyes stalked from the room. On the other side, she recognized Connie's murmured voice.

"Can we fucking get rid of her already?" Connie asked. "It's not like we need her around. Let's put a bullet between her eyes and dump her in a fucking bear cave or something."

"That's not the plan," Blue Eyes answered.

"Plans fucking change, Mace. We're the ones with all the fucking power right now. Start acting like it."

Something crashed against the wall, rattling the windows.

"Let's get one thing straight right now." Blue Eyes' threat was nearly inaudible through the door. "*I'm* the one with the fucking power. No one lifts a finger or twitches their fucking nose until I give the go-ahead. Do I make myself clear?"

Isa couldn't hear Connie's response, but Blue Eyes—Mace—must have been satisfied enough by it. The wall shook again and footsteps faded down what sounded like a long hall before disappearing completely.

"I've got to get out of here," Isa whispered to herself.

With renewed fervor, and ignoring the blood dripping down her wrists and hand, she tugged on her restraints. It hurt like hell, but the slickness created a small bit of give and made her all the more determined to not be tied up when Blue Eyes—or Connie—came back into the room.

* * *

Roman squared his shoulders and faced off against his brother. Ryder hadn't said anything that he didn't know or wouldn't have pulled himself if the situation were reversed. No one liked being the one left behind, but there wasn't another choice.

"You realize we're in Alaska, right?" Ryder glared from across the map they'd been studying for the better of the last two hours. "There's at least four of them—probably more, because there's always a few hiding in the background. And you're three people…one who's—"

"If you say *a woman*, I will kick your scrotum so hard it flies up and tickles your tonsils." Jaz looked prepped to follow through on her threat in the blink of an eye.

Ryder subtly shifted his pants and grimaced. "I was about to say one whose head may not be completely in the game, but good to know."

"My head's in the game," Roman disagreed. "Hell, my whole damn body is in this."

"Then you really think splitting up is the way to go? We need more hands on deck, not less. Transporting the samples can wait until we get Isa back."

Roman shook his head. "If we wait, Jaz's threat to your scrotum will be nothing compared to what Doc will do to us if she finds out we didn't get those samples to where they needed to go. Tony confirmed that the GHO will be here by daybreak. Now you need to escort him back to DC and get him to Tru Tech."

As much as it killed Roman to send the extra help away, it was what needed to happen. That little girl, Abby, could very well be the first—and potentially only—person to ever survive an FC-5 exposure. If shit really hit the fan, what those blood samples could tell everyone could be a matter of life and death.

Literally.

"Fine," Ryder gritted out. "But how are you planning on dealing with the fact that there's three of you and countless square miles of Alaskan wilderness?"

That was the question of the damn hour.

A knock on the door prevented Roman from answering that question.

Tony stood on the porch. "Can you guys come out for a second?"

Roman exchanged looks with King before following the older man outside to where a dozen or more Beaver Ridge residents stood, bundled up, in the quickly dropping temperatures.

An older woman stepped forward. He recognized her as the little girl's grandmother.

"Is everything okay?" Roman asked, immediately concerned. "Abby?"

"She's improved even more." She glanced around to her friends and neighbors. "We're actually here about Dr. Santiago. We want to help."

"I appreciate it, but—"

"Help how?" King cut in. He shrugged off Roman's glare, his eyes fastened on the locals.

A group of about eight people, varying in age from twenty-something to mid-fifties, stepped up, but it was the oldest of the group who spoke up. "We were all born and raised next to this mountain. There isn't a bear we can't track or a rock we won't recognize. If they have Dr. Santiago out there somewhere, *we'll* be able to find her. Like Edith said, she risked a lot in coming here to help us. Helping her now is the least we can do."

Jaz's, King's, and Ryder's gazes fell on Roman like a damn anvil.

He wanted to find Isa more than his next breath, but...

"The men we're after aren't friendly neighborhood type of people," Roman warned. "If you do this, I can't guarantee that there won't be casualties."

The men and two women glanced around at each other before murmuring to their spokesman. He nodded and turned back. "It's a risk we're willing to take. If something happens to Dr. Santiago, we're dead anyway...including our families."

Roman couldn't fault them on that logic in the least. It was painfully close to what he'd told her before, but her abilities to kick FC-5's ass wasn't what made Roman want to storm into the Alaskan wilderness and turn over every damn rock that he found until he located the bastards that took her.

"Then your help's greatly appreciated." Roman nodded in agreement. "But you and your people help track, steer my team in the right direction, and then you fall back. No questions and no hesitation. I know you say you're willing to put it all on the line, but I'm not. Your families need you, too."

"It's a deal."

Two hours later, with Ryder and Tony headed back to DC, Roman counted himself damn lucky to have the people of Beaver Ridge. They knew these woods *better* than the back of their hands. Using maps, they'd pinpointed the three most likely areas where people could get in and out relatively easily but unseen.

They'd come up empty with the first two, and as they approached the third, Roman's skin itched. Wind howled through the trees, masking their twelve-person team. According to Bruce, the leader of the Beaver Ridge residents, this had to be where they were holed up with Isabel.

Roman signaled for everyone to wait...which went against everything his body was telling him.

"Breathe, man." King's hand dropped on his shoulder as if reading his mind...and he probably was. After countless missions and their assignment in Burundi, they'd quickly developed their own silent language.

"You know it's killing me to wait, right?" Roman murmured.

"It's not like you're sitting on your ass, Ro. Let Jaz do her eagle eye thing, and I promise you, if Dr. Sexy is down there, we'll get her back."

"I know we will." *Because he wouldn't accept anything else.*

On cue, Roman's ear mic crackled.

"Eagle eyes here, you read?" Jaz's voice came through the comms.

"I read. What do you see?"

"The nest full of fucking vultures."

They'd found them. They'd found *Isabel*.

"I count three on patrol," Jaz said. "One on perimeter, and two on the north and south exit points. It's not exactly Fort Knox. Hell, I'm surprised the building hasn't collapsed in this wind."

King grunted. "So we have three outside, one probably inside with Isa, and then the brain of the operation, because we know his ass isn't walking perimeter lines in this fucking cold. That's five men *at least*. Five men, three of us...unless..."

"No, the locals stay out of it. They already have enough on the line."

Jaz grunted her agreement through their comms. "I could take two of them out right now. I have a pretty solid line of sight."

"Not with this wind working against you. One slipup and they'll know we're coming."

"I'm going to pretend that you didn't just question my abilities, but yeah. You're right."

Roman ran through the possible scenarios in his head and was on the last one when a shot rang out, echoing loudly through the trees. Everyone ducked, and Roman cursed. A second was quickly followed by a third.

"Jaz!"

"Wasn't me! *Fuck!* There's another vulture...in the sky and about twenty yards from your six!"

A split second later, the ground inches away from Roman's feet exploded as a bullet dug into the earth. "Jaz!"

"On it...give me one...little...second..."

Another shot ripped through the air, and this time it came with a low groan off to their left.

"Got the bastard," Jaz announced proudly. "Good news is that he won't be performing any activities involving hands anytime soon, but the bad news is that there's no way his friends didn't hear our little tiff."

Roman signaled to Bruce and his group. "Fall back! Fall back and retreat! King."

"On your six, buddy."

King and Roman hustled to Jaz's location just as she dropped down from her perch in the tall pine. The Marine sniper didn't usually wear a smile on her face unless she was being a pain in Tank's ass, but her current frown didn't give Roman the warm fuzzies.

"What wrong?" Roman demanded.

"I saw Isa...so she's definitely in there. I think she

heard the commotion and somehow managed to rip the cover off the far back window."

Roman's heart slowly lifted to his throat. "And...?"

She handed him her scope and pointed in the direction of the asshole's cabin. It took him a second to spot the window she mentioned, and when he zoomed in, it was more than his heart that lifted to his throat.

The cringeworthy taste of bile rose, coating the back of his tongue.

A red handprint.

A bloody handprint...and it had been left there by Isabel.

CHAPTER
SIXTEEN

The window had been wishful thinking. As soon as Isa had yanked off the cover, she'd known there was no way in hell she'd fit through. A kindergartener would be hard-pressed to squeeze out of the small space, which meant she needed to find another way.

Her wrists, gouged and bleeding, burned as if doused in gasoline and set on fire, but at least she was free—until someone else came through that door.

She scanned the room for anything she could use as a weapon but, other than the chair, came up empty-handed. *What self-respecting criminals don't leave crap lying around these days?*

A loud crack froze her feet to the ground.

Was that...?

Two more rattled off, followed by a third. She'd learned enough in the Army to recognize gunfire when she heard it. In an instant, the quiet cabin burst into a flurry of activity and shouts. Footsteps pounded as someone ran across the creaky floorboards, the sound getting louder by the second.

Chair it is. Isa grabbed the wobbly chair and plastered her back along the wall next to the door. As it opened, she counted to three—and swung.

Her female captor cursed and ducked, fending off the worst of her blows with her arm. "And I thought you were a weak little mouse. Consider me wrong."

"Looks like you were also wrong about how smart you are," Isa taunted, sidestepping with the hope of sliding closer to the exit.

"Oh, I know how smart I am, honey."

"Really?" Isa took a page out of Roman's book and hiked up a single cocky eyebrow. "Do you and your team usually celebrate your smarts by running around cursing? Funny. Your celebration sounds a lot like panicking."

She stepped again, but this time, her captor countered it.

"You know, Mace didn't want me playing around with you, but as you pointed out, he's a little preoccupied right now." The woman sneered. "You're more trouble than you're worth, and frankly, that pisses me off. There's nothing I hate more than wasting my time."

"Then by all means, step out that door and don't look back. I sure as hell won't stop you...but it sounds like my friends will." Isa pushed a smile onto her face that she hoped looked more confident than she felt. "That's what all the commotion is about, right? Did my friends find us a little sooner than you were expecting?"

"If I walk out that door right now, hon, you won't like where I'm going next." The woman stalked closer, her eyes wild and threatening. "What's the name of that cute little ranch in Texas where you grew up? Golden Plains? Your sweet old grandfather runs a horse sanctuary, right? I've always liked ponies. After dealing with the Alaskan cold, I could definitely use a change in weather."

"Don't you fucking dare," Isa growled as she stepped right.

"What? You don't think Grandpa dearest would be up to helping us win our investors over? I think it's the least he could do considering his granddaughter fucked up our plans here in Beaver Ridge."

"You go anywhere near my family and there won't be a rock big enough for you to crawl under."

Connie chuckled and stepped left, and before Isa realized it, nearly had her pinned into a corner with nowhere to go. "The doctor's got some spunk after all, huh? Too bad it's not going to help you...or anyone else. Thanks to your meddling, we realized that we were thinking too small with Beaver Ridge. We're moving on...to *bigger*...and more...*populated* places. The bigger the punch, the bigger the payout, don't you think?"

"Lina! We got to get the fuck out of here! Now!" someone shouted seconds before a door crashed open and more shouts ensued.

The woman in front of Isa—Lina—shifted her attention for a split second, but it was all Isa needed. She kicked out, her boot snapping against Lina's knee.

"You bitch! I'll make you so fucking sorry you were ever born!" The other woman struck out with a jab.

Isa blocked it—barely—and delivered a hard kick to the torso. "And you'll be sorry you ever threatened my family."

With a grunt, Lina stumbled back. As she teetered, she snagged Isa's bleeding left wrist and dug her nails into the tender flesh.

Isa screamed.

"If you can't play with the big kids, then get off the playground, sweetheart," Lina chided.

"Couldn't say it better myself." Isa swallowed every ounce of white hot pain, wrapped her fingers around the broken chair leg, and swung like a professional baseball player. The cracked wood thudded against Lina's head, and she dropped, heavy and unconscious, to the ground.

Cradling her injured hand against to her chest, Isa sunk to her knees just as the door to the room burst open. Roman stood in the entryway, gun drawn and face furiously scanning the area until it fell on an unconscious Lina...and her.

"Doc." His look of fury was quickly, replaced by something that looked a lot like relief. He called to someone out in the hall as he dropped to the ground in front of her, gently cupping her face in his hands. "Are you okay? Where are you hurt? *Talk to me.*"

"They threatened my grandfather." Adrenaline coursed through Isa's veins. "They know exactly where he is, and they blame me for screwing things up for them here in Beaver Ridge."

"I'll get people on it right away, baby." Roman caressed a stray hair off her face. "But are you okay?"

She shook her head. "They're planning something bigger than Beaver Ridge. You were right. This is all a show in the hopes of finding buyers...and they want to show people exactly what it's capable of doing."

And if they did that, no one would be okay.

* * *

Roman dropped into the plush chair on the Steele Ops jet and released a string of curses his mother would've chastised him for had she heard, but one swear word wasn't enough after last night.

Two dozen wouldn't do the fucking job.

He couldn't even wrap his head around the feelings that had ripped through him at seeing Isabel hunkered on the ground, bleeding and exhausted. If she hadn't already knocked that Lina woman unconscious, Roman wasn't sure what he would've done.

"You did the right thing." King lay sprawled on the couch, watching Roman like a damn hawk.

"What thing is that?"

"Not doing anything stupid."

Roman shot a glare at his friend that didn't do shit. "You saw what those assholes did to her, right?"

"Yep. And I saw what your woman gave right back to them. Kick-ass through and through. The two of you are a match made in heaven. And now that the authorities have that Lina chick in custody, we can all hopefully get some damn answers."

"We?" Roman wasn't about to let his friend's play on words go.

King shrugged. "I got nothing else to do at the moment, and as pitiful as it sounds, I'd rather stare at your ugly mug for a few more days than stare at Garrett's. You're a few degrees more pleasant since Dr. Sexy came along, but *that* poor bastard hasn't gotten laid in probably three years."

Roman snorted and shifted in his seat. His leg ached, and he rubbed it subconsciously. The fact that it only bothered him now was saying something, considering he'd hiked up and down a fucking mountain. He made a mental note to give his designer buddy a two-thumbs-up rating when all this was said and done.

Jaz pushed King's legs off the couch and sat. "I called Ryder. He and Tony are an hour out of Manassas, and Isa's friend Maddy is already waiting for them and the samples at Tru Tech."

"Good." Roman nodded. "At least one thing is working in our favor. Now if I could only change Doc's mind about this family reunion."

"Well that's just not going to happen."

At Isabel's voice, they all turned to see her standing just outside of the bedroom. Dark circles framed her eyes, and bandages covered her wrists. She looked like hell warmed over but was still able to drill him with a disapproving look.

"I'll go to DC," Isabel said adamantly. "I'll finish what I started, and I'll give those bastards a reason to be worried about me. But before I do that, I'm going to make damn sure my family is safe."

Roman crossed over to her, and as much as he wanted to touch her, he kept his hands to himself. "Do you trust me?"

"Is that a trick question?" She took a moment to

think about it. "To keep me safe? Yes. To find these jerk-offs and stop them before they do something horrible? Yes."

Fuck. Roman wanted to ask her what exactly she didn't trust him to do, but it wasn't the time or the place. "Then why can't you trust me when I say that we're not letting anything happen to your grandfather. Knox already sent someone from the team to Texas, and I can have Jaz on the way there in a matter of hours as backup."

"And I appreciate that. I do. But you don't know my grandfather. If he thinks for one moment that anyone is there to babysit him, he'll run them off with the shotgun he keeps above the mantel...and I'm not joking. I *have* to be there to explain it to him. I *have* to make him see reason."

"Phones really come in handy nowadays, and they can operate pretty much anywhere. Even safe bunkers."

Fuck. Roman realized it was the wrong thing to say the moment the words left his mouth.

Isa's glare turned molten as she stalked forward, stopping only when the faint trace of shampoo filled his nose. "That woman threatened my *family*. There is nothing—and no one—on this earth that'll prevent me from doing whatever I can to protect him. And that includes you. And I would think you of all people would understand that."

Isa stormed back to the bedroom, slamming the door behind her.

Jaz glared at him.

King's mouth opened and closed again before he finally shook his head.

"What?" Roman demanded of his friends. "What the hell are those looks for?"

Jaz rolled her eyes. "Because you're a freakin' moron."

"I'm a moron?"

Jaz glanced to King. "Isn't that what I just said?"

King shrugged. "Sounded like it to me."

Roman's fists clenched at his side. "I'm a moron for wanting to keep her *safe*?"

"No. For thinking there was the slightest chance Isa would let you get away with your I-am-caveman routine," Jaz clarified. "You two are primo examples why, much to my mother's dislike, I choose to stay single and free to mingle."

"You won't be single and mingling once we get to Texas," Roman couldn't help but throw out. His comment earned him a glare from the Marine sniper. Petty payback for her moron comment, but he'd take it. "You have a problem with playing a part to keep Isa's grandfather safe?"

"You know I don't…as long as it's Ryder who's playing my co-pilot. I'd even take *him* over the other choice." Jaz jabbed her finger at King.

King laughed. "Don't look at me. I'm not an official part of the team."

Roman smirked. "And Ryder *has* been out in the field for a while. He could use the rest."

Jaz leaned forward. "I'm telling you right here, right now, if anyone other than Ryder is waiting for us at that Texas airport, I'm putting hazard pay on my time sheet. Feigning a relationship with your brother is one thing. Feigning one with Tank is something entirely different."

"Not my choice. That's all on Knox, but whoever it is, you need to make it work, because Isa's said multiple times that her grandfather won't take being watched over very well. To make your job easier, you better sell the whole engaged friends of Isabel looking for a wedding venue spiel. Even if your *co-pilot* is Tank."

Jaz emitted a low growl. *She* was irritated. *Isabel* was pissed. So far he was batting one hundred, and that was just fine with him. If it meant getting shit done and keeping Isabel safe, he'd do whatever it took.

Even transforming back into the assholish prick he'd been before he met her.

CHAPTER SEVENTEEN

Before getting off the plane, Isa had spent no less than four hours on the phone with Maddy and Tony, walking them through the step-by-step process required to receive the new samples from Beaver Ridge into the Legion. As much as it killed Isa to relinquish some of that control, the rest was up to them. They knew what they were doing, and Maddy was more than able to prep samples and initiate trials. The GHO had gotten boots down in Alaska to help the people of Beaver Ridge.

Now Isa needed to focus on her grandfather, because no way would she leave him vulnerable to Blue Eyes, aka Mace, and without Jaz and Tank watching over him, that's exactly what he would be. If he didn't tell them to get lost altogether.

Tilting her face skyward, Isa soaked up the warm Texas sun. Scents of hay and clean, fresh air permeated the air and immediately transported her back to a time when the weight of the world wasn't balanced on her shoulders. On either side of them, rolling fields filled with herds of Angus cattle stretched as far as the eye could see. It was a gorgeous sight, one Roman hadn't spared a second glance since the plane touched down.

She had that in common with the fields.

Roman no longer looked at her like the woman he couldn't wait to devour. He barely looked at her at all, and when he did, an odd detachment glazed over his eyes, making it difficult for her to breathe. And talk to her?

Forget it.

He'd effectively buried her Roman in some untouchable place and brought back the broody, cocky Steele Ops operative from their first meeting. He'd barely said anything on their drive, and when he did it was to bark out a command or a warning.

No, Isa mentally scolded herself. *He was never* my *Roman... or* my *anything.*

He'd been the man to give her a few toe-curling orgasms. That was it. That was all it *could* be. She knew it logically, but something inside was reluctant to agree.

"You guys are clear about why you're there at Mari's Sanctuary?" Isa snuck a glance at the "happy" couple sitting in the far corners of the back seat. "Because I wasn't kidding...if my grandfather gets the slightest whiff we're trying to pull something over on him, he'll send us right out the door."

Tank slid a mischievous look toward his seat partner. "We're here because my wife-to-be is in bridezilla mode and keeps changing her mind about the wedding venue. A month ago, it was a beach wedding. Three weeks ago, it was a cruise ship. Last week, it was a vineyard. Now we're here."

Jaz drilled him with a glare. "Maybe instead of changing the venue I need to change the groom."

"We're in steer country." Tank gestured out to the vast golden field flying by the window. "Now's your chance, chére."

Isa muttered, "Maybe we should take the risk he'll run us off the sanctuary."

Roman shot his teammates a warning glare. "They'll be fine...and if they're not, they can consider themselves working this assignment pro bono."

That seemed to shut the duo up for the moment. Truth was, Isa wasn't worried about Tank and Jaz giving something away. It was *her*. The smart thing to do would be let the professionals keep her grandfather safe while she went back to DC and the Legion, but she needed to *see* him.

She needed to hug him, to tease him for not keeping his beard kempt, and harp on him for eating regular bacon instead of a low-fat turkey variety. That meant putting on her best acting hat and praying he'd lost some of that all-knowing power he'd possessed when she'd been a teen.

Roman turned off the main road and onto the pot-holed dirt lane that led the way to the sanctuary. Her smile came reflexively as a gorgeous black mare galloped along the left side of the fencing, keeping up with the bouncing car. On the other side, horses grazed in the open fields, and far off in the distance, someone led a group of trail riders, the small, thin line looking like a collection of nesting dolls on the horizon.

Home sweet home. White with golden shutters that matched the fields, the two-story farmhouse was adorned by flower boxes at each window, their contents blooming with vibrant purple and red blossoms. Her grandmother's favorite colors.

The veranda where they'd sit every evening, cold glasses of lemonade in their hands, still housed the handmade swing and a handful of the world's coziest rocking chairs. She couldn't even count the number of times she'd sat on that swing with Olly, their gazes tilted up to the starry sky.

"Focus on the present, Isabel," Isa murmured as a reminder to herself.

As they pulled to a stop in front of the house, a plume of dirt and dust rose around the car, but it didn't obscure the view of her grandfather stepping onto the porch, his hands shoved deep into his pockets.

Pushing a smile to her face, Isa leapt from the car and rushed the steps, straight into a waiting hug.

"You look like a breath of fresh air, sweetheart." Carlos Santiago smiled down at her. That familiar twinkle in his eye never ceased to put a real smile on Isa's face. "So beautiful. And so much like your grandma."

"And you..." Isa sniffed before locking her grandfather in a stern glare. "Have you been smoking cigars again? What did your doctor tell you about that?"

Her grandfather's grin was partially masked by his white mustache. "When company brings a gift, I can't refuse. That would be rude, and we're all about manners in this house. Speaking of..." He stuck his hand out in greeting—to Roman. "Carlos Santiago."

Roman shook it. "Roman Steele, sir. It's good to meet you."

They made their rounds of introductions, Jaz and Tank sticking to their script.

"It looks as though everyone's had quite a day." Her grandfather nudged them all to the house. "Why don't we get everyone set up in their rooms before seeing about dinner?"

Isa's grandfather led them into her childhood home, where he made a point to show Roman his room—conveniently on the opposite end of the hall from Isa's. Tank and Jaz got one to share, and it took everything Isa had not to burst into laughter at the look of pure disgust on the female operative's face.

"Isa." Jaz's hand caught hers before she slipped into her room.

"Breathe, Jaz." Isa took a deep breath. "One baby step at a time. Freshen up for dinner. Eat. And then make Tank sleep on the floor. If it's any consolation, I think my grandfather still keeps that barn cat around that likes slipping into the house and leaving presents on the floor."

"Tank would be sleeping in a litter box." A slow smile crept onto the operative's face. "I like that."

"Good. Now hold on to that thought."

As Isa jumped into a hot shower and changed into clothes that didn't scream road grunge, she *almost* forgot about what happened during the last forty-eight hours. She'd *almost* convinced herself this was a regular, everyday visit, and that she had brought friends home to see where she'd grown up.

Her grandfather hadn't touched her room throughout the years. The canopy bed had been replaced by an older, more sophisticated version, but the rest of the furnishings were the same. A white oval mirror hung over the dresser, photos from different times of her life tucked into its wicker frame.

Smiling faces beamed into the camera, but Isa's was always the brightest when the person standing next to her was Olly. She scanned the timeline of their relationship, from preteen birthday parties to high school graduation. In one, taken on a hot summer weekend during his first R&R weekend, she sat on his lap, her arms tangled around his neck as if unwilling to let him go.

That's how they'd been for most of their lives.

Inseparable. Comfortable. *Safe.*

Isa felt anything but safe and comfortable at the moment, but she put on a smile she hoped looked authentic and headed downstairs, where she found everyone on the back patio, her grandfather transporting a plate of stacked steaks to the table.

"Let me help you with that, Abuelito." Isa rushed forward, noting the patio was already set up for them to eat outside.

"Nonsense. I got it. Sit down. All of you."

Isa was the last one to obey her grandfather, which meant she had no choice but to take the empty seat next to Roman. An enormous amount of food was passed around, and soon their plates were heaping—Tank's more than anyone else's.

"This is incredible, Mr. Santiago," Tank gushed through a mouthful of food.

"Carlos, please." Her grandfather casually spread apart a roll and slathered on an unhealthy amount of butter. "I figured we should all have full stomachs while you tell me what kind of trouble has followed you all the way out here to Texas."

Everyone froze, Roman with a juicy piece of steak an inch away from his mouth. Jaz's gaze shot to Isa, and Isa simply stared at her grandfather.

"I'm sorry, sir," Roman said carefully, "but what do you mean, *trouble*?"

Carlos Santiago slowly set his roll back on his plate, his gaze sliding over each of them before slowly transferring between Roman and Isa.

Crap-*tastic*. Isa wasn't sure how, but he *knew*. "Abuelito, I—"

"Ah-ah." Her grandfather shushed her with a wave of his finger. "There's no Abuelito-ing yourself out of this one, Isabel. I may be an old man, but I'm not oblivious. These two"—he pointed to Jaz and Tank—"look like they'd rather tear each other's heads off than their clothes."

"And you..." He drilled a look at Roman. "You haven't stopped looking around, even when your head is turned straight ahead. The only two types of men who do that are paranoid ones or ones who are expecting trouble to pop up around any corner."

Finally, Isa's grandfather turned his attention to her. "But I think *you* were the most obvious, sweetheart. I've been begging you to come home for a visit for months and always get the same excuse. *Work.* And you show up *now*? With only a few hours' warning? Like I said, I'm old, but I still can smell a bullshit story from acres away."

Isa exchanged a look with Roman.

"It's up to you, Doc." Roman put the decision in her hands.

Sighing, she turned back to her waiting grandfather. "Before I tell you anything, you have to promise to listen. Not just *hear*, Grandpa. *Listen*. Jaz, Tank, and Roman know what they're talking about when it comes to keeping people safe."

"People?" Her grandfather latched onto her words quickly. "Or you?"

"*And* you." Isa told him everything—minus details about her scuffle with Lina. And with every additional piece of information, her grandfather's frown grew. "But I don't want you to worry. Jaz and Tank are staying here at the ranch to watch over things—and you—and I'll be DC-bound in a few days to help Maddy in the lab. I'm not letting these people use FC-5 to terrorize anyone."

Her grandfather soaked up everything she told him before finally nodding. He looked at Roman. "If Tank and Jaz are staying here at Mari's Sanctuary, I'm guessing that means you'll be the one watching over Isabel?"

Roman nodded. "Yes, sir. I am."

"And you've done this sort of thing before?"

"I have. Trust me, sir. I'm not letting anything happen to your granddaughter."

"I'd like to believe that, son, but she's already been taken once by these people. In Alaska. Who's to say it won't happen again?"

Isa opened her mouth to intervene, but Roman cut her off. "*I* do."

Isa counted to ten until her grandfather finally looked somewhat appeased. "That's what I hoped to hear."

"Mr. Santiago. Sorry to interrupt, sir." One of the ranch hands stepped up to the porch. "Henry arrived with the dance floor. Do you want me to have him put it alongside the grain feeder until the boys are finished prepping the barn?"

"Sounds like a plan, Ben. I'll be down in a half hour or so to see how things are coming along." Carlos dismissed the young cowboy with a nod.

Henry Walton. Dance floor. Barn.

All those words slowly reformed in Isa's brain until it came out with one vividly clear memory that involved all of them. "Grandpa, what weekend is this?"

His smile moved his bushy mustache. "It's Founder's Week...and tomorrow's the barn dance right here at Mari's Sanctuary."

His knowing gaze landed directly on Isa, and her stomach dropped to her knees.

This was the price she paid for staying away. In twenty-four hours, people she hadn't seen in years, some since Olly's funeral, would be at the ranch.

"Excuse me for a second. I just need some...air." She stood from the table, taking her uneaten plate inside.

Before the screen door closed at her back she heard Tank's response: "Don't people usually stay outside to get fresh air?"

The *oof* and muttered curse immediately following indicated that Jaz brought an end to the conversation.

Leaning against the kitchen counter, she took a series of deep breaths and hoped one of them settled her rolling stomach. As much as Mari's Sanctuary and the entire town of Golden Plains fueled some of her best childhood memories, it also held some of her worst.

* * *

By the time Roman finished the last-minute tweaks on Carlos Santiago's existing security system, the farmhouse was dark and everyone was already fast asleep. It was just as well. He wasn't in the right frame of mind for small talk, or any conversation that went beyond *things that go boom*.

After dinner, Isa had locked herself away in her room and, according to Jaz, teleworked with Maddy and Tony back in DC. One thing he'd come to know about Isabel Santiago was that like him, she used work as an escape from the real world.

You couldn't see shit flying at you from all directions if you had your head buried in the sand, and at the mention of this Founder's Week dance, she'd practically shoved her head in the hole up to her shoulders. He'd only barely stopped himself from following her into the house, not realizing until that moment how much he'd gotten used to their talks—the serious, the funny, and yeah, the naked ones.

Even now, his first instinct wasn't to go to his room upstairs.

It was to go to *hers*.

He found himself standing in front of the fireplace mantel, where a small army of pictures was lined up from one end to the other. Most included Isabel, and in all of them she wore a bright, happy smile that made Roman's chest ache all the more.

"That's some pretty deep thinking you're doing." Carlos Santiago stepped into the living room.

"That's why I get paid the big bucks," Roman joked. "And speaking of money, I didn't think ranches—especially equine rehabs—usually had top-of-the-line security tech. Cameras. Motion sensors along the perimeter. It's impressive."

"They usually don't, but before we became a rehab, we bred thoroughbreds. High-end animals require high-tech precautions. I complained about it to my wife when we had it all installed years ago, but I find myself being thankful for it now."

Roman didn't know what to say, so he kept quiet.

Carlos plucked a picture off the fireplace, his face softening as he stared at a picture of Isa and someone he guessed was her grandmother. "I don't think there was a person Isabel idolized more than her grandmother, and really, they were like the same person. The same strength. The same stubbornness and need to help others...to make others happy. Isabel took it really hard when her grandmother got sick. I think it's actually the reason she wanted to become a doctor."

Roman couldn't help but listen raptly, and although the depth of her caring didn't surprise him, the fact that her grandfather was sharing it with him did. "Isabel's still looking after people."

Carlos smiled wistfully. "She is...and I think that's why she's held on to Oliver for so long."

At the mention of Isa's fiancé, Roman stiffened. "Why do I get the feeling you're trying to tell me something, Mr. Santiago?"

Carlos sighed. "Because I am...and I'm trying to do so without breaking any trust, or stepping on any toes, because I know you care for my granddaughter. I see it plain as the nose on my face. Olly cared for her, too—deeply—and while he may have seemed like the perfect man, I don't think he was the perfect one for *her*."

"Isabel must have thought otherwise. She was going to marry him, right?"

"Oliver proposed, and Isabel accepted only a few days before my sweet wife joined her family in heaven." Carlos smiled sadly, replacing the picture on the mantel before turning his eyes on Roman. "I know Isa loved Olly. They grew up together. They were damn near inseparable. But I think—between you and me—that her acceptance of his proposal had more to do with making my wife's finals days happy than they were about the rest of her own life. Oliver's unfortunate passing just won't let her see that for herself."

Yawning, Carlos stretched his arms and headed toward the stairs.

"Sir?" Roman called out, and the older man stopped. "Why did you tell me all of that?"

A mischievous grin came onto his face. "Because when my Isabel's right guy *does* come around, I want him to be prepared and have the right ammunition to fight for her."

Inspected. Scrutinized. *Studied.* None of those words

quite explained how Roman felt watching Carlos Santiago climb the stairs. Somehow the older man read his thoughts in a way even his brothers couldn't.

With Isa's grandfather's words still rumbling in his head, Roman headed upstairs. A faint light coming from under Isabel's room illuminated the hall. Knowing he should drop face-first into his own bed and leave her alone didn't stop him pausing at her door.

"Asking for trouble, Steele," Roman murmured. He turned to leave when he heard a faint, undecipherable mumble followed by a slightly louder cry. *Screw it.*

"Doc?" He knocked softly. "You okay in there?"

Something dropped to the floor, and Isa cursed. "Yeah. Come...come in."

Isabel sat at a desk that had definitely been picked for a teen girl. White with painted pink and blue flowers, the only thing sitting on top of it was a laptop...and Isa's head.

Her eyes opened as he stepped in the room. "Hey."

"Hey yourself. You know that flat surface over there is a bed, right?" Roman teased.

Isa yawned and sat up. "Maddy and I made some headway on those viral samples, and I didn't want to stop. By the time we did, I was too tired to get up."

"You made progress?"

"Yep." Isa stood, stretching her arms above her head. Her taut stomach peeked out from beneath the hem of her shirt. "There's something in the way Abby's blood responded to the virus that's unlike anything we've seen in any samples *ever*."

"You think you can duplicate the reaction? Make

a vaccine from it? That's what they do with the flu vaccines, right?"

"That's a tall order with one sample. But if I can spend more time monitoring the way her immune system fought off the virus, we can try to duplicate the effects with the right combination of antiviral medications. That's what I'm hoping at least."

Roman was impressed. "That's good."

"It will be if we can figure out the biologics of it. Thank God Maddy knows as much about FC-5 as I do. I don't trust anyone to run all these tests more than her."

"That's good." Roman stood awkwardly in the middle of Isabel's bedroom and shoved his hands into his pockets.

Holy shit. Did he not know any word beside *good*? Feeling this off-kilter around a woman threw him off his game and left him unsure what to do next. And the way Isabel fidgeted with the bottom hem of her shirt didn't help.

They'd barely said a few sentences to each other since leaving Alaska, and a large part of that had been on him. He regretted it now, and he was physically aching to reach out and touch her.

"It's obvious you love it here and that you love your grandfather. Why haven't you been here in so long?" Roman heard himself ask. "Why go MIA? What about this Founder's Week made you get up in the middle of dinner and run into hiding?"

Isa turned her back and yanked the covers down on the bed. "Maddy and I will be up early and working on the samples again for most of the day, so I'm calling it a night."

"You're not answering my question," Roman said.

"Nope. I'm taking a page out of the Roman Steele handbook and avoiding subjects that leave me uneasy." She tossed a glare over her shoulder, lifting one delicately arced eyebrow. "Unless you suddenly want to talk about why you've been acting as though I'm persona non grata?" At his silence, she scoffed and turned back to fixing her bed covers. "Didn't think so. Good night, Roman."

His feet didn't move.

Did he want to tell her? Surprisingly, he did. But the second he came out with his concerns about not being able to keep her safe, she'd call him out on his bullshit. Hell, she'd have him reversing his mind with the snap of her delicate fingers, and he'd be in that bed with her—naked or fully clothed. It didn't matter which, because holding a fully clothed Isabel Santiago was just as dangerous as making love to a naked one.

The only way to make sure that he didn't screw them both over was to stay on course and walk away.

Which was exactly what he did.

"That's it?" Isa asked as he reached the door. She sat upright in bed, the covers over her lap. Anger and hurt were evident in her dark eyes. "You're just going to go?"

"That's exactly what I'm doing." Control was Roman's middle name, yet he couldn't let go of the door handle. The second he did, he'd be across that room and next to her bed. "Like you said, you have an early start in the morning…and then there's a party to prepare for. Good night, Doc. Sleep well."

Because he sure as hell wouldn't—and didn't. His time in Burundi leaked out of his memory vault and played in his dreams like a movie reel. Except this time, it wasn't a duo of innocent children he'd purposefully stepped on that active IED to save.

It was Isabel.

CHAPTER EIGHTEEN

After working remotely with Maddy the entire morning, it was time for Isa to perform her granddaughter duties. No backing out. Nowhere to hide. She stared at her reflection in the mirror and was transported to the past, because the lacy yellow and white sundress she'd plucked from the back of her closet was one she'd worn a million Founder's Weeks ago...the last one she'd shared with Olly.

She'd be the only one to remember that, but that was the only thing that would be forgotten. Small towns were a lot like young children—long memories and no filters. People who didn't look at her with pity over her loss would shoot her glares from a distance at her noticeable absence from Golden Plains. A brazen handful would no doubt make their displeasure known face-to-face.

By now the feed barn had been cleaned out, and the temporary dance floor laid down. White lights had been strung from the wooden rafters, and if they weren't already here, Old Man Eddie's band would soon be set up in the small gazebo off to the right of the pond.

Isa couldn't hide in her room much longer before her grandfather came looking for her.

A frantic knock pounded on her door. "Isa, you got to help me. *Pronto!*"

Isa opened the door an inch, and Jaz pushed the rest of the way through, in obvious freak-out mode. Wearing a halter-style kerchief dress, her shoulders were left bare. The bodice hugged her breasts and slender waist before flaring out and stopping about mid-thigh.

She looked gorgeous.

"Wow, Jaz. You look..."

"Ridiculous? Half-naked? Like a girl playing dress-up?" Jaz grimaced and glanced to her cowboy-booted feet. "These are not the kind of boots I'm used to wearing. This isn't the kind of *anything* I'm used to wearing."

"You mean camo and T-shirts?" Isa struggled not to laugh.

"And sports bras." Jaz looked down, cupping her boobs. "I can't even wear a bra in this thing, Isa, because *it has no back*. Please tell me you have something else in your closet. *Anything* else."

This time, Isa couldn't contain her laughter. "Sorry, but that dress is the only thing that wouldn't swim on you. I think you're stuck with it...or with a horse blanket. We have more than a few of those in the tack barn."

Jaz's eyes looked hopeful. "You think that will work?"

"No." Isa steered the operative in front of the full-length mirror. "I think you look beautiful. Look at you."

"Do I have to?"

"Yes!"

Jaz's twisted look of pain slowly melted away the longer she looked at her mirror image. Twisting her hips, the full skirt swayed around her toned legs. "I guess I don't look *too* bad."

"That's the underestimation of the year, my friend. Not that you're not stunningly beautiful in Steele Ops fatigues, but wow. He'll swallow his tongue."

"Good. Maybe he'll choke on it." Jaz froze, catching her slipup. "I didn't mean Tank. I meant a metaphorical someone. Some rando guy. A cowboy. Oh, freaking hell."

Isa pulled Jaz into a side hug. "Your secret's safe with me. But I hate to remind you that even if you do have any interested suitors out there—and I'm sure there will be many—your dance card is already filled by your *fiancé*."

Everyone had agreed—even her grandfather, surprisingly enough—that it would be best to keep up the charade for the people around town. They were a well-meaning bunch, for the most part, but nosy as hell. If anyone got wind about bodyguards floating around Mari's Sanctuary, the rumor mill would explode in a scale large enough to be seen from space.

"Dance?" Jaz's face paled. "Oh no, no, no. I can't dance. Not with Tank. Not with anyone. Like seriously, Isa. Shoot a target from a million yards away? I'll get it done. Grapple with a man double my size? He isn't getting up anytime soon. And I can make mouth-watering pancit while blindfolded, but I do *not* dance."

"If you can do all those things, I *know* you can dance."

"I'll look like I'm having a seizure while standing upright," Jaz complained.

Isabel laughed. "The good thing about the Founder's Week dance is there will be a lot of out-of-towners mixed in with the locals. They won't know what they're doing, either. You'll blend right in."

A few minutes later and Isa's prediction for a crowded dance was proven right. Cars and trucks, each one more beat-up than the next, filled the far field and almost spilled into the next. Any car sporting less than an inch of Texas dust no doubt belonged to a tourist.

People roamed the grounds of Mari's Sanctuary, the men decked out in Western shirts adorned with bolo ties and women in light, airy sundresses designed to show off their year-long tans. The sun, barely hanging above the horizon, illuminated the near-cloudless sky in pretty patches of dark blue and peach, and when paired with the clear white lights decorating the barn, turned the ranch into a magical realm.

Jaz's mouth fell agape as she was taken in by the beauty, too. "Wow. You don't get these kind of views in DC. Tell me again why you're living in a Foggy Bottom apartment when you could live *here*?"

Jaz hadn't meant it as a dig, but it didn't stop the reality of the answer from hurting less. Once upon a time, that had been her plan. That had been *her and Olly's plan*. In the Army, she'd build up her clinical skills enough to open up her own small practice in Golden Plains. While he served his country, she'd prepare their home for when he hung his uniform up for good...and then they'd start the next phase of their lives.

Together. Like they'd done everything else while growing up.

After he'd died and she'd switched gears from practicing medicine to research, that plan had no longer felt right...including coming home to Golden Plains.

People's heads turned as Isa and Jaz closed in on the barn. The locals were easy to spot. Gazes that at first slid right over them snapped back. A few gave polite nods of recognition, and a steady trickle stopped them for hellos and small talk. Seeing fictional grandbabies, Betty Hanson from the diner had not-so-subtly snatched her single son and dragged him over for an introduction to Jaz, and for the first time, the operative proudly flashed her fake engagement ring. Twenty minutes later the poor woman still looked crestfallen.

"You okay?" Jaz watched her carefully as they stepped into the barn.

"I'm fine. Why?"

Jaz flashed her a look of disbelief before glancing down to where Isa's arm had hers in a death grip.

"Crap. I'm sorry." Isa released her grip and chuckled. "Guess I'm more nervous than I thought. The last time I've laid eyes on most of these people was at Olly's funeral...which played out a little bit like a daytime drama."

"Don't worry about what they think. Anyone who judges you for stupid crap like that has a special place in hell dedicated just for them."

"Spoken like someone who's had to deal with it."

Jaz half-shrugged. "The second I decided to become a female sniper in the Corps, I painted a target on my back. People accused me of earning my high rank in accuracy by sleeping my way up the chain of command...because how could a woman handle a sniper scope better than a man?"

"That's asinine." Isa was pissed on her behalf.

"That's a woman's life in uniform. But it's getting better...gradually."

Isa couldn't imagine struggling with that kind of animosity every day. In the lab, she didn't have to constantly prove herself, at least to no one but herself. Maybe that's the real reason why she stayed away from home for so long.

"You have celebrities here in Golden Plains?" Jaz nodded toward the other side of the barn, where a growing crowd at least three women deep huddled in pack formation just off the dance floor.

But it wasn't an actor or even a country singer that had stolen their attention.

Tank's familiar shaggy blond head stood in the center of the crowd, and right next to him was Roman. Dressed in black jeans and a dark Western shirt, his hair loose around his jaw, Roman looked the perfect combination of rugged cowboy and bad-boy rocker. No wonder he had a fan club. Isa was half tempted to hip-check all those other women away and take the president position for herself, and judging by the way Jaz studied Tank, she felt the same way about him.

As if sensing he was being watched, Roman looked up. His gaze collided with hers before going on a slow stroll over her body, and what first started as a butterfly feeling in her stomach turned into pterodactyls the longer he stared.

Jaz chuckled. "Guess Tank isn't the only one who's about to lose his tongue."

Isa wasn't sure if she meant her or Roman. It could go either way, because while the desire in Roman's gaze was impossible to miss, she had to think hers was the same.

"Isa!"

Without thinking, she turned toward the sound of her name and immediately turned to stone. She couldn't breathe. She couldn't move. Her head spun, tilting her world on its axis as she laid eyes on her fiancé in the first time in years.

Oliver, his dark hair cut short and styled away from his face, strode in her direction like a man on a mission. Like the other men in attendance, he wore jeans and a Western shirt, though his shoulders didn't look quite as broad as she remembered.

And then he smiled, making her heart stumble.

Isa blinked twice before she climbed out from the hallucination...

Olly had had a scar on his chin that dimpled when he grinned. This man didn't have the scar, or the biceps. This man was what Olly would've looked like if he hadn't joined the SEALs.

This man was Michael. *His twin.* And one of the only people who blamed her for his brother's death more than she did.

More than a few sets of curious onlookers gawked as if waiting for a repeat performance of the show at Olly's funeral. Her head spun, practically hearing the accusations ringing in her head all over again, and they took her breath away now as easily as they had back then.

Jaz stepped close, her dark eyes narrowed in on Michael. "Do I need to intervene? I have a gun holster strapped to my thigh."

"No. He's a...friend."

"Most people don't look for exit routes when their friends show up."

She wasn't wrong. "You don't have to stick around for this, Jaz. This isn't bound to be a pleasant conversation."

Jaz crossed her arms over her chest. "All the more reason for me to stay."

Knowing there was no changing her mind, Isa waited for the inevitable blame to fly her way. Olly joined the Navy *because of her*. Olly had requested the extension at the forward operating base *because of her*. He died on that last op because *she'd broken his heart*.

All Michael's accusations hadn't been anything she didn't blame herself for, too.

Michael's light green eyes, so much like his brother's, flickered over to Jaz. Before Olly's death, he would've greeted her with a joke and a hug that spun her in circles until she got dizzy.

This Michael kept his hands tucked deep in his pockets and stopped three feet away. "You're here. I'm surprised Carlos didn't announce your trip home in the *Gazette*."

Isa cleared her suddenly dry throat. "I didn't give him a lot of advance notice. It was just one of those times when the stars aligned. It won't be a long visit, though. I'll be out of your hair before you realize it."

Something flickered over Michael's face, but it was there and gone before she registered what it was.

"I guess I deserved that." He nodded. "And a hell of a lot more. I know this is a few years too late, and in no way makes up for anything I said, but I *am* sorry, Isa. I don't really have an excuse except that I'm an asshole, and during Olly's funeral I was a drunk asshole."

Isa wasn't sure what he expected her to say. "We both did things we regret back then."

"You shouldn't regret being honest with him."

Biting the inside of her cheek, Isa held tightly on the whir of emotions rising quicker by the second. Her last conversation with Olly was one she hadn't told anyone about, but it was obvious that Oliver had shared it with his brother. And it made sense. The two of them had been halves of the same coin, so much more alike than just their looks.

Michael took her silence as the end of their talk. "Anyway, I just wanted you to know that I'm an ass. I'm sorry. And you don't have to avoid Golden Plains because of me. Your grandpa misses you, and neither one of you should have to suffer because of something I did."

Isa's skin vibrated, alerting her to Roman's presence moments before he stepped between them and shoved Michael into the nearest support pole. "And what exactly did you do to her?"

"Roman, no!" Isa cried.

"Shit," Jaz cursed.

Roman stepped closer to Michael, his eyes hard. "You going to answer me?"

Michael, near the same height but with nowhere near the muscle mass, stood upright and didn't so much as blink. "I don't think that has anything to do with you."

"If it has something to do with Isabel, then it has something to do with me."

"Is that right?" Michael asked. He looked at Isa over Roman's shoulder. "Is that how it is now, Izzy? You never let anyone talk for you before. Hell, I remember you ripping Olly a new one when he thought about trying."

"It's not like that," Isabel stated before glaring at Roman. "And *you* need to take a step back. Literally and figuratively."

They'd started to draw attention despite the fact that the band had worked themselves up into a full swing. Stares burned into the back if Isa's head from all directions. More fuel for the gossip mill. She couldn't stand there and give them any more.

"You know what? Have at it. But don't expect me to stand here and watch." Without a word, she left the madness with no real destination in mind.

Somewhere behind her, she heard Roman call out her name, but she ignored it and kept walking, realizing after a minute or two that she was being tailed. "I really just want to be alone right now, Jaz."

"Totally get it, Dr. Sexy, but now isn't the time to go stalking off." King stepped out from the shadows.

"I either walk off now, or I wrap my hands around your friend's neck. Which will it be?"

"Neck-ringing or ass-kicking, Ro could probably use one of each."

"Glad we're in agreement."

"Just do me a favor. Don't cut him out of the running just yet."

"I don't know what you're talking about," Isa lied, but she saw King's meaning all over his face.

"Shit happens to the best of us, and Roman's had to deal with more than his fair share. He is the way he is because he cares too much and doesn't know how to channel it in the right way." There was no sign of King's usual playful tone. "But I think you can help him channel it, Isa. Or at the very least, show him that he's capable of doing it himself. Just…don't give up on him entirely."

As she digested his words, he grinned, nodding to the far barn closed off to guests. "If you want somewhere to stalk away to, may I suggest over there? Far enough away to stew, close enough to be heard."

She glanced toward the barn her grandfather used to rehab the newest sanctuary residents. "You going to tell him where I am if I go there?"

"Sweetheart, I don't need to tell Roman Steele shit when it comes to you. He'll find you regardless."

* * *

Roman's hand twitched with the urge to whip out the weapon on the holster beneath his shirt, but he kept cool—barely. If this guy had been a true threat, Jaz would've dealt with him before he had even gotten there. Still, Isabel's body language had indicated this had been far from a friendly interaction.

"Ro." Jaz's voice barely drilled through the red haze of his anger. "Roman!"

"What?" he growled, head spinning to face the sniper's don't-fuck-with-me look.

She gestured to the curious sets of eyes watching them. He grudgingly stepped away from the asshole in front of him. "Don't expect me to apologize."

The blond man chuckled, fixing the front of his shirt. "Didn't even cross my mind. And trust me, I get it. But can I give you a little advice? Isa doesn't do protective very well. First, because she doesn't need it. And second, because she feels like it's *her* job to do the saving."

Then they had that in common.

Roman had the sudden urge to see her. He turned, stopping when Michael Park grabbed his arm.

"You want Isa to be happy," Park stated. It wasn't a question.

"I do."

"Then make sure she doesn't sacrifice her happiness for someone else's…because that, my friend, is Isabel Santiago's MO."

Roman didn't know what to say to that as he walked off, circling the crowded dance floor before realizing Isabel wasn't anywhere to be seen. He found Jaz by the exit, leaning against the wall.

"She's in there." She nudged her chin to the darkened barn next door. "But before you go over there, you need to take your head out of your posterior and not be *you*."

"What the hell's that supposed to mean?"

"Growly and demanding."

"I don't growl," Roman growled. *Fuck.*

She pointed at him. "See. Growly. And it doesn't take someone with a genius IQ to realize something changed. One moment a girl could get third-degree burns standing next to the two of you, and now I'm afraid frostbite's about to set in. I'm placing my bet that *you're* the reason for the climate change."

"If I am, it's for the best."

"Yeah?" Jaz stared him dead in the eye. "Whose? Hers or yours?"

Roman couldn't blame Jaz for her protectiveness over Isa. She seemed to draw that out in everyone on the team. "Help Tank and King keep an eye on Carlos. I got Isa."

Roman only heard one soft neigh as stepped into the barn.

"You're missing one hell of a party, Doc." Roman looked up toward the hayloft, knowing she was there without seeing her.

"I'll be back in a few minutes. I just need some time alone. Please."

He almost left, but then Jaz's words hit like a freight train. *Don't be you.*

Don't be the guy who avoided being alone with her because it scared him to hell how much he craved it. Don't kiss her one moment and avoid her the next. Don't expect her to talk about her feelings while he bottled his up in an airtight vault.

A muffled sniffle took his decision out of his hands.

"Fuckin' A," Roman muttered to himself as he braced one boot on the ladder and hoisted himself up one rung at a time. His prosthetic buckled once, but he pushed on until he breached the top.

Isa sat in the open hayloft door, her back turned toward him. Hearing him, she brushed her hands against her face. "When was the last time you had a physical? Because I think there's something wrong with your ears."

"My ears are fine. It's my judgment I seem to be having a problem with."

"Ah. Well. Then welcome to the second-guess yourself party." Isa scooted over and made room for him. "Have a seat and grab a party favor."

He dropped his legs off the edge, his thigh touching hers. "This is quite the view."

"It was my grandmother's favorite spot. She always claimed she could see straight to the Gulf of Mexico...a gross exaggeration, I know, but as a little girl I ate it up and wished my eyesight was as good as hers."

"Your grandmother sounds like a great woman."

"She was the best. She and my grandfather were made for one another." A wistful smile fluttered onto Isa's face.

"Like you and Oliver?" Her fiancé's name slipped off Roman's lips like sandpaper before he could stop himself.

He'd never thought himself capable of being jealous of anyone, much less of someone who wasn't alive. The past shouldn't dictate the future, but it did. Hell, he'd let his own history define every relationship choice he'd made since.

"Forget I asked," Roman added, his voice gruff with unnamed emotion. "It's none of my business."

"I loved him," Isa answered softly. Her voice wavered as she stared out into the starry night, tears welling in her eyes as she refused to meet his gaze. "He was the dutiful son. The encouraging brother. The thoughtful boyfriend. He was perfect in every way imaginable except one."

Roman shifted his gaze to her face. "Which way was that?"

"He wasn't perfect for *me*." His face must have showed his surprise, because she smiled wanly, biting her lip as she sifted through her thoughts. "We'd just gotten the news that it wouldn't be much longer until my grandmother passed when Olly proposed... right in front of her and on bended knee. She'd had such a big smile on her face, the first one in close to a month... and I couldn't make myself say no. I couldn't take away what little joy she had and then..."

"Then you couldn't take it back."

"By that point I think I'd sufficiently talked myself into thinking that what Olly and I had was a mirror image of what my grandparents shared. And Olly knew it." A tear slipped down Isa's cheek, quickly followed by another. Roman ached to wipe the moisture away, but he sensed she wasn't done... crying or talking. And he was right. "He'd called me out on it right before he went out on that last detail with his unit. He'd been distracted. Unfocused. And rightfully angry. If I had loved him as much as I should have, he might still be alive today."

It twisted his stomach into knots hearing her blame herself for Oliver's death. No longer able to keep his hands to himself, he gently angled her chin toward him, brushing an errant tear off her cheek in the process.

"You loved Olly the exact amount you were *meant* to love him. Everything else isn't your fault. It's *no one's* fault. The sooner you can realize that, the sooner your past doesn't have such a death grip on your future."

Isa scanned his face as she whispered, "You sound like you know what that's like."

"Because I do," Roman said honestly. "Only in my case, it was very much my fault."

Opening up didn't come naturally to him. Far from it. And especially when his story didn't paint him in the best light. Still, the words were on the tip of his tongue, and if it had been a month ago, or hell, weeks ago, he would've swallowed them back down and gone about business as usual. Right now, he didn't want to choke it back. Sharing this with Isa right now and in this moment felt *right*.

He just couldn't do it while touching her.

He pulled away and forced his hands to himself. "You once told me that I was the kind of person to sacrifice myself for others, and you may have been right. To an extent. But I also risked what wasn't mine to risk."

Isa sat patiently while he collected his thoughts. "You don't have to—"

"I want to. It's just...it's not something I've talked about for a really long time."

Roman pulled his thoughts together while simultaneously fighting to keep the anger that always came with

Burundi at bay. And damn, it was fucking hard. But he did it, not wanting Isabel to think she'd been the one to conjure it.

"A few years back, King and I were selected as part of a team to be stationed at a CIA black site in Burundi, Africa. A lot of times, the government used Special Forces to run their security, used us as backup in case things went to hell in a handbasket. It was a tense assignment. Little to no reward. The area was located in a region of Africa that was in civil upheaval and had been for as long as anyone who had lived there had even been alive, but we weren't allowed to get involved. Our only orders were to protect the *base*."

Roman slid a look to Isabel and pushed through. "While I was there, I got close to one of the CIA operatives. Kat. It wasn't anything revolutionary. We were bored, there wasn't much in the way of selection, so we kept things easy. We had to work together, after all, and being as secluded as the base was, there was no avoiding each other if things got ugly. We were transporting ammunitions off the site to a waiting military convoy a few clicks away when I drove us straight onto a fucking minefield. The damn thing hadn't been there twenty-four hours earlier, but those rebel cartels were notorious for setting up pop-up fields."

Roman snorted, a small smile forming on his lips. "Kat was *pissed*…called me every name in the book and then some for not paying attention. And normally it wouldn't have been a big deal. I could've backtracked our route easily enough and gone around…but those bastards had put their field right next to a village.

They'd planted bombs where the local kids play soccer every damn day."

Next to him, Isa sucked in a breath. "Oh my God."

"I hopped out of the Humvee, tried flagging the kids down before they stepped onto the field, but they were too far away. Kat laid on the horn. They just looked and ignored us." Roman blew out a breath and momentarily closed his eyes. "There was a little girl, barely four or so, with them that day. One of the older ones kicked the ball and she took off like a bat out of hell after it...right onto the field. Kat and I knew what would happen if we didn't *show* the kids that it wasn't safe to be out there...but we didn't have anything to trigger the IEDs...except ourselves."

Roman blew out a breath and momentarily closed his eyes. Even after all this time, when he thought about that day it felt like he stood there all over again, faced with having to make the same choice. If it had been just him out there, he would've done it in a heartbeat.

With Kat less than five feet away from him, it had taken him two.

"Do it, Ro," Kat had begged him. "We can't let those kids run out here. Either you do it or I will."

A sniffle had Roman opening his eyes.

"You stepped on that IED on purpose," Isa whispered.

"It was either let the kids become casualties or become a casualty myself. It worked—at least that's what King tells me. He was the first on the scene after the explosion. But while the IED took my leg and fucked me up pretty good, Kat had been standing too close to the Humvee full of weapons to be that lucky."

Pain filled Isa's eyes, and Roman knew it wasn't for her, but for *him*. And he didn't deserve it.

He got to his feet, that damn shot of phantom pain ripping through his knee in the process.

Roman gritted his teeth and used it as fuel for what he needed to do next. "I'd failed Kat that day. Instead of saving her life out there, I took it. I *deserve* to feel guilty as hell because I *am*. You just deserve to be healthy and happy...and that's what I'm damn well going to make sure happens."

No matter what it cost him.

"What does that mean?" Isa's question stopped him at the top of the ladder. "Does that mean a repeat occurrence of the caveman routine like back at the dance...or something else?"

"Answer me one question, Doc."

"What?"

"Where were you and who were you with the last time you felt truly, and completely happy?"

Roman waited for her answer with bated breath.

"Here at Mari's Sanctuary, and with my grandfather." She gestured to the sunken sun. "It's peaceful here. Uncomplicated. It makes me feel safe in a way that I can't even wrap my head around what's waiting for us outside."

"Then that's what I'm going to make happen for you," Roman forced himself to say despite the fact that the words tasted like ash on his tongue.

Isabel Santiago deserved happiness…more than anyone he knew.

He'd made it to the ladder when his ass vibrated, his phone belting out some Celine Dion song. *Leave King alone with his phone one damn time…*

Roman glanced at the caller ID. *Liam.* "What's up?"

"You and Isa need to get back to DC," his brother said cryptically. "Now."

Roman's eyes immediately found Isabel's. She was already getting up, her gaze cautiously watching him. He let Liam tell him everything, meanwhile silently cursing at what it meant. By the time he hung up, Isabel was on alert.

"What happened?" Isabel demanded. "And don't tell me nothing, because I can tell by your face that it's a very big something. Heck, the fact that I can tell anything from your expression tells me that it's worse than bad, so just come out with it already."

"There was an accident at the Legion." He waited a beat. "Maddy was exposed to FC-5."

Instead of the news sending Isa to her knees, she lifted her shoulders and hit him with a look that said there was no use arguing. "Then we're going back to DC. It's time I put my house in order."

CHAPTER NINETEEN

From behind the multi-layered glass, Maddy noisily blew her nose. The wad of tissues sitting next to her on the isolation room's bed had grown exponentially in the thirty minutes Isa sat outside quarantine. At this rate, they'd need to be restocked in another hour... probably less.

"I'm so sorry, Isa," Maddy cried out her twenty-third apology. "I'm *so* sorry. I still don't know what happened. One minute we were fine, and the next, Tony spotted the hole in my suit and I *freaked* out. When *I* freaked out, *Tony* freaked out. The vials ended up on the floor. *All that work.* Gone."

"Maddy, it's okay," Isa said soothingly.

"No, it's not. I *panicked.* You always tell me to take a deep breath and a few seconds to think, but I'd gone completely blank."

"It happens to the best of us, Mads," Isa said truthfully. "But if you want someone to blame, blame me. It was unfair of me to put all this pressure on you. *I'm* the reason you've been working such long hours in the Legion. If I had been here in DC instead of—"

Maddy lifted her hand. "Instead of trying to save people's lives? Please. Your apology is *so* not needed.

It actually borders on ridiculous. You were exactly where you needed to be. If we'd have waited for those corporate suits at the GHO to become interested in Beaver Ridge, we'd be waiting for them to send out a team a month from now. And that's if we were lucky."

"You're starting to sound a little like Tony." Isa smirked.

"He's not wrong."

For Maddy's sake, Isa remained calm...and hopeful. "Well, at any rate, you decontaminated properly. You took immediate action, making sure the ratio of water particles to virus was minute. Any chance you came into contact with any FC-5 virus is minuscule."

Maddy gave her a watery smile. "I love you, Is, but lying doesn't become you. Give me a distraction. Any distraction." She glanced over Isa's shoulder to where Roman sat in the far back corner, a magazine propped in his lap. "You can start with your sexy gargoyle loitering in the corner of the room."

The sound of Roman turning a page froze. He'd heard, and judging by the wicked smile curling up her friend's mouth, Maddy knew he would. The two-way microphone didn't allow for whispering of any kind.

Isa bit her lip. If she didn't laugh, she'd cry. A huge question mark hovered over Maddy's head, and there she was teasing Isa about her love life...but if this was what her friend needed to focus on instead of the next round of blood draws in an hour, then that's what she'd give her.

"There's nothing to tell," Isa said.

"Uh, no. There's everything to tell. The man saved you from a psycho bitch."

"Actually, I kind of saved myself. He just showed up afterward...although I did appreciate the warm coat on the hike back to town," Isa teased.

"And then you took him home to your *grandfather*."

"I didn't take him so much as I went and he supervised. That was all it was, Maddy. After hearing that woman from Alaska threaten my grandfather, I had to make sure he was going to let Roman's friends keep him safe."

"He doesn't look at you like a chaperone, Isa."

Actually, he didn't look at her much at all since they'd left Texas. After he'd told her about what happened to him in Africa, something had shifted between them. In being more open with her, he'd also closed himself off. It almost felt as if he'd been saying goodbye without actually coming out and saying the words.

"You're about to head down to the Legion to work yourself ragged, aren't you?" Maddy asked knowingly. "I know that look, Isabel Santiago. When shit's going through your head, you work."

"I also work when my best friend has given me an awesome advantage. You've done an amazing job while I've been gone. Thanks to you, we're that much closer to nailing this treatment cocktail."

A blush rose on Maddy's cheeks. "I only did what you told me to. It's like congratulating a puppy for using the puppy pad and not the carpet. It's easy to do when it all laid out right there in front of you."

"You keep believing that, but I'll know the truth."

"Hey, Mr. Visual Vacation?" Maddy called out to Roman. "Hide the Red Bull tucked into the far back left corner of the employee lounge and make sure she sleeps. *Please.* I won't have my best friend jeopardizing her own health in the name of mine."

"Maddy..." Isa warned.

"Got my word," Roman agreed.

"Hey!"

"Good." Looking appeased, Maddy feigned a huge yawn. "Get the hell out of here so a girl can get her beauty rest. Seriously. All the in and out all the time. It's like people are counting down the hours to my last day or something."

Isa frowned. "That's *not* funny."

Maddy smirked. "It was a little morbid, but it was funny, too."

"Call me if you need anything."

"Uh-huh."

"I mean it, Mads."

"I will!"

Isa hated leaving her friend there alone to wait and wonder. No amount of reading material or binge-watching of *Downton Abbey* would take her mind off the long list of what-ifs. Isa attempted not to think about them as she exited into the hall and walked toward the Legion.

"She's right, you know," Roman murmured, walking by her side. "I know you want to pick up right where she left off studying those samples, but you're not helping anyone if you run yourself into the ground. Trust me, I know."

"Yeah, but with Maddy in quarantine, I'm down one more person who knows nearly as much about FC-5 as I do. Have you checked in with Jaz and Tank? My grandfather's okay?"

"Safe and subjecting Jaz and Tank to manual work around the ranch—*together*. Pretty sure your grandfather's using it as some form of team-building exercise. It's pretty genius, actually. I wish I would've thought of it sooner."

Isa smiled. "Leave them to the devices of my abuelo, and they may come back to DC engaged for real."

Roman barked out a laugh. "If that happens, I'll run naked across the National Mall."

"I'll prep my camera," Isa teased.

Knox joined them at the end of the corridor, and the two brothers became her unofficial guards as they headed to the Legion. With others positioned around the entire building, Tru Tech had never been safer.

Mark, her backup assistant, bounced his nervous gaze between her and her armed escorts.

"Hey, I was thinking..." Isa kept her voice calm. "Is it okay if I go into the lab alone today? Call it OCD, but I want to make sure I'm able to document each step as accurately as I can, and I can do that better if I'm just recording my own actions. But you can be my spotter, though. How does that sound?"

He nodded a little too exuberantly. "Yeah. Sure. That's cool."

Isa badged into the door that would take her into the prep room, but before she stepped through, Roman's hand caught hers.

Concern filled his eyes as his gaze dropped to her mouth and back.

She surprised them both when she lifted to her toes and pulled him down for a soft, quick kiss. Her heart rate kicked up a few notches, wondering if he'd push her away, but he didn't.

His arm now wrapped around her waist, he held her close. "Be careful, Doc."

"I'm always careful." She flashed him a confident smile that in no way showcased the turmoil happening inside.

Less than twenty-four hours ago, they'd trusted each other. They'd each bared their soul and shared things with the other that they hadn't with anyone else. And she had no clue what he thought about it. They hadn't had time to talk it through or for her to ask just how he'd make sure she'd get her happy ending.

And they wouldn't have time to talk about it until she played into those bastards' fears and made sure FC-5 was no longer a threat to anyone. But when it was done, all bets were off. She'd tell him how much his honesty in the barn had meant to her...and she'd admit that her happy space didn't just include Mari's Sanctuary and her grandfather.

It also included him.

"Time to work some magic." Isa forced her head and her body away from Roman and back on the task ahead of her. "Go brood in a corner somewhere and let me work."

The second the door hissed closed behind her, she donned the first level of protective gear. Paper jumper.

Boots. Hair cover. Once that was done, she slipped through the second door with Mark, where he helped her step into a hazmat suit.

She did as much as she could herself, and then turned for Mark to connect the air tubes. Only after a triple check of all systems did she enter the lab. He left the way he came, and Isa proceeded ahead.

Alone.

Before stepping into the Legion, Isa released a slow, deep breath.

Head in the game, Roman had told her, and that's what she did.

Bringing up the last few weeks' files, she scanned Maddy's previous reports and tagged the samples showing the most hope. Then, she got down to business.

Isa lost track of time. She jumped between the samples collected from the infected patients in Beaver Ridge and the ones Maddy had made with the antiviral meds. The first six medications seemed to have no effect on FC-5 virus at all, and after making that note, she jotted down the observations and moved on to the next.

Samples subjected to both an inhibitor and a reducer made her pause, go back to the initial single-med samples, and look again. *It slowed*. Although the virus continued to duplicate, the rate of replication wasn't as severe.

Her heart lurched into the throat. *This is good.*

This was better than good. It was *fan-freaking-tastic*. Isa forced her hands to still as she shifted to the next batch of samples.

Any excitement she felt evaporated.

"Now *why* are your friends over there doing something while you guys are being sticks in the mud?" Isa murmured softly.

She brought up the fact sheets of all the medications and compared them. Six samples. Twelve different medications. And only one of the combinations showed any promise, and she didn't know why. They were all the same class, same equivalent doses.

"Doc?" Roman's voice burst though the intercom. "It's about time, don't you think?"

Isa's gaze flickered from the computer to where he stood next to Mark. The younger man shifted anxiously in his seat, steeling an occasional glance at Roman's gun holster.

"I just need a few more," Isa stated.

"Minutes?"

She grimaced. "Hours."

Roman was already shaking his head. "I don't think so. Do you realize how long you've been in there already?"

"An hour? Two?"

"Try eight. Without so much as a damn piss break."

Isa glanced at the clock and cursed. "Give me one more hour."

Roman opened his mouth to argue.

"I *promise*. Just sixty minutes. I want to set up another six samples with a different group of medications. We're getting close."

"*One* hour," Roman reluctantly agreed. "Then you're

coming out, even if I have to put on one of those space-suits and drag you out myself."

"I don't think we have one that would fit you."

"Doc," Roman growled.

"If I only have sixty minutes, then you need to close your trap and let me do my job."

Tuning out distractions and keeping the previous samples in mind, Isa hunted for the proper meds in the cabinet. The new samples were made, cata-logued, and inserted into the holding tank with five minutes to spare before Roman could make good on his threat.

As she approached the decontamination room, Isa suddenly felt every single one of those nine hours. Her muscles ached as if she'd run a marathon, and her head blossomed with a headache that throbbed right behind her eyes.

Her body felt half run-down and half hopeful.

It wasn't the full-blown cure she'd hoped to find, but at least they had something. Something that could potentially give them more time, which was more than what they had before.

Roman stood outside the level 1 door when she stepped out.

"I need to make a few phone calls to the GHO in Beaver Ridge." Isa's gaze slid hesitantly to her assistant.

Roman's eyebrows lifted. "With good news?"

"Not with news that I wanted, but I'll take it none-theless. I think I bought us and everyone else a little bit of time. I just don't know how much."

He nodded as if understanding. "We'll take whatever we can get."

* * *

By the end of the day Isa hadn't gotten the miracle cure she'd hoped for, but they did get other good news. Clean bloodwork had meant springing Maddy from quarantine, and her one and only request was to go somewhere and get mind-fogging drunk. Since Isa was still on a tight leash, that meant hitting up Iron Bars.

"I didn't realize how much I like whiskey until this very moment," Maddy announced to no one in particular, dropping her empty glass to the counter. "Barkeep! Another!"

Behind the Steele Ops wet bar, Ryder chuckled. "You have another and we'll be mopping you off the floor, sweetheart."

"Screw it," Maddy's words slurred slightly. "Leave me where I fall, because anywhere is better than that isolation room. Do you know how difficult it is to sleep when someone's watching you on a video screen? It's some fucked-up crazy shit, let me tell you."

"Definitely not one of the fun reasons to be videoed, that's for sure."

Maddy let out a drunken snort-laugh. "I hear you. Hey." She glowered at Isa from over the rim of her glass, pointedly looking at Isa's nearly untouched drink. "Why aren't you on your fourth one by now? A good friend never lets her bestie drink alone."

"A good friend also remains sober to make sure her bestie crawls into her own bed and not the bed of a serial killer."

Maddy sighed comically. "Fine. You got me there. But could you do me one tiny, itsy bitsy little favor?"

Isa was almost afraid to ask. "What?"

Maddy started to hum the chorus to "Secret Agent Man" and looked across the room to where Roman talked to Knox and Zoey. As if sensing he was being talked about, he looked up.

Even from a dozen or more feet away, Isa felt his gaze as if he stood next to her.

"You need a vacation, Isa." Maddy practically shoved her off her barstool. "And babe, you deserve it. Thanks to your crazy smarts and ridiculous work ethic, we'll have a brand spankin' new treatment plan for FC-5 within the next few days."

"I don't know about a few days, but I do feel like we're really close."

"Which means you need to go somewhere that is not here and way over there." Maddy pointed across the room. "Away with you. Be gone."

"I'll be on Maddy duty." Ryder grinned. "No serial killers for her tonight. Besides, I don't think you're the only one who could probably use some relaxation."

Isa followed his gaze to Roman, who stood rigid just off the dance floor. That's how she felt, too. Tense. Uneasy. Antsy. They all deserved a little break, and she crossed the room, hoping Roman felt the same. He saw her approach and met her halfway.

"Everything okay, Doc?"

"I've been told I need a vacation, and I was hoping that you'd be able to help me with that."

"Yeah? And how would I help sweep you away?"

"Dance with me?" She skated her hands up his chest and around his neck. Just when she thought he'd maybe pull away, Roman's arms eased around her waist, pulling her flush against him.

Isa closed her eyes on contact, her body melting against his as she dropped her cheek to his chest. The loud thump of his heartbeat created the beat to their very own dance.

She didn't need a cement bunker in the ground to feel safe. Or armed guards. Roman Steele's arms did that just fine. They lost track of time, Isa barely recalling Liam attempting to cut in and Roman telling him to bug off but in less polite terms.

"It's getting a little crowded up here, isn't it?" Isa scanned the filling dance floor before meeting Roman's heated gaze. "Or is it just me?"

"Definitely not you."

"Maybe it's time for a change in location?" She swallowed the lump that had formed in her throat. "Somewhere a lot quieter. With a lot less interruptions. Anything come to mind?"

"The only place that fits that bill is my bedroom downstairs."

Somehow they made it down to the basement, through Steele Ops, and into Roman's room in record time. Mouths fused and hands already pulling off clothes, Roman kicked the door closed behind them.

"I don't think you realize how badly I've been wanting

to touch you today...or hell, for days." Roman glided his mouth over the curve of her neck before pausing to nibble at the patch of skin just below her ear.

Isa nearly melted into a puddle of goo right there. "Probably as bad as I've wanted you."

Roman Steele—fully clothed or completely naked, smirky or growling—had more than gotten under her skin. He'd somehow burrowed his way into her needs and desires.

When they'd started this, she never would've thought the man in front of her would become as vital as breathing, and yet here she was, breathless and aching for him to kiss her.

To touch her.

To love every part of her body.

She wasn't sure when that had changed, and as Roman shifted his gaze all over her face, she could see him trying to figure out the answer himself.

Cupping her cheeks, he lowered his mouth to hers in an achingly soft kiss. It was the barest touch of lips, and yet it sucked out every breath she had in her lungs.

Worried she'd collapse if she didn't hold on, she wrapped her arms around him and pulled him closer, but Roman didn't change his pace one bit. Keeping the kiss feather-light, he backed them toward the bed until the backs of her knees hit the mattress...and then he slowly lowered her naked body down, his following.

"You're so damn beautiful, Doc." His lips gently kissed a path from her shoulder to her mouth. "So. Damn. Beautiful."

Isa arched her body against his, every inch of her

begging to be touched. She wanted more. She wanted everything. And as Isa slid her palms down his back and guided him between her legs, she realized she wanted *him* most of all. She didn't have much doubt left—if any.

She'd fallen head over heels in love with Roman Steele...and it could either build her up the highest she'd ever been or knock her down into tiny, fragmented pieces.

CHAPTER TWENTY

A warm, weighted blanket nestled against Roman's side. He snuggled into it, wrapping his arms around it, and held it close. A flowery scent, mixed with hints of vanilla, filled his head, a pleasant invasion that reminded him of Isabel.

"I hope that smile means you're thinking about me." Isabel's sultry voice rumbled through his body.

Roman cranked one eye open, then another, to see her chin propped on his chest. Her gorgeous brown eyes peered up at him with a heady mixture of sleep and drowsiness. And it was the best thing he'd ever seen.

"Morning, beautiful." Roman eased her closer, dropping a kiss on her bare shoulder. "And yes, definitely thinking about you."

And everything they'd shared the previous night.

Never in a million years had he thought himself capable of being that open with someone else. It scared the shit out of him and made him hopeful in a way he didn't think possible before...

Before *Isabel*.

Part of him was afraid to blink and find it a dream— or a nightmare. Or worse yet, to have this glimpse of what life could be like and have it yanked abruptly away. He didn't think there'd be any coming back for him after something like that.

"Hey now." Isa slid up his body, her leg easing over his waist until she straddled him. She pinched his chin in her fingers and held his attention ransom. "Where did you go just now?"

"Beneath you," Roman tried joking, but it fell flat.

Isa frowned, obviously not amused by his attempt at humor. Hell, he wasn't thrilled with it, either. This happiness thing was something he wasn't used to.

He slid his hands up her back and into her hair, holding her close. "I guess I'm just waiting for the other shoe to drop. And I guess I also feel a little guilty. Shit's still happening out there, and yet, right now...I'm happier than I have been in a long time."

Fuck, that took a lot for him to say. He attempted to shift his gaze, uncomfortable and exposed, but Isa brought her face to within inches of his, the determination in her eyes fueling his own. "The shoe might drop...but at least we have *this* to fall back on when we need reminding what we're fighting for."

Them. A future. Hopefully together.

That's what they were fighting for. Well, at least he was, because Isabel Santiago was the woman he could see himself with for the rest of his life.

Next to his bed, Roman's cell rang. He ignored it, not wanting to give up even a moment of this time with her. It stopped when his voice mail would've kicked in, and then wailed again.

"I think someone really wants to talk to you." Isa kissed a path over his chin and to the corner of his mouth.

"Too bad it doesn't go the other way around." Roman took her mouth in a slow, deep kiss. Right around the time his head went dizzy, his cell rang again.

"Roman," Isa chuckled.

"Fine. I'll answer it." Roman grabbed his cell, not bothering to check the caller ID, because it could only be one of a select few. "This better be fucking good, asshole."

A beat of silence, and then, "Did I call you at a bad time? My mother always said I had the worst timing of anyone she knew."

"Who the fuck's this?" Roman asked the unfamiliar voice.

"I'm sure your pretty little doctor is close by, right? Put me on speaker phone, and I'm sure she can verify it for you. I'll wait."

Something in Roman told him to hang up, but instead, he put the phone on speaker.

The voice addressed Isabel, "Hey there, Dr. Santiago. Tell me, have you learned your lesson yet? Wait, don't answer that. I already know you didn't, because you went ahead and got my special lady friend arrested."

Isa's eyes narrowed as she glared at the phone and confirmed his suspicions with a nod. *It's him.* "If she didn't want to be arrested, maybe your special lady friend shouldn't have threatened to put a bullet between my eyes. Or hell, taken up with the likes of you."

Roman squeezed her leg to get her attention. Grabbing the pen on the bedside table, he wrote on Isabel's hand: *Get Liam.*

Isa leapt from the bed, practically diving into her

panties and grabbing one of his extra-large T-shirts on her way out the door. Roman slipped into his prosthesis before tracking down and tugging on his pants. "So you're the bastard with the big brass balls who stole FC-5 from Tru Tech, huh? Gotta say, man, that was a pretty fucking stupid move."

"Oh, I don't know about that. It's paid off so far, hasn't it?"

"You said it yourself. We already have one of yours sitting in a jail cell. I'm not so sure I'd call that being in your favor. Staring at the possibility of life behind bars tends to make people awfully chatty."

The asshole chuckled. "Nice try, but she's not going to talk. Now me, on the other hand? I'm willing to have a nice little chat."

"Yeah? If it's to turn yourself in, I accept. Why don't I personally come pick you up? Tell me where you are, and I'll be there in a jiffy."

"Turn myself in? And here I thought you'd been a soldier, not a comedian."

"I see no other reason for why you'd be calling me."

"I have a proposition you'll want to hear."

"Somehow I highly doubt that." Footsteps padded on the cement floor as Isabel returned with not just Liam, his computer in hand, but Knox and Ryder. Hell, even Cade and Grace. *Good thing he wasn't naked anymore.* "But for shits and giggles, go ahead and tell me."

Liam, with an already booted up computer, signaled for him to keep the bastard talking as long as possible.

"I want you to hand over Isabel Santiago."

Roman snorted. "You may as well be asking for flying

pigs, because you'll get those before you lay another hand on Isabel."

"You see, I thought you might say that, so I made myself a little insurance policy. Did you know, that at this very minute and well into the night, there's a street carnival happening right down the block from that gothic-looking building you're holed up in? All the people. The families. The little kiddies holding their cotton candy and balloon animals."

Next to him, Isa looked like she was prepped to jump through the phone and kick the bastard's ass.

"Did one of your brothers ping my general location yet, or would you like me to keep talking?"

Everyone froze.

"You'll find I'm a lot closer than you realize, and I'm not joking, Steele. I want Isabel Santiago at the festival. *Alone.* In one hour. If I see you or anyone from your team, I expose the festival. If I see any cops, I expose the festival. If I see anything I don't like, I expose every last fucking person at that damn festival. And when you send Izzy my way, give her your phone so we can catch up on what we've been doing since parting ways in Alaska."

The line went dead.

"Fucking hell," Roman growled, barely refraining from throwing his cell against the wall. "Where was he?"

"He wasn't lying. The cell pinged off the nearest tower less than a mile away." Liam brought up a map that looked eerily familiar. "He's practically in our backyard."

"That means he's already at the festival. We need to suit up and canvass the area...be on the offensive rather than playing defense. No way is this bastard slipping through our fingers this time."

It was time for *him* to be the one pulling the strings.

Roman led his brothers to the commons and straight to the gear closet. None of them hesitated to pick out their favorites, Roman's being a set of throwing knives and a taser with the highest legal capacity to shock someone's balls off of their rocker.

"Can we hold on a second?" Isa stepped into the cage, now fully clothed in his T-shirt and a pair of his boxers. "We need to step back a bit and think this through. The FC-5—"

"That's right, Doc. He *has* FC-5, which is all the more reason to go all-out."

"But—"

"That bastard's a threat to every living person who walks this earth—and that includes you. I'm ending the threat today."

"Everybody stop what you're doing right the hell now!" Isa shouted.

Roman and his brothers stilled. Grace watched with interest and a whole lot of concern, but he was only concerned about one person, and her glare practically drilled him to the core.

"Doc..." He reached out to touch her, but she stepped back, shaking her head. He felt the move like a stab to the gut.

"I *have* to go to the festival. We have to do exactly as he says," Isa stated firmly.

"No, we sure as hell do not," Roman growled. "We have no idea what his ultimate goal is with you, and I'm not putting you in that kind of situation. No way. Nohow. Never."

Isa came to him, and he took her hand and tugged her close.

"Is there any doubt in your mind he won't do what he threatened?" She paused for him to answer, and when he didn't, she added, "No, there isn't. Because they've already done it once to Beaver Ridge. *This* could be their grand show, Roman. We're right at DC's back door. Do you have any idea the kind of fallout that could happen if he follows through on his threat against the festival?"

"If this is his closing number, then he's going to expose the festival regardless of if you turn yourself over or not."

"Are you really willing to take that chance?"

Fuck, Roman's chest hurt even thinking about letting her go. "I can't let you do it. Don't ask that of me. You...you of all people know..."

It was like Kat all over again...except losing Isa wouldn't just fuck him up. It would destroy him.

Her hand slid against his cheek and held him captive. "I know, Roman. I do. But I looked into the eyes of every sick person in Beaver Ridge, and I told them that I'd do whatever it takes to make this right. This is our chance. This is the shoe, Roman. And you're my reminder."

Grace said, "There has to be a way around the ultimatum."

"He was pretty clear," Cade added. "If he sees any-one, it's over."

If he sees anyone.

"Fuckin' A." Roman wanted to kick himself in the ass. "He's got people on each of the entry points... *that's* how he'll be alerted if Isabel doesn't come alone. If we take them down first, they can't throw up an alarm."

"How are you identifying them before they spot you?" Isa asked. "They probably have the faces of everyone who was in Alaska ingrained in their memory vault."

She was right... except for one thing. "But we weren't all in Alaska."

Roman turned to Knox, Cade, and Liam. Grace waved, getting his attention, his cousin not one to be left out.

"Seriously," Grace scoffed. "Why do you guys always forget the one with the actual federal badge on her hip?"

"You think your bosses would be okay with you taking part in an operation like this?" Roman asked.

"I think in this case it's easier to ask for forgiveness than permission."

Knox grunted in agreement. "Then we're doing this?"

Roman nodded. "You four are going to be the first wave. You'll identify this asshole's men and take them down so the rest of us can get safely inside."

Cade looked as eager as any of them to get in there and bust some fucking heads. "Just to clarify here, but we *are* working two men short with Jaz and Tank still in Texas. I mean, it's not impossible, but I think the saying the more hands the better is pretty damn fitting, don't you?"

"King," Isa and Roman said at the same time.

There's no way Ethan wouldn't want to be part of this, and unlike last time, Roman wouldn't have to appeal to his deeply hidden good nature. He'd simply mention it was for Isabel's safety, because like she'd slipped her way into his heart, she'd made his hard-ass friend that much more malleable.

* * *

With only thirty minutes to go before she needed to make her festival appearance, Isa's earlier bravado had finally started to fade and nerves had taken its place. Knox and the rest of team one had already started scoping out the festival, but the takedown couldn't happen until Isa made contact with Mace.

In order for this plan to work, everyone needed to perform their individual tasks with no flubs and no miscommunications. If they didn't, they'd jeopardize hundreds of innocent lives.

A soft touch on her arm jolted Isa from her worries.

"You okay, Doc?" Roman eased her to the side, where it was only a bit quieter.

"Yes. No. Is both an option?" Isa asked, half serious. She chuckled to lighten up her concern, but it didn't work.

Roman's frown grew. "It's not too late to change your mind. We'll find another way."

"We both know that's not true. There's too much at stake for us not to do it this way. Besides, my part's easy." Isa shrugged, playing it cool. "There's countless things I'd like to hash out with this asshole. I'm more worried about you guys hunting down the virus. A family street festival isn't lacking for different types of food. It could be anywhere."

"We'll just look for the shady-looking goon selling meat products. I don't think that'll be as difficult as you think." His mouth twitched.

"Seriously." She huffed, annoyed. "How the hell can you joke at a time like this?"

"Because if I don't joke about it, I'm throwing you over my shoulder and locking you in the back vault." Roman dropped his forehead to hers. "It's killing me not to be going with you."

"I know." She rubbed the dark stubble on his cheek. "But he's not doing anything to me while we're standing there in the middle of a crowd. Your top priority has to be tracking down the virus. Once you guys have it in your hands, then you can help me kick his ass."

This time, Roman chuckled. "You're going to kick his ass?"

"I'll kick it so hard he won't be able to sit in his jail cell for a month."

He kissed her, and Isa held on to him as long as she could. "You're something else, Isabel Santiago."

"When this is all done and over with, you'll have to tell me what that something is."

"Awww," Liam, with team one already at the festival, cooed via their comm links. "That just made my heart go all aflutter."

"Fuckin' A, Liam," Roman growled, making his youngest brother laugh.

"This is me, announcing that team one is officially looped in on your comms, so now we can communicate like one big happy family. This is also me officially warning you that if any of my toys end up with so much as a scratch while I'm not there, there will be hell to pay."

Ryder, sitting in Liam's usual position behind the computer, snorted. "Right back at you. And while you're at it, make sure Knox shows you which end of the gun the bullet comes out of. We wouldn't want you shooting your nose off your face and making it any uglier than it already is."

Roman whistled, earning him a handful of curses from team one on comms. "Quick operation rundown: We're looking for six assholes. Team one will locate and disarm the four men stationed at each of the festival's entry points...and only then will team two breach the festival grounds. Everyone's *first* priority is the *virus* and our fifth asshole. No distractions. No detours. The virus is this bastard's fail-safe. If *anything* goes wrong in his plan, he's striking the match. We don't want there to be any gasoline."

Isa took a deep breath and reiterated what they'd already gone over earlier. "It's a festival, so there'll be a lot of food, but our biggest bet, and your focus, needs to be on stands selling meat products. Burgers. Hot dogs. Mystery sausages coated in batter and deep fried."

"If you have questions, now is the time to ask them." No one did. "Great. Then let's get this shit done and over." Turning to Isabel, Roman slid his phone into her back pocket. "For you, as the asshole requested. Ryder? Double-check her shoe mic for me?"

"Sure thing." Ryder ran a handheld scanner over her sneakers until it flashed green. "All's good. Just remember you're not alone out there. You may not be able to hear us, but we'll be able to hear you."

"Got it." Isa shook her hands and arms as if warming up for a marathon.

"Doc—"

She cut him off, unwilling to second-guess herself now. "No. You stay here. No goodbyes. No good lucks. *I'll* go have a chat with our friend. *You* find the virus."

Isa glanced at her watch and knew she needed to move it.

With every step she took toward the exit of Iron Bars, her stomach roiled a bit more. And the fresh air didn't do her any good. Up a block and a half, the sound of music and laughter filled the street. Someone on a microphone announced the commencement of a contest in the parking lot of Mama Jo's Diner, and the heavy fried-food-and-sugar-scented air indicated there were definitely a lot of food stalls inside.

"Just another day at the office," Isa muttered to herself and everyone listening on her fancy shoe mic.

She reached Main Street and hung a left. Seeing the first entry point to the festival, she headed toward the short line and waited her turn to get inside.

Everyone Isa looked at, she wondered if they belonged to Blue Eyes' group. Maybe the older gentleman at the coffee shop sipping the largest travel mug she'd ever seen, or the younger guy, baseball hat turned backward, playing on his phone.

As her attention slid to the next person, Isa recognized Grace. She looked like any other young mother, smiling as children sprinted from ride to ride and pushing her—empty—stroller. She flashed Isa a quick wink and walked past. Almost immediately after, Roman's phone vibrated in her pocket.

"Didn't anyone tell you it's rude to be late?" Mace quipped when she answered.

Isa sidestepped a group of kids and scanned the area. "There's a lot of people here. I'm not exactly sure how the hell you expect me to spot you."

"Aw. Feeling feisty this afternoon, are we?" he purred. "Don't worry, hon. I'll make sure I fix that. Dump this phone in the garbage can on your left, and then cross the Cloud Bridge. Oh, and Dr. Santiago? My watch says you have five minutes to get there...or else you know what's going to happen."

Isa barely refrained from snapping back. She tossed the phone and hustled over the bridge, apologizing as she bumped into a couple stopping to take pictures from the higher elevation. When she set foot on the other side, Isa saw Mace right away.

The jerk wasn't even hiding.

Sunglasses perched on his head, he casually sipped something in a tall cup. He'd threatened the lives of everyone here and he'd stopped to grab a damn iced coffee.

Mace smiled when she approached. "It's so good of you to join me. Do you want something to drink? I highly recommend the salty macchiato. My insides are practically tingling in delight...oh wait. No. I actually think that tingle is because you're about to make me a very rich man, Dr. Santiago."

Not even close.

If Isa had anything to say about it, she was about to make him a very jailed convict.

CHAPTER TWENTY-ONE

Roman wasn't built to wait. Kick asses? Yes. Punch faces? Definitely. Eat his ma's cookies? You bet. But *wait*? No way in fucking hell. And judging by the occasional murmurings coming from his brothers' comms, the dislike was definitely a familial trait.

"You're making me twitch," King grumbled next to him.

The two of them stood in the alley to the left of the pharmacy, a half block away from the eastern entry point. Close enough to see; far enough away to not *be* seen.

"Just make sure you're ready to move the second Knox gives us the green," Roman warned.

"Oh, I'll be ready, but will you?"

"What's that supposed to mean?" Roman scanned the entry's surroundings with the binoculars. *Why couldn't this asshole's little bastards wear neon yellow vests or some shit?*

"You're raring to get in there to Isa. I get it, man. I do. Just remember what we have to do first."

Roman locked his friend in a hard glare. "You think I don't know what I need to do?"

"I think you'd move hell or high water to get the

woman you love to safety, but this is one of those times where you have to trust her to do her thing while you do yours."

Roman didn't balk at his friend's use of the word *love*. He didn't snort or punch him. But just because he didn't kick King's ass for using the term didn't mean Roman was ready to use it aloud. Hell, he had nothing to compare it to.

What he felt for Isa was totally different from how he felt about his family, or Tank, or Jaz. He'd never felt this way before, vulnerable and strong at the same time. It didn't make any fucking sense. He cared about her. He'd move heaven and earth or step on a hundred land mines if meant she lived a long and happy life—with *or* without him.

If that was love, then yeah. He loved her. And the fact that he wanted inside that damn festival wasn't because she couldn't take care of herself. He'd place money on Isabel any day. She was trained. She was determined. And she was fucking pissed.

But it still went against his grain to let her walk into danger.

"This is west gate," Knox's gravelly voice announced via their comms. "West gate is green to enter. I repeat, west gate is green to enter."

"Entering west gate now," Ryder announced.

Roman's grip tightened on his binoculars, and it took everything in him not to run to the other damn entrance. They needed to stick to the plan. They needed to take down *all* these looming assholes or risk someone sounding an alarm.

"South gate green," Grace announced. "Headed toward east now."

"North down," Cade added. "I'll meet you over at east."

"Now the ball's rolling," King muttered, clapping him on the back. "Won't be too much longer."

Never taking his gaze off the festival perimeter, Roman slid his attention from one person to another, looking for one that never seemed to move from the same position. It took a hell of a lot longer than he'd wanted, but he finally spotted a middle-aged man sitting on a bench.

"East gate, check out the guy on the blue bench. Bald. Black shirt," Roman announced. "He's doing more people watching than reading that paper in his hands."

"Making an approach now," Grace said.

"You see something?" King joined Roman at the mouth of the alley.

"Guess we'll find out in a second." Roman glued himself to the binocs as the man in question held the paper out in front of him—upside down—and pretended to read. "That's him. That fucker's too stupid to even blend in well."

Grace approached, wheeling her empty stroller like a woman on a mission, and turned the corner. Cade purposefully stepped off the curb and directly in her path, the two of them colliding in a spectacle right in front of their last target. The asshole jumped up, but not before realizing that Cade had dropped some kind of drink in his lap. He leaned over to help, and whispered something in the older man's ear, making him turn to a statue. When the ass reached for a gun at his hip, Grace stepped up with her own.

"And that's a bingo," Roman announced.

"East gate clear," Grace announced. "We'll hand this one off to Nat outside and be right back."

King and Roman didn't waste another second. They entered the festival together and, with a silent nod to each other, fanned out on opposite ends of the street, sticking closer to the larger crowds. Crowds camouflaged, which was why this bastard wanted Isa to meet him there, but while it worked in his favor, it also worked in theirs.

Cotton candy. Pretzels. Roman skirted around a group of kids waiting in line for something on a stick, covered in chocolate, but there was no meaty beef station of any kind he could yet see. His gaze scanned the other side of the street and froze at the restaurant directly across from him.

He didn't need his binoculars to verify he had just found Isa and the asshole. They were so close. He could come up on their six and take that bastard down before anyone realized.

It would all be over.

The end...and then maybe he and Isa could finally form a beginning.

* * *

Isa stared at the man across from her and had to remind herself on a repetitive mental loop that she was a doctor. She saved lives, not took them. But seeing Mace up close again and knowing he was responsible for the attack on Beaver Ridge—and would eagerly launch a second one—really pissed her off.

"You know..." He grinned at her as if knowing her thoughts. "You keep glaring at me that way, and I'll think this friendship of ours isn't working out."

"I told you back in Alaska, I don't associate with homicidal maniacs."

"Yeah, about that little scene in the cabin. I feel as though I should reiterate the rules of this little outing for the people I'm sure are listening in as we speak. My guys have specific orders to start handing out our special product should anything happen to me, if any of us see *you*, or if you just piss me off too much."

Isa ground her teeth until they ached. "Trust me, we don't need reminders."

Keep him talking. All she had to do was buy Roman and the others time to ferret out Mace's team and locate the virus. Once the immediate threat was contained, Isa could jump back into her lane... one that didn't involve sneaker comms and a strategic operations manual.

Mace leaned in, dropping his chin on his hand as if they were just two friends catching up. "You have to tell me... what's it like fucking half a man? Doesn't it freak you out? Or ruin his *thrust*, so to speak?"

Anger burned through Isa's veins as she balled her hands in her lap to keep from throwing a punch. "You really have no moral compass, do you? You have no remorse for the things you've done and the lives you could've destroyed?"

"Owning a moral compass doesn't make a guy rich.

And I honestly have nothing against those idiots in Alaska, or the oblivious ones here. This is just a simple matter of consumerism 101, Izzy. It's why car dealerships have you drive before you buy. But I have to say that for being so deadly, I expected massive death and destruction right off the bat, not this wait and wait and wait some more. But oh well. I'll gloss over that little statistic when I meet with potential buyers and just play up the fact that the longer they're sick, the more people they could potentially infect. They'll eat it up like candy."

A small click alerted Isa to the fact that he'd drawn a gun on her, and to prove it, he nudged the muzzle a bit farther under the table, directly into her thigh.

The smile never left his face. "We're standing up and seeing what this little festival has to offer...and you know what will happen if you're nothing but a good little girl, right?"

Movement caught Isa's attention as her gaze flickered across the street. Roman stood on the sidewalk, body tense and fists clenched at his sides. But reality doused her rising hope like an ice bath.

He couldn't make a move. He couldn't intervene. If he did, hundreds of people's lives would be put in danger.

Roman's heated gaze flickered to hers just long enough to give him an almost imperceptible shake of the head. His jaw hardened as he comprehended what she told him.

He needed to stay away. He needed to let her do this on her own. He needed to walk in the other direction.

CHAPTER TWENTY-TWO

At the idea of turning around and walking away from Isa right then, a searing knifelike pain ripped through his chest. He couldn't breathe, much less move. It took everything in him not to cross the street and take that bastard down right then and there.

But that small shake of the head and the pleading look in Isa's eyes froze his feet to the ground. Roman may not have known what love felt like before, but he was damn positive he did now.

Love was the warmth that settled into the core of his body when he held Isa in his arms.

It was the fierce pride that surged inside when she selflessly fought for her patients.

And it was the fear in watching Isa walk down Main Street with the one person on this earth that could destroy that love—and him—in one single heartbeat.

"Roman," King's voice echoed into his ear mic. "Dude, I know you want to go after her, but—"

"I'm not." Roman found his friend in a thicket of tourists across the street. He'd had an even better view of them sitting at the table than he had. Swallowing the jagged lump that had formed in his throat, Roman winced. "Virus first. And then we're getting the woman I love."

King grinned. "About damn time."

Roman took one last look down Main Street as Isa grew smaller...and then suddenly stopped. "What's going on? Why'd they stop moving?"

He shifted up a bit further, knowing King did the same. "Bastard's looking off to the left."

"What the fuck's he looking at? Did he make someone?" Panic tightened his chest. "Who the fuck's on Main Street? Roll call now!"

"It's not one of ours," Knox confirmed.

Roman quickly crossed the street to get King's better viewpoint...and he saw it, too. The food stand. *Burgers*. It was small. It was brief. But that blond-haired bastard *definitely* locked eyes with the attendant behind the burger counter.

They found their virus.

"Burger stall. Corner of Main and Deer. Everyone but Eagle into fallback mode. I repeat, we're entering fallback." Roman nudged King, and the two of them hustled off the main thoroughfare to Grubb Avenue, the street running parallel to the main drag.

Grace had abandoned the stroller now that the façade was just about over, and she and Cade, along with Ryder, met them around back while Knox remained on Main Street with eyes on their man behind the counter.

Roman made eye contact with everyone. "We have the element of surprise here. That asshole has no clue we've taken out the rest of his guys, but we still need to make this as quiet—and safe—as possible. Grace, hang back and circulate the area just in case there's anyone floating around we haven't anticipated. Cade, you fly as Knox's second set of eyes. King, Ryder, and I will make the final approach on the burger joint."

King clapped him on his shoulder. "You ready for this?"

"I'm ready for this shit-show to be fucking over."

Everyone immediately got into their positions. While Ryder and Cade took the left side of the block, King and Roman went right. At the corner, Roman stayed close to the redbrick wall and slowly closed in on the food stand. They bypassed a neighborhood bakery, and a stand selling antique dolls.

Roman saw the man from the burger counter from ten feet away. His gaze nervously skirted around, and he looked annoyed when someone came up to his counter to place an actual order. "King, you're looking awfully hungry right about now. Sure you couldn't use something to eat?"

King chuckled. "Actually now that you mention it, I am feeling a bit peckish."

Roman snorted as his friend made his way around to come at the stand from the hungry festival-goers' side of the street. They needed to tread carefully. They'd already deduced the tainted burgers were probably out of reach, but easily accessible...probably the bright red cooler sitting on the ground by the guy's feet.

The *vial* of FC-5 was a different story.

They didn't know where this fucker had it and couldn't risk the damn thing breaking.

"Let's close in," Roman ordered.

When they made a tight three-feet perimeter, King stepped up to the counter. "Give me a hot dog. No. Wait. Make it a burger. Do you have sweet pickles to put on the side?"

"Does this look like a fucking restaurant to you, asshole?" the man growled.

"No. But you know what it does look like?" King moved so fast, he blurred. Grabbing the back of the guy's shirt, he yanked the goon face-first into the counter. Bones crunched and blood splattered on the counter from the asshole's broken nose. "It looks like a really bad day for you."

"You guys will fucking pay for this! Just you fucking wait!"

King smacked the asshole's face into the counter a second time. "This is a family-friendly area, asshole. Stow the foul language."

Roman couldn't help but chuckle.

"Found them," Cade called out. With a gloved hand, he opened the cooler to find at least fifty or more burgers, all double-bagged and waiting for use. "On second thought...hold on."

He held out the bag toward their new friend, and the man practically did a somersault to avoid touching it.

Knox snorted. "Yeah, I think it's pretty safe to bet that those are our burgers."

But no vial.

"Where's the virus?" Roman hauled King's new friend halfway across the counter, nearly spilling him off the other side. "Where's the damn virus? The vial!"

Blood dripped down his face and into his teeth as

he smiled. "You really think he'll let it out of his sight? Mace is nothing if not a control freak."

Roman's stomach sank like a lead weight. They'd got all the bastard's men. The tainted burgers were taken out of the equation. The festival was safe.

Now the only threat out there was to the woman he loved.

* * *

Isa walked straight ahead, not wanting to give Mace any reason to make good on his threat to the festival. But every step she took, she felt like she'd just stepped a little farther out on a rickety pirate's plank.

Isa hoped talking would distract him enough to slow him down, "So you take me, and maybe you even dispose of me. You sell FC-5 to the highest bidder. And then what? You realize that virus has the ability to wipe out a huge portion of the population."

Mace dug his gun deeper into Isa's side. "That won't be my problem. I'll be long gone by then."

"Really? Where are you escaping to? Because unless it's freakin' Mars, nowhere will be safe. How do you not get that?" Isa snapped.

Mace yanked her back and immediately got in her face. A few people around them paused to stare, maybe to possibly intervene or maybe to just sit back and watch the show. "You're *really* getting on my nerves, Izzy. If you don't watch that mouth of yours—"

"Do what?" Isa challenged. "You're already planning on *disposing* of me."

"And maybe I'll do it sooner rather than later." His gun whipped up, no longer hiding it against her side.

Isa pushed his hands to the sky and it discharged. Around them, people screamed. A flurry of movement caught her attention. Nat, leading a team of black-suited DCPD, quickly cleared the area, hustling families in the opposite direction from where she stood with Mace.

"Doc!" Roman, flanked on either side by King and Ryder, were the only ones heading her way. "The vial! He's got the vial!"

Mace dropped his hand to his hip, hovering it over the left side of his jacket pocket. She didn't think. She struck. Twisting his wrist in one direction and the gun in the other, she disarmed him and tossed the gun aside.

In an instant, Roman was there right along with King and Ryder.

"It's in his pocket! Do *not* crush his jacket!" Isa warned, seconds before they man-handled him into cuffs. Donning a pair of gloves she'd pulled from her pocket, she carefully frisked him until she pulled out a fragile glass ampule. "You had it in your fucking pocket?"

Roman left Mace to his brother and nearly tugged her into his arms, but she stopped him, dangling the FC-5 from her fingers. "I wouldn't if I were you. Did you locate the tainted food? And what about the rest of Mace's team?"

"Confiscated. All of it." Roman looked about a second away from not caring she held a deadly virus in her hands. "Are *you* okay?"

"As good as I can be while holding something that could kill everyone on this street," Isa half-joked.

"So what do we do with...that?"

"Me!" Maddy sprinted down the sidewalk, a metal biohazard box swaying in her hands. "I can't wait to hug you, but first let's get the infectious material safely tucked away in its little hidey hole and take it home, shall we?"

"That sounds like the best idea ever."

Nat gestured to the cop on her left. "We'll give you guys an armed escort back to Tru Tech."

"Thank you."

"Not a problem. And you"—Nat not so gently nudged Blue Eyes in the opposite direction—"get an armed escort to a six-by-six jail cell. At least until the feds come and pick your sorry ass up."

Isa turned to Roman, torn between following Maddy and never letting him out of her sight.

"Go." He eased her into his arms and dropped a soft kiss on her forehead. "I know you need to go. Do your thing, Doc."

CHAPTER
TWENTY-THREE

Roman could hardly see straight, he was so damn tired, but it wasn't just physical exhaustion. He was mentally drained. Emotionally wiped out. Hell, he couldn't even bring himself to celebrate with everyone at Iron Bars despite the fact that they couldn't have asked for the operation to go any smoother than it did.

This job may be done, but there'd always be a next. And one after that. It wouldn't be the theft of FC-5, but something would come along equally as dangerous, and Roman would do whatever he could to make sure it didn't happen, because that's what he did. It's who he was.

But that kind of stress, the constant unknowns...it wasn't who Isabel was. And it sure as hell wasn't what she deserved.

Standing on the rail by the dock, he stared across the Potomac. The DC lights reflected off its surface, rippling the glowing river as if it housed thousands of blinking fairies.

"Pretty man. Pretty view. I'm not sure if there's anything that could make that sight any better to be honest." Isabel's warmth coated his back as she wrapped her arms around him. "King told me you were hiding out here. Just curious why when the party's happening up there."

"Guess I'm just not in the mood for a party."

"That doesn't sound like a positive." She slipped under his arm and around his side until she stood in front of him, her brown eyes staring up at him in full concern mode. "What's wrong?"

"You're not at the lab, so things must be looking up. Good day?" *Coward.* By deflecting her question he was only delaying the inevitable, and judging by her frown, she knew it.

"We're closer than we've ever been before, and all because of Abby. There's something in her body's reaction to the virus that's the missing link I've been needing. As much as I wish Beaver Ridge had never been targeted, we're only a week or so away from finding a cure because they did."

Roman pushed a smile to his face. "That close, huh? Then I guess it *is* a good day."

"It's looking up, but we're just not quite out of the clouds just yet."

"You'll get there. I don't have a doubt in my mind."

"But you do about something...don't you?" Isa's voice faltered as she watched him carefully.

No one had ever been able to read him so accurately before. Not even his brothers.

"Talk to me, Roman. No matter what it is you have to say, I deserve more than this silence. Is it me? Do you not want...me? I mean, I know we never discussed how things would go once we—"

"*None* of this is about you." Roman cursed at her small flinch.

He ripped his hand through his hair and pulled away. Being close to her like that made it hard to remember what he needed to do, and that was put her first. "This is me. Doc. Everything we've gone through in the last couple of weeks? The danger? All the unknown variables coming from every which angle? That's my daily fucking life...and it is as far from Mari's Sanctuary as you'll ever want to be."

She tucked her arms across her chest. "It's different, I'll give you that, but—"

"It's not just different, Isabel. It's not compatible." Fuck. It hurt to breathe, a five-hundred-pound weight settling on his chest. "*We're* not compatible. I won't gamble with anyone's life but my own. Least of all yours. I told you before that I'll do whatever it takes to make sure you get your happy ending, and that's what I'm doing. I'm doing this for the both of us."

The tears that had slowly welled in Isabel's eyes stalled, giving way to anger. "That's the biggest bunch of bullshit I've ever heard."

He blinked, taken back. "Excuse me?"

"Oh, you heard me. You know who gets to decide what I need to make me happy? *Me!* Yes, the Sanctuary makes me happy. So does my work at Tru Tech. And the pupu platter at Lin's China Bistro. And right until about ten minutes ago, so did you."

"Doc, I—" He reached out to her, but she stepped away.

"You know what doesn't make me happy? As a

matter of fact, do you know what downright pisses me off?" She didn't wait for him to answer, drilling her finger into his chest so hard it pushed him backward. "When someone comes along and thinks they know what will make me happy better than I do. Well guess what, *Mr. Steele*? You don't."

"I only mean to—"

"To use me as an excuse to keep you from reaching your *own* happiness?"

"That's not what I'm doing."

"Oh, that's right...you're using *Kat* as an excuse."

Roman bristled, balling his fists at his sides. "You don't know the first thing about Kat."

"No, but I know that just like I didn't cause Olly's mission to go sideways, you didn't ask for those rebels to plant their very own IED garden, and if *I* deserve to be happy, so do *you*." She left him by the river and walked away, pausing after a few feet. Her anger melted away, leaving behind raw emotion. "You know what would make me happy, Roman? When you realize that you don't just have *something* to give...but *everything*."

Roman watched as Isabel walked away, and for every foot of distance that she put between them, it felt as if he stepped on that land mine over and over and over again.

* * *

Roman lost himself in the methodical sway of the sparring bag, drilling it with a series of punches each time it veered toward him. Judging by the frayed state of his hand wrap, he'd been at it for a few hours and hadn't had even one interruption—a huge perk of using his own gym and not the one at Steele Ops.

Another plus was no pitying looks from well-meaning family or, God forbid, unsolicited advice. He didn't want to see it. Didn't want to hear it. And he'd spent the last forty-eight hours avoiding it.

Eventually, someone would come pounding on his door, and he hoped to hell it was a brother, because one of those bastards he could punch. His mother or cousin, not so much.

Two feet away on the bench, his cell vibrated. Ignoring it, he tugged the sparring bag close and drilled it with a short series of knee pounds. His prosthesis protested the move, pinching him behind the knee, but he finished the set and stepped away.

Sweat poured down his face and chest, soaking the waistline of his shorts. He'd mopped himself up with a towel when his security alarm beeped with deactivation.

Fucking visitors.

Liam stepped into the gym with King, and neither one looked very happy. "You owe me twenty bucks. He's still breathing."

"Barely." King's brow furrowed. "Fuck, man. How long have you been at this?"

Roman panted. "I can still move my arms, so not long enough."

"Instead of beating your body up until it's entirely black and blue, why don't you go to fucking Tru Tech and get your woman?"

"Why don't you fuck off?" He scowled at his

youngest brother and best friend. "And why the hell are the two of you even together? Is this supposed to be some kind of intervention or something? If so, I think you're missing about a half dozen nosy-ass people."

Liam snorted. "We're the first wave. Or varsity team. Or whatever you want to call it. Basically, if we can't talk sense into your sorry ass, you'll have another visit in thirty minutes. And just so you're warned, Mom and Grace are next."

Fuck. Roman downed his water bottle before tossing the empty container in the corner recycling bin. "You're all wasting your time. Besides, even if I wanted to go after her, there's no way I can make it right. You didn't hear her before she left the other night."

"I did," King told him. "Actually, not there at Iron Bars, but I took her home and heard plenty. As a matter of fact, I heard it all night long."

One minute Roman was sitting on his ass, and the next he was sprawled on it. Seconds before getting in his friend's face, King had sent him flying right onto the mat.

"What the fuck do you mean, you heard it all night long?" He got to his feet as quickly as he could, something in his prosthetic jamming into his skin. "And what the hell were you doing taking her home?"

"Someone needed to look out for her after you ripped her heart from her chest. I just happened to be the bastard in the parking lot when she came looking for an escape." King shook his head at him, his disgust palpable. "Do you really believe any of that shit you spouted off about? I mean, compatibility? Fuck that, Ro. I can tell you from having known you pre-amputation and seeing you with Dr. Sexy these last few weeks, there's no one out there more compatible with your sorry ass than her."

"She deserves more—"

"Say she deserves more than you can give her, and I will fucking conjure Kat's spirit, let *her* take possession of my body, and have *her* kick your fucking ass." King looked like he wanted to lay him out on the ground again. "And you know she'd do it if she found out you were using her death as a reason to stop living your damn life."

Some of Roman's annoyance leaked away. He dropped onto the bench as if a two-hundred-pound barbell had been dropped on it. Reliving the sight of her tears clawed apart his insides all over again.

He loved Isabel more than he thought himself capable of loving another person. In a time when he fought to breathe, she made each breath come easier. When he couldn't see even two feet into his future, she lit up the way like a beacon.

"I fucked up," Roman admitted. "After everything I said, I'm not so sure she'll believe me if I tell her how I really feel."

King muttered to Liam. "Why the hell did they send the single guys to teach him the way of the female mind?"

Liam shrugged. "Hell if I know, but I think I actually know the answer to this one. Ro, as nice as words are, sometimes you also need to *show* people how much you care."

"And if that's not enough?"

"Enough of this whining shit." King pushed his shoulder, nearly toppling him off the bench. "Get the fuck up and *try*. You two are like two puppies hiding under the bed during a thunderstorm."

"Excuse me?"

"You heard me. Well guess what? You guys survived the damn storm. It's time to climb out. If you tell her how you feel, show her what she means to you, and *you're fucking honest about it,* and she *still* tells you to fuck off, then you're both morons."

This time when Roman jumped to his feet, *he* clocked *King*.

Ethan stumbled backward, tripping over a dumbbell.

Pain radiated from Roman's knuckles and up to his wrist, but he didn't care. White hot fury soared through him at the thought of anyone—even his best friend—giving Isabel less than the respect she deserved. "Talk about Isabel like that again, and I'll do more than loosen a few teeth."

Isabel Santiago deserved more than respect. She deserved unflappable support. Friendship that could withstand the test of time. Someone to challenge her. Someone to love her.

Someone ready to make her happiness his own.

And that was *him*.

It hit him like a freight train until he almost landed on his ass right next to King. "What the hell was I thinking?"

"You weren't." King's already swelling lip curled into a grin. "So don't you think maybe it's time you change that?"

Definitely.

Roman's cell rang *again*. He stopped himself from throwing it across the room seconds before seeing the DCPD caller ID. "Steele."

"Hey," Nat greeted him warily. "I know you guys did your job, and I won't blame you in the least for wiping your hands of this entire thing, but…she's saying she wants to talk."

"She?"

"Lina Doe."

"That's not going to happen, Nat. No fucking way."

"Roman, I wouldn't have called you if I didn't think we needed it. None of those guys from the festival are talking. Not a damn word. And this woman? She's pissed off enough that I think we can flip her on them."

"Who cares if she flips on them? We've got her and her entire team locked up. We got the virus. It's game over. She has no cards to play. Anything she's trying to pull is simply to keep everyone jumping through hoops."

"Roman…"

"No."

"She said it has something to do with Isa…and I really think she's telling the truth."

Fuck. Nat wouldn't say that unless she meant it…and it also meant that he couldn't blow this off. He'd already risked losing Isabel in so many different ways he refused to risk losing her yet again.

"I'm on my way."

CHAPTER
TWENTY-FOUR

Isa pulled another slide out from the microscope and barely resisted the urge to chuck the damn thing against the wall. She, Tony, and Maddy had been at this for the better part of the morning, and they were still empty-handed.

"This one isn't working, either," she growled. "I thought we were onto something, but these three samples look as if the meds had no effect whatsoever! What the hell?"

"Okay. Whoa. Take a deep breath and step back from the microscope." Maddy barely hid her amusement. "Alexa, play some soothing meditation music."

Throwing her friend a glare in their bulky protective suits was difficult but not impossible, but Maddy wasn't fazed, raising her gloved hands in mock surrender. "I love you to pieces, Is, but you have to chill out. The promising samples outnumber the shoddy ones... by a lot."

"But they weren't what we're looking for."

"No, they weren't. But now thanks to them we know what we're *not* looking for. *We learn as much from failures as we do successes.*" Maddy tapped her chin, feigning deep thought as she flicked her attention to Tony. "Tony, help me out here. Where did I hear that before? Hmm. Wait. It's almost on the tip of my tongue."

"Minus a few words, it would be from Bram Stoker," Tony retorted.

But Maddy was right. She continually went on tirades about no failure being a real failure. Things in history were discovered by pure accident: Silly Putty, Post-it Notes. Failures gave you data and make you better informed for the next try. The stress of knowing the people in Beaver Ridge were counting on her to make good on her promise was making it difficult for her to remember her own lessons.

Having narrowed down the premier cocktail to four different medications, they were so much closer than they'd been yesterday. All they needed to do now was calculate the medication to viral load ratio and apply it to the human samples.

And then sit back and watch.

"Last batch cooked up," Maddy announced the completion proudly. "Let's put these babies in the incubator, take a break, and come back and see what they got for us in an hour or two."

"You go on ahead. There's one more thing I want to check out before I call halftime." The lab suddenly got ridiculously quiet. Both Tony and Maddy, wearing matching worried expressions, watched her cautiously. "What?"

"You're doing it again," Maddy accused.

"Doing what? My job?"

"Burying shit under test tubes. Isa, *come on*. You know I can't stand seeing you so...sad."

Or so pathetic. Or so grumpy. There was a lot of *so* the last couple days. Less than an hour ago, she'd been ready to take her aggravation out on an innocent bottle of saline, for crying out loud. "I'm not burying myself under test tubes. I made my feelings clear. I was dumped. It happens. It's time to move on."

"Yeah, but did you really?"

"Did I what? Get dumped?" Isa's heart still ached whenever she replayed Roman's words. *Not compatible*. "Yeah, he made himself pretty clear."

"But did *you*?"

"I told him—"

"That you're in love with him? Did you actually say the three little words: I. Love. You?" Maddy turned to a silently listening Tony. "You're a man. Tell her that unless you look them point blank in the eye and enunciate those three words loudly and clearly, in the man's psyche, you most definitely did *not* make your feelings clear."

Tony shrugged. "For what it's worth, men can be pretty dense."

"Exactly." Maddy turned back to Isa. "So unless you told Roman in explicit detail how much you L-O-V-E him, he most certainly did *not* get your message."

"I don't know what difference it would've made," Isa said honestly.

Oh, Roman had *almost* succeeded in making her believe he really meant every syllable of the words coming out of his mouth, but she'd seen the pain in his eyes. But *because* she loved him, she knew any attempt to show he was deserving of happiness would fall on deaf ears until he was ready to hear it and *believe* it.

No three magical words would make that happen any faster, and until Roman realized it on his own, all she could do was wait and pray she didn't die from a broken heart in the process.

"So that's it?" Maddy demanded, less than enthused by her answers. "You're seriously going to just let the man you love walk away without putting up some kind of a fight? Who are you, and what have you done with my best friend?"

"Your best friend is trying to do the best she can in the situation." Isa squeezed her gloved fingers with her own. "But she loves that you're always looking out for her...and she'd love you even more if you went to the employee cafeteria and got her a plate full of those soft-baked macadamia nut cookies she loves so much."

Maddy pointed an accusing finger at her. "That's blackmail."

"No, because I didn't offer anything in exchange. It's actually a guilt trip." Isa pushed a shaky smile to her face. "Is it working?"

"Damn you, yes. Tony? You want anything?"

"Maybe just a coffee."

She squinted her eyes through her hood. "I'll get you a water, too. You're looking a little peaked."

Fifteen minutes later, when Maddy was safely tucked onto the Legion elevator, Isa turned her back on Tony and let the first tear fall. Then the second. By the time the third slipped down her chin, all she could do was pray she emptied out by the time Maddy got back with those cookies.

* * *

Roman glared through the one-way mirror to where Lina Doe sat in interrogation, her wrists and ankles shackled to the anchor on the floor.

"Looks like she's been the model inmate, huh?" Roman joked without a speck of humor.

Nat grunted. "We didn't bolt her to the table the first time and quickly learned our lesson. Two guards with broken noses, and I'm pretty sure Duke won't be able to give his wife that boy they've been talking about anytime soon. The State Department cannot take these guys off our hands fast enough."

"When's that?" King asked.

"Supposedly this afternoon." Her gaze flickered toward the window before landing on Roman. "What do you think?"

"I think," King interjected, "that you need to turn off the cameras and leave me alone with her for ten minutes. Fuck that. Five."

Nat drilled the former black ops soldier with a hard glare. To say the detective and Roman's buddy hadn't hit it off on their first meeting was a vast understatement. "And if this were a corrupt nation, that might fly, but we have rules and laws and something called the Bill of Rights. Whatever the hell you want to do in five minutes isn't allowed."

King shrugged, seemingly unaffected by her disapproval. "Maybe not, but it *is* effective, princess."

Roman shifted closer to Nat, and Liam shifted to King, as if prepping to pull him to safety. There wasn't a doubt in Roman's mind his friend hadn't used *princess* in reference to Nat's former life as Miss USA.

"Why the hell is he here again?" Nat shifted her ire to Roman. "I extended the invitation to Steele Ops, not low-level criminals."

King leaned back in his chair and smiled. "You may actually hurt my feelings if you keep that attitude up."

She rolled her eyes. "As if you have feelings to hurt. Please. I know your type. Hell, I've arrested too many of your type to count."

"Can we get back to Lina Doe over here?" Roman intervened. "She's really not in any facial recognition system? Fingerprints?"

"Nothing that we've come across yet, although fingerprints would actually be kinda helpful. She's either burned them off or poured acid on them or something, because she doesn't have any." Nat glared at the woman Isa had tussled with in Alaska. "And she's not exactly chatty...except when it comes to Isa."

Roman knew there was a big possibility this was nothing but another twisted game, and he was done playing it. "Then let's get this over with." He tossed a look at King. "You in?"

"Hell yeah, I am." He dropped his boots to the floor.

Nat stepped in front of the door. "I don't think—"

"Don't worry, princess. I'll keep Roman here in line." King flashed her a shit-eating smirk.

Nat tossed a pleading look at Roman. "Roman."

"He'll behave, Nat. I promise."

"Killjoy," King muttered as they stepped into the holding room.

Lina's head snapped up when they entered the room. "Oh look. A reunion."

King grunted. "You wanted to talk. We're here, so start talking. You have five minutes."

"Is that any way to talk to someone who's looking to right a few wrongs?"

"A few wrongs?" Roman interjected. "You infected an entire town with a deadly virus, and God only knows what you guys planned on doing with Isabel Santiago the two times you attempted to abduct her. You've now got four minutes and thirty seconds."

She bristled and shifted in her seat, unable to move far due to the chains. "I'm about to do you a favor, so you may want to rethink that time limit."

Roman slammed his palms to the table, making her jump. "I don't need any fucking favors from you! In case no one has told you, we have your entire fucking team *and* the virus. You. Are. Done."

"You have the virus and my crew, but you may want to rethink that other boast."

"Sorry to rain on your parade, sweetheart, but there's more than sufficient evidence to put you and your friends away for a very long time. Your money stream has officially been cut off."

"I want a deal," Lina demanded. "I get a plea deal in exchange for telling you something that you really want to know. That's how this works, right?"

The door to the interrogation room opened.

"What the hell do you have?" Nat asked.

"She's got nothing, Nat." Roman shook his head. "I've seen this kind of shit before. She's afraid of getting tossed in the federal pen, and so she tries to make herself indispensable."

Nat leaned against her, her green eyes locked furiously on the other woman. "I'm going to ask this one more time. What do you have?"

"Deal first, then info," Lina demanded.

"That's not how this works, Lina. You only get a deal if and when I decide the information you're giving me is worth it."

With a growl, Roman headed to the door. "I'm done with this shit."

"Me and my crew didn't target your girlfriend's stupid virus all on our own," Lina called out.

Roman's hand froze on the door handle. "What the hell are you talking about?"

"None of us had even heard of the damn thing much less would've known where to find it if we didn't have a little help. And abducting your little doctor? Not our idea...at least not originally." An evil, all-knowing smile crawled onto her face.

"You expect us to believe this?"

"I don't really care if you do or not. Just know that if you don't, it's going to be your little girlfriend that pays."

"And you're suddenly ready to tell all, huh? After being cooped up in here for a few days?"

"Well, like you pointed out, me and my team are now all locked up in here...and I'll give you one guess who's not."

CHAPTER
TWENTY-FIVE

Blinking, Isa pushed her hood closer to the microscope. "No way. No. Freaking. Way."

"What's up?" Tony hovered near her shoulder, waiting for her to share. "Something exciting?"

"You tell me." She flipped on the monitor linked to her scope, and the image on the slide came to life on the much larger screen over their heads. "What do you see up there?"

Tony studied the monitor. "I see FC-5. I see red blood cells. I see...what exactly am I seeing right there? On the bottom left?"

Excitement had her nibbling on her bottom lip. "So you see it, too. I applied two different antivirals from the same class, and two inhibitors, each from a different class...and it slowed down the FC-5 replication. I mean, it's not a full reversal, but the fact that it's slowed down that much could be huge!"

"It gives us more time to explore our options."

"*And* it gives the patient's immune system more time to heal so it can hopefully help fight the infection right alongside the medication!" Isa laughed, giddy for the first time in days, and pulled Tony into as tight a hug as their suits allowed. "It's happening! It's finally happening!"

"I knew if anyone could do it that it would be you."

"Oh, it wasn't just me. It was you and Maddy. It was Roman and his family. We never would've gotten to this point if it hadn't been for everyone involved." Isa sighed, glancing back up at the screen and the slowing FC-5 cells. "I need to notify the GHO. They need to start implementing this in Beaver Ridge right now."

Isa reached for the phone, but Tony's hand beat hers there. "Don't you think we should maybe verify it with another test or two?"

"If we weren't in a pinch for time, definitely. But this could help ease some of the suffering happening in the more extreme cases in Alaska." Isa frowned, glancing down at Tony's hand still wrapped around hers. "You don't think we should jump on this?"

"I know you, kiddo. You'd be destroyed if we didn't test the theory out more thoroughly and something ended up happening to one of those patients."

He was right. She'd be devastated. The last thing she wanted was to make anyone suffer more, or to get their hopes up only to watch them spiral down in a horrible crash. Yet as Isa studied her mentor, something unsettled her stomach. The feeling was one that, after meeting Roman, she knew never to ignore.

Tony, as much as she loved him, had never been the cautious sort. It's what made him a good epidemiologist, unafraid to go into hot zones deemed too hostile for even the most experienced medical personnel. It's why the GHO had both hired him and cringed at his reports.

That man wasn't the one standing in front of her now.

Isa slid her hand out from Tony's and inched left. "So you think we should run the test again?"

He nodded. "At least once. Maybe twice."

"That'll take at least two, maybe three days until we actually see the chemistry behind the process. That's a long time for Beaver Ridge."

"It'll best for everyone involved in the long run. Trust me."

He stepped closer, and Isa's feet automatically countered his movement. "Waiting longer means we're dealing with higher viral loads. How is that best for everyone?"

"You realize what we're up against here, right, Isa?"

"More than anyone. FC-5 is—"

"I'm not talking about FC-5. I'm talking about the Global Health Organization. I'm talking about the corporate greed that has absolutely no business being present when it involves the lives of the world's population." With eyes locked on Isa, Tony shuffled closer, his suit squeaking against the floor. "Medical decisions should be based on science . . . on actual case studies and analysis obtained by experts in the field. They shouldn't be made by someone pushing papers and running a calculator while sitting behind a desk."

"I . . . agree," Isa said carefully. "And yet, if it wasn't for those people who push those papers, there isn't a lab anywhere who would get the funding needed to run their research programs. Mine included."

He gripped her arms, his gloved fingers digging painfully into her biceps. "It shouldn't be like that, Isa! I'm trying to show them that it *can't* be like that without *serious* risk. Risk to ourselves. Risk to our communities. Our families. Once we let corporations have control of our own humanity, there won't be any humanity left."

Isa grimaced. "Tony, you're hurting my arm."

"I'm sorry." He let her go, and she bumped into a tray of empty vials, the glass crashing onto the floor. "It wasn't supposed to be like this. It wasn't supposed to... damn it, Isa. I'm so sorry."

"What... what did you do?"

"I needed to show them that they couldn't wait for the next big thing to happen." Tony paced, his breathing erratic. Each heavy pant fogged the inside of his mask more, until all she could see were the heavy dots of moisture. "They left me with *no* choice. I had to do it. I *had* to."

Tony ripped at his suit.

"No! Don't!" Isa lurched to stop him, but it was too late.

He'd tugged off his hood, the oxygen funneling to his mask from the canister on his back, hissing loudly. Without the barrier, Isa saw just how far gone her one-time friend really was. His hair stuck up at all angles, and dark circles framed each glassy blue eye.

"Tony." Isa kept her voice calm. "What did you do?"

His glazed blue eyes locked on her. "I did what I had to, Isabel. I did what I always do, and I looked at the big picture. The GHO needs to be shown the error of their ways, and I need to be the one to do it. I can't let you interfere, kiddo. There's too much on the line, and it's far more important than you or me."

Isa's gaze shifted down to his hand and immediately

saw that balled up in his tight fist was an uncapped needle...and it was filled with nearly ten milliliters of yellow-tinted liquid that looked a hell of a lot like the undiluted FC-5 serum.

* * *

Roman stepped on the gas, staying close to the bumper of Nat's squad car as she weaved in and out of traffic, her police siren wailing. If it weren't for her as an escort, there'd be no telling how long it would take him and King to get across the river to Tru Tech.

Or what he'd find.

King hung up from his call, his face grim. "Guess when they say the lab is run by a skeleton crew after hours, they mean it. No one's answering the damn phones. Got nothing on Dr. Sexy's cell either, or the friend."

"Or Winter," Roman growled.

Fucking bastard. He couldn't believe he let the man walk away with Isabel, and on more than one occasion. When he got his hands on him, he'd make sure the bastard couldn't walk again. Period.

"I don't get it," King thought aloud. "Winter claimed to serve the people, right? Be some protector against the evil viruses or some shit. Then why the fuck would he work with mercenaries to unleash FC-5? It seems counterproductive to the way he's lived his entire life."

Roman asked himself the same question ever since they'd run out of the prison, and he'd come up empty. "None of it makes sense. Any man willing to potentially kill an entire town shouldn't give a rat's ass if his one-time mentee lives or not."

And if Lina Doe was to be believed, that had been Winter's one stipulation to their crew: *Take Isa, but take her alive.*

But that was before every single one of his accomplices had been tossed in a jail cell. It was before they'd ratted him out. And it was before he'd realized that they were onto him. If the man was willing to kill an entire town, one woman wouldn't even register on his radar if he felt Isa stood in the way of him and whatever goal he had.

"Call the Legion again," Roman directed King, his fists tightening on the steering wheel. "And keep trying until you get hold of someone."

He never did. Five minutes later, Nat cut off a line of cars waiting to turn onto the main road and pulled right up to Tru Tech's front door. Roman screeched to a halt right next to her, jumping the curb seconds before he jumped out from the car and ran into the building.

He'd barely reached the center lobby when Maddy nearly crashed into him.

Her eyes widened before narrowing into daggers. "*You.* It's about damn fucking time. What the hell took you so long?"

"Is Isabel okay?" Roman's breath froze in his lungs.

"Is she okay? Okay?!" Maddy stepped closer, drilling a finger into his chest. "No! No, Roman Steele, she is definitely *not* okay! Actually, she's as far from okay as one could get!"

"What happened?"

Maddy's look would've killed him if she had the power. "What happened is that the man she's head over heels in love with is a cowardly jackass! You would only be so damn lucky to have Isabel in your life. You'd be the luckiest man on earth...*ever!*"

Roman gently gripped her arms before she drilled her finger through to his spine. "Maddy, I'm not disagreeing with you. I'm the stupidest man for not telling her how I feel. Trust me, I plan on rectifying that as soon as I make sure she's safe."

"Safe? What are you talking about?" She blinked, concern overshadowing the anger, and fisted Roman's shirt. "Damn it, man, talk to me!"

King gently extricated her grip from his shirt. "Easy there, kitten."

Nat scoffed. "Do you have pet names for *all* women?"

Maddy waved her hands for attention. "Why does Isa need to be kept safe?! I swear to God if someone doesn't talk soon—"

"Where is she?" Roman asked.

"She's in the lab—working—as usual."

"Alone?" Fuck. His chest tightened as if Maddy still had a grip on him.

"No, she's with Tony. I tried convincing her to come up here with me for a little break, but in case you haven't already noticed, she likes working through pain. And you, asshole, hurt her really damn bad."

Roman spun on the detective. "Nat? Surveillance. Get eyes on that lab."

"On it." Nat hustled off.

Maddy folded her arms across her chest. "Is someone

going to tell me what's happening at some point, or am I going to have to guess?"

Roman steered her toward the lab elevators. "Right now you're taking me and King to the Legion, you're going to put yourself in one of those spacesuits, and then you're going to stay as far out of the way as possible."

"Roman!" Nat yelled, flying across the lobby, her gun drawn and at her side. "Video's grainy, but it's rolling and Winter is definitely in the lab with Isa...and it doesn't look like he's empty-handed."

Roman's heart stopped in his chest, the abrupt sensation buckling his knees. He couldn't be too late.

He needed to make things right.

He needed to keep her safe.

He needed to make her *his*.

CHAPTER TWENTY-SIX

Tony's hand shook as his fingers clenched around the syringe.

"Tony." Isa kept her voice low and calm. "You really don't want to do this, do you?"

"I don't, kiddo. I really, really don't." His voice cracked. Sweat dotted his forehead and dripped down his face. "I'm so close to making the GHO stand up and take notice. I'll finally have their attention and their—"

"Money?" Isa finished. "That's what this is about, right? Your bank account?"

"No." He shook his head adamantly. "Not *my* money. Funding for the *field*. For research programs like yours all over the world that are struggling to understand these horrific viruses with practically no money."

"You're doing this for funding? Tony! If you want a damn grant, you put in the paperwork and—"

"And it sits on a fucking desk until one of those paper pushers deems it a worthwhile cause!" Tony screamed. He stepped forward again, his gait slightly unsteady. "You were never supposed to get this close to figuring out FC-5 until *after* I shook them up...until after they finally started taking me seriously."

Isa took a small step back, but Tony took two forward. He stumbled before righting himself, his fingers clutching the syringe even tighter.

"You don't look very good, Tony," Isa said truthfully, hearing him wheeze even from their four-foot distance. "Why don't we sit down so I can take a listen to your lungs? Or I could take you to the nearest emergency room. I think you need a chest X-ray and maybe a—"

"That's not necessary."

"It is." His usual tan complexion looked more pallid by the second. "I'm sorry I ruined your plans, but you don't need to resort to drastic measures. You saw yourself, FC-5 is still a killer. What I found isn't a long-term solution. It's a Band-Aid on an artery bleed."

"But it's enough. It's enough of a leap that the GHO will shift their notice right over it. It's enough that they once again won't see the threat looming right over all of our heads."

The blinking light of the Legion elevator caught Isa's attention, and when it opened, four figures stepped out, all crouching low and immediately fanning out. Isa immediately recognized King, and Nat from the DCPD. Maddy crab-walked toward the back room, where they stored extra gear.

And Roman was the fourth.

His gaze caught hers from the distance, and he held a single finger to his lips before motioning for her to keep Tony talking.

"You can help me, Tony." Isa drew his attention back toward her. "You and I can work together in fine-tuning this treatment plan. We can help the people of Beaver Ridge, and the GHO will see that. They'll see what kind of good we can do when we have the right tools."

He scoffed. "It won't work, kiddo. They don't communicate in successes. Threats and decay and death are the only ways to get—and keep—their attention." The hand holding the filled syringe lifted, and Isabel's heart lurched into her throat.

"DCPD! Drop your weapon! Now!" Nat shouted from the clean room, her gun aimed directly at the glass...and Tony.

Tony spun around and, seeing the three forms advancing, quickly hauled Isa in front of him.

"Don't move!" He held the needle three inches away from her neck. "Don't you fucking dare move!"

Roman froze, his gun aimed, and King and Nat followed suit. "This won't end well for you if you keep on this route, man."

"Things are already not ending well...for me or for anyone."

Tony's chest rattled. Isa was able to feel the vibrations at her back.

"Anthony, please." Isa's voice wavered. "Please don't do this."

Something dripped onto her arm.

Blood. It rolled off the back of Tony's hand and onto her suit, and just as she registered its presence, another trickle slid down the side of her mask from where his cheek pushed against her hood.

His words of warning and all his physical symptoms set off every internal warning bell she possessed.

"You're sick," Isa whispered, more for her own ears than anyone else's.

Tony wheezed into her ear. "It took you long enough to figure it out."

She didn't need to ask him to confirm her suspicion. He wasn't sick from the flu or a case of pneumonia. Fever. Loss of equilibrium. Pallor. And large-scale capillary hemorrhaging.

"How did you become infected with FC-5?" Isa's heart broke as she spoke the words. Based on the severity of his symptoms, she'd guess him to be near the final stages of the illness.

"Does it matter? It's done."

The finality of his words sent a shiver through Isa as she locked gazes with Roman through the thick glass and wished with everything she had that she'd had the chance to tell him how much she loved him.

* * *

Roman knew that look, and he'd be damned if he'd let Isabel say goodbye to him through a fucking double-paned window. "Maddy?"

Isa's friend stuck her hooded head out from the back room. "Yeah?"

"Let me into the lab."

"You're in the—"

"No, the *lab*. Right now."

Her eyes widened. "You can't go in there without a—"

He shot her a hard look. "Do you see what that bastard has in his hand right now? Do you know what'll happen to Isabel if he decides to use it? Get me in that lab *now*."

Maddy cursed under her breath, but she slipped out from the back room. "She's going to kill us both for this, just so you know, but since she can only do us in one at a time, I'm shoving you toward her first."

"Noted. King? Distract him for me."

Ethan glanced into the lab and back. "Maybe you should hold on a second, man."

"I've already waited too damn long. I'm not waiting a damn second more," Roman growled. "Maddy? Get me inside."

He followed her along the perimeter of the room, and so far, King and Nat did a good job keeping Winter's wavering attention on them.

"You sure about this?" Maddy asked, stopping in front of a door much like the one around front, her badge hovering over the security scanner.

"More than anything." And Roman meant it. He'd risk this and a hell of a lot more to keep Isa safe.

With a nod, she swiped her badge and entered her code. The door slid open with a hum, and it was when he eyed the white lockers and fresh clothes that he realized she'd taken him through the back.

She tipped her head to the door on the far end. "You'll be entering the lab how we normally exit. That door leads to decon, and the door on the far side of decon takes you directly into the lab. It's air-sealed, so when you hit the button, it's *going* to make noise."

And Tony will realize that he and Isa are no longer alone. "Thanks."

She nodded, already looking regretful. "Just bring my friend out safely. And yourself, too."

Roman had every intention in doing both. With every door he opened, he heard Tony and Isa's voices more clearly. She'd never stopped trying to talk him down.

He took a deep breath at the last door, his gun clenched tightly in his hand as he visualized the layout of the lab inside...and pushed the last button. The door hissed open.

Tony spun both him and Isa around, the needle still hovering over her neck. "Don't you dare move!"

Isa's wide, panicked eyes found Roman's. "No. No, Roman go back. Don't come in here."

He took a small step forward. "That's not happening, Doc."

"Please." Tears slipped down her cheeks from behind her hood. "Roman, he's sick. He's *infected. Please* go back."

Isabel was trying to protect them. To protect *him*. But he wasn't sitting back and doing nothing. One wrong move. One twitch. One startle and that syringe Winter held could would slide right through her plastic hood and into her delicate flesh.

Six steps. Four. At three steps away, voices echoed through the clean room and two more uniformed DCPD cops barged into the clean room side of the Legion.

Winter's attention snapped back and forth before finally falling and staying on Roman. "I said don't fucking move!"

"Do you not see that it's over?" Roman gestured to the room of waiting cops. "Come on, man, know when to quit. You've made your point. Bureaucracy sucks. All you're doing at this point is making things worse for yourself...and for Isabel."

Tony blinked at the mention of Isa.

"I know you care about her, Tony. Or at least I thought you did."

"I could say the same about you, and yet I've done nothing all morning but listen to how you took her feelings and trampled the shit out of them. Guess we're both good at hurting the people we care about."

Roman forced himself not to react at the rough jab. "I plan to make it up to her the second I can hold her in my arms again."

Tony wavered...ever so slightly. Movement from outside the window snagged his attention, falling on one of Nat's men, and in a snap, he was back on alert, the syringe raised. "I have a job to do here, just like everyone else...and I can't let my affections get in the way."

Tony raised the syringe, his grip tightening on Isabel. Roman didn't hesitate. A mere inch from the point the needle would've breached her suit, he fired. The noise of the gunshot ricocheted through the lab like a roar. Tony's grip on Isabel relaxed and he spun, crashing into the counter from the momentum.

Red blossomed on his shirt, just below his shoulder, but the bastard still held on to that damn syringe. Roman rushed him, and they collided in a tangle of arms and legs. For a sick man, Tony sure as hell put up a fight. They exchanged blow after blow until Roman finally captured his syringe hand and slammed it onto the ground once, twice, and finally a third time before the older man released it. With a final move, Roman swiped an elbow straight across Tony's nose, and Tony Winter finally lay there unconscious.

A half dozen people rushed forward, some to help Isa, one to check on Tony.

"No one come any closer!" Isa's scream brought them all to a standstill.

Blood poured out from Tony's gunshot wound despite Roman's effort to miss hitting anything vital. Isa dropped to his side. Her suit hindered her efforts to stanch the bleeding, and she cursed.

"Roman." She nodded to his knuckles and the front of his shirt. Both coated with a slicky wet substance. Her brown eyes met his, and even though she tried to suppress it, he saw the panic. "You need to get yourself into quarantine."

"I'm not going anywhere without you."

"Don't worry. I'll be there soon enough, too." She reached around the back of her hood and tugged it off.

"What the fuck are you doing?" Roman rushed forward, stopping a split second before touching her when he remembered the blood on his hands. "Isabel. *No.*"

She ripped off her gloves. "I'm a doctor, Roman. I can't..." She swallowed her words and took a breath before meeting his eyes. "I can't let anything happen to him. I can't *not* try. Just...maintain your distance."

Just in case he hadn't already been exposed. Roman hands were specked with trails of blood that could've been his own—or from the sick man on the ground.

CHAPTER TWENTY-SEVEN

Roman couldn't sleep. Sterile and way too quiet, the solitary confinement at Tru Tech was worse than any hospital he'd ever been in or visited. And he'd been in a lot of them between his own surgeries and rehab, and then adding in visits to service buddies.

After he and Isabel had been deconned and placed in side-by-side observation rooms, he'd thought they'd have time to talk, but that hadn't been the case. Isabel had spent most of her time talking Maddy through the next steps of their FC-5 research, and when she wasn't doing that, she was coordinating their own quarantine.

He was starting to think she was avoiding him.

It had to be somewhere close to midnight or after, and he couldn't help sneaking a peek at the shared window separating their rooms and wondering if she was awake, too. Now they were in a waiting game. Any minute, they'd get news of their latest batch of blood samples, the ones that would either clear them of FC-5 exposure or officially hurtle them into the next countdown.

He really fucking hated waiting.

He sat up, scrubbing his palms over his face, and

caught movement from the other side of the blinds. Isa paced back and forth, obviously as restless as him. He pushed the intercom button that allowed them to talk freely through the glass.

"Keep pacing like that and you'll wear a hole in the floor, Doc."

Isa's blind flew open and suddenly she was right in front of him. He needed to be closer, so he half-walked, half-limped over to the window.

"You're limping." Her graze dropped to his leg. "No one told me you hurt your leg."

"Because I didn't hurt it. It's just the prosthetic. Guess I'll be writing my friend and complaining to him that it didn't hold up to the test of taking down a biological terrorist."

She frowned. "Was that supposed to be funny?"

"Not really, no." For the first time in an hour, Roman got a good look at her.

Wearing the lab's pale blue linen PJs, she looked healthy and fit and like a force to be reckoned with . . . and he couldn't help but worry that her vitality was about to be taken away. He'd nearly had a damn heart attack when she'd ripped off her protective gear, but in true Isabel Santiago form, she hadn't thought twice about helping her old friend despite everything he'd done and everything he'd hoped to do.

Thinking about what could be in their future, Roman's stomach churned.

He'd fucked up before because he didn't make the right decision, so he fought like hell to find the right words now. Or at least ones that didn't entirely suck.

"You mean a lot to me, Doc." He inhaled, hearing the quiver in his own breath.

"Roman, you don't have to—"

"Yeah, actually, I do, and I know I don't deserve a second chance here, but I'd really appreciate it if you'd zip those beautiful lips of yours and let me say what I need to say."

She pantomimed zipping her mouth and gestured for him to continue, making him chuckle.

"I was an ass the other night at Iron Bars, and I have no other reason for what I said than I was a fucking idiot, and you were once again very much right. I do deserve to be happy...and I know without a doubt that you do it for me. Until *you* came into my life, I hadn't realized how much I'd just been *existing*. When you came into my life, I realized just how much I was really missing."

Roman swallowed a forming lump of emotions, the knot reforming when tears floated in Isabel's eyes. The sight of them gutted him, making him wish he could reach through the glass and wipe them away.

"I know my life isn't for the faint of heart, Doc. I know it's a lot. But I also know I love you, Isabel Santiago. I'm *in* love with you." Roman braced his palm against the window and felt his chest throb when she laid hers on top. "And if you taught me one thing, it's that there isn't a damn thing you can't do if you do it with the person you love."

"Roman, I..." Tears now poured down Isa's cheeks, but the rest of her words were cut off by the faint buzz of the door.

The air lock in Isabel's quarters disengaged, and in stepped Maddy. No hazmat suit. No protective equipment. She smiled warmly and glanced between them. "Sorry to interrupt, but..."

"Well?" Isa asked, her nerves showing.

Maddy wrapped her into a hug, her happiness the only thing rivaling Roman's own relief. "You're clean, Isa. No exposure."

On cue, Roman's own air lock disengaged. The door slid open, but instead of a friendly smile, the person entering quarantine wore the all too familiar yellow-hooded biogear that he'd come to hate.

"No," Isa gasped.

Roman shifted his gaze to her, and this time, the tears pouring down her cheeks definitely weren't because he'd poured his heart out.

"No!" Isa cried out, shimmying out of Maddy's restraining hold. She pounded against the glass as if trying to burst her way through to him. "Roman!"

"It's okay, Doc." Roman smiled wanly.

No one needed to tell him what was expected of him. He sat back on the bed and extended his arm for another round of blood tests. As the tech hung his next bag of meds, Roman closed his eyes.

If he looked at Isabel through the glass, she'd see he was a few thousand miles away from okay. He'd finally had his own happiness at his fingertips...and now it slipped away with every tick of the clock.

* * *

So much for Tru Tech being closed to civilians. Roman had no sooner gotten prodded for the twelfth time in as many minutes than the small waiting area outside his personal bubble filled with Steeles—literal and honorary.

If it weren't for the pass-coded sealed doors, Roman was pretty sure his mother would've charged into the room, infectious or not, the second they'd arrived. But thankfully, one look to Knox or his cousin Grace, and they managed to steer the conversation—and Cindy Steele herself—in the other direction.

Now Liam stood on the other side, shaking his head at Roman's stark surroundings. "I know some people go to extreme measures for attention, but seriously, Ro. Don't you think this is a bit overkill?"

"What can I say? Go big or go home, right?" Roman shrugged playfully.

He appreciated his youngest brother's joking nature much more than the doom and gloom that had been the theme when they'd first arrived. It had taken a lot of verbal assurances and hours of seeing it for themselves, but they were all finally believing that he felt fine.

And he hoped to hell they left before realizing that that was no longer one hundred percent true. Maybe it was a little hypochondria, or way too much time thinking and questioning, or hell, maybe it was being stuck in this damn room. But his muscles developed that faint unused ache, and the room felt a little cooler than it had before.

"I'm not gonna ask you if you're doing okay," came King's voice.

He'd taken up the window spot that had been temporarily vacated by Liam.

"Good... because I'm getting sick of hearing that question," he said truthfully. "And what's up with the constant pop-ups, man? This is getting to be a habit. Soon you'll be sniffing around Steele Ops looking for a job or something."

King laughed. "Yeah. No. I'm so fucking done with organized groups. No offense, man, because your brothers are kick-ass, but I'm way too fond of answering only to myself."

"I know of a few others who felt that same way, and I'm signing their paycheck."

"But unlike them, I mean it." King glanced around as if making sure he wouldn't be heard. "She's doing okay... just so you know."

Roman didn't need to ask who he was talking about. On King's first visit to quarantine after hearing of his status, he'd asked him to make sure Isabel didn't run herself into the ground trying to find a cure for him.

"How do you know this?" Roman asked.

"I may have run into Maddy in that cubby they call a cafeteria and gently requested that she make sure to take care of Dr. Sexy."

"And she didn't tell you to fuck off?" Roman half-teased. No one in Steele Ops would ever be on the doctor's friend list after the way things played out.

"Actually, no. She simply said she was already on it... and I believed her."

Chills abruptly sucked away all Roman's air, his teeth

reflexively chattering. Taken by surprise, he searched for the nearest sturdy object and held on tight. "Well, shit."

"Hey, man. You okay?" King's concerned voice barely reached his ears. "Dude. Ro?"

"Yeah." Roman cleared his throat and slowly released his grip on the nearby chair as he stood upright. He blinked until King's face was no longer blurry. "I'm good."

"You sure about that?"

He wasn't so certain. "I think...I think I may need to sit."

He reached for the chair and then the one chair split into two. He blinked, hoping to clear away the sudden double vision, but it only made his head spin more. "Fuck me."

"Roman?" He heard an anxious voice call out his name.

His mom? Grace?

Roman stumbled. Someone shouted, the loud bark sending a stabbing pain through his head. "Don't... yell."

"Someone get Isabel! Now!"

"No," Roman ordered weakly. "Don't...worry... her."

Fuck. Was his speech slurring? He reached out for the chair again, and this time, he missed entirely. His body fell forward with nothing to stop his fall but his overexerted muscles...and his face.

CHAPTER TWENTY-EIGHT

"This one's a dud," Isa announced, sliding her latest viral sample from the microscope and putting it with the ever-growing shelf of other rejects. As she set it down and closed the shelving unit, she barely refrained from smashing the entire thing with a sledgehammer—not like she had a sledgehammer.

They'd been at this for hours—how many she didn't know. Not like it mattered. She didn't care how long she had to stay in this damn suit. She wasn't going anywhere until they found a drug combination that eradicated FC-5 completely.

The problem was in Roman's blood.

His viral load was too damn high, way higher than it should be for twenty-four hours after exposure.

"Is, look at this," Maddy called her over to the other side of the room, where she worked with samples that had been taken from Tony.

Roman was still unconscious, the meds they were giving him around the clock the only thing keeping him alive. For now.

As Isabel got to Maddy's station, her friend slid over. "Take a look at that viral load."

Isabel peered through the lens. "Whoa."

"*Right?* Those numbers are like nothing we've seen before. I mean, it's not natural. It's like... hell, I don't know what it's like. Isn't that a bit extreme for a run-of-the-mill exposure? How did Tony say he exposed himself?"

"He didn't. But there's no way he has that kind of viral load with a simple proximity exposure. It's almost like..." A horrible thought occurred to Isabel, and her stomach churned. "It's almost like he injected the undiluted virus into his system."

Behind her hood, Maddy's eyes widened to saucerlike discs. "No. Fucking. Way. He *wouldn't*!"

"Before what happened, I'd think the same thing, but now? I think there wasn't much Tony wouldn't do to get his agenda seen." Isa hated to admit it. "And it would explain why we're seeing such high levels in Roman's blood, too."

"Is this going to speed up the clock? Our current anti-virals are helping to give us a little extra time, but—"

"We're almost there," Isa interjected. "We need to keep our noses to the grindstone and we'll have it locked in before we know it."

She wouldn't accept anything less.

They were already thirteen hours past exposure. The fact that Roman hadn't yet shown any physical symptoms of FC-5 infection was a good sign, and Isabel was holding on to that shred of good with both hands.

"Dr. Santiago." One of the Legion spotters waved at her through the window. "We need you in quarantine."

"What's wrong?"

"It's Mr. Steele, ma'am. He's taken a turn."

A thick-gloved hand caught Isa's arm as she teetered on her feet.

"Is, look at me. Isabel!" Maddy grabbed her hood and forced Isabel's gaze on her. "You with me?"

Isabel nodded. She was. Now. But the inside of her mask was fogged, evidence of her sudden panic.

"Good. Keep your head in the game, okay? You'll focus. You'll sleep, eat, and you'll fucking take one breath at a time. If you don't continue to do any of those things, you're worthless to him. Do you hear me?"

"I can't lose him, Maddy," Isa heard herself whisper. "I can't..."

"We're doing everything in our power to make sure that doesn't happen. Now go. You have two patients to go look after. Him...and you. I got things here. You go be where you need to be."

She gripped her friend's fingers as tightly as the gloves allowed. "Thank you, Maddy. I can't tell you how much—"

"Will you stop kissing my butt already and go be with your guy?"

The ten minutes Isa spent hosing off her gear in decon and going through checkpoints never felt so damn long. By the time she finally stepped into the Legion's lobby, she was ready to crawl out of her skin.

Isa sprinted toward the clinic's quarantine wing. She didn't even stop when she hit Roman's viewing room. She burst through the door and was instantly swarmed by well-meaning Steeles and their barrage of questions and worries.

Someone—King—grabbed her hand and paved her way.

At Roman's window, she pushed her face to the double-paned glass and watched as one of the clinic staff attempted to help Roman, who lay sprawled on the ground, apparently refusing any kind of assistance.

Isabel punched the mic button on the wall to allow two-way conversation. "Stop being such a pain in the ass and let Ben get you into bed."

Roman's gaze snapped to her, and something flickered over his face and left way too quickly for her to decipher it. "I told them not to call you."

"Thankfully, they didn't listen. Now, are you letting Ben help you, or do I need to get gowned and drag you there myself?"

She counted to five before Roman very reluctantly put his hand into Ben's gloved one and accepted the help to his feet. Once there, he wavered slightly, but the five-foot-eight tech caught him.

Isabel's stomach threatened to empty its contents. What contents, she didn't know. She couldn't remember the last time she'd put anything in her mouth more substantial than the Red Bull she'd commandeered from Maddy's hiding spot.

She waited until Roman was safely tucked into bed before heading toward quarantine's clean room.

Roman followed the movement. "Where the hell do you think you're going?"

"To do my job." Ten minutes later, fully garbed, she stepped into his room. Ben stood off to the side, readying his next dose of antivirals.

"Thought you said you were going back to work." Roman frowned as she approached.

"I am. Maddy kicked me out of the lab, so now *you* are my job." She lifted a lone dark eyebrow and hoped he could see she was serious. "You have a problem with that?"

"No, he does not." Cindy Steele's voice came though the speaker. She glared at her son through the window, her mom scowl no less lethal. "I'm telling you right now, Roman Wallace Steele, you will let Isabel help you, or with as God as my witness, I will come into that room and give you a spanking like you've never had before."

Roman burst out laughing. "You've never spanked us a day in our life, and you're going to give me one now?"

She huffed. "Now is when you're acting like a spoiled child. Don't test me, son. I will do it...in front of the woman you love or not."

A small smile formed on Isa's face. She couldn't help it. Just like she couldn't help wondering if Roman had told his mother about her...about what he'd shared with her before they'd been hit with the news. But judging by the slight color that rode high on Roman's pale cheeks, she didn't think so.

Roman may have laughed and made a joke, but it hadn't been without cost. Even without listening to his breath sounds, she could tell he was breathing a bit too fast and a lot too shallow. His skin, dotted with a faint dew, looked overheated.

Roman turned his eyes to her, and it was right there in front of her. *He was barely keeping himself together.*

He swallowed roughly and murmured for her ears only, "Make them leave."

"Roman, they're worried about you. They—"

"Won't be any less worried if they stand there and watch me like I'm a rat in a maze. Please, it's bad enough I'm not getting rid of you. I can't let *them* see me like this, too."

"I'll try not to take offense to that," she joked lightly.

He didn't mean it harshly, but he was right. He wasn't getting rid of her.

"I'm sorry, folks." She turned toward his family and friends. "I have to give Roman a physical and it might get a little...personal. Then he needs to get some rest."

"You're kicking us out?" Cindy looked affronted.

"Of course not. I'm *relocating* you." Isa chose her words carefully. "Tru Tech has a small sleeping quarters for staff on the other side of the building. It's almost like a small apartment, and it's already been readied for guests. When you want to see Roman again, find the nearest employee and have them pick up the phone to set it up."

Roman's mom didn't look thrilled, but she accepted the news and turned to her son. "You make sure they call us if you need anything."

"Will do, Ma."

"I mean it, Roman. That means you actually have to tell them you want to see us."

A real smile slid onto his face. "I promise, Ma. You have my word."

She looked as if she was about to lose her battle

against her tears and aimed a motherly look at Isa. "Take care of my boy, sweetheart."

"With everything I have, Cindy. I promise."

With everyone gone, the only sound to be heard was the steady drip of Roman's IV.

"You need anything else from me, Dr. Santiago?" Ben asked.

"No, thank you. I'll check his vitals and take it from here." She waited until the air lock hissed and the tech stepped into decon.

"What do I have to do to get you to walk out the door and follow my family?" Roman asked. His hands clutched onto the side of the bed as if trying to prevent the room from spinning.

"You'd have to know how to perform miracles, because divine power is the only way I'm leaving this bedside."

He grimaced and let out a body-shaking wet cough. "Yeah, that's what I was afraid of."

"Roman, I never would have left you in the first place if it weren't for the fact that we're so close to getting the cocktail right. Now that I'm here, I'm not going anywhere." She stepped closer to the bed and wished she could climb in right next to him. He looked a little more winded, and according to the oxygen monitor on the wall, wasn't experiencing the high oxygen levels expected for a man of his general good health. "Tell me everything you're feeling."

His lips twitched. "So we're bringing up yesterday now? Wait…was it yesterday? I've kind of lost track of time."

"I'm a firm believer in the order of basic necessities, but in order for us to have a conversation about our future together, there has to be a *you*. So start talking."

"Future, huh?"

"Spill it, Steele."

As they ran through a complete body systems check, Isabel forced her face into the blank mask that Roman excelled at. She asked questions, and he answered honestly, only needing prodding a few times. He got winded talking, and it was evident by the goose bumps erupting across his skin that his fever was wreaking havoc with his body.

Once she was finished playing Dr. Santiago, it grew more and more difficult to keep her face impassive. Her shoulders dropped and she released a deep breath, temporarily fogging her hood.

"Come here," Roman demanded softly, crooking a single finger.

"Are you...beckoning me?"

He smirked. "Don't make me ask again, Doc."

She closed in on the bed, wishing with everything she had that she could take off her garb and slide her fingers through his. He must have felt the same thing, because his gaze dropped to the thick rubber monstrosities on her hands.

"Guess there's no copping any feels in this get-up, huh?" he teased.

"Roman..." She fought against the tears. No way was she feeling sorry for herself when it was the incredible man in front of her who facing ridiculous odds.

"We're finding a treatment. I'm not stopping until I do. I bet that by the time morning rolls around—"

"Isabel."

At the use of her full name, Isa stopped. "Yeah?"

"I need you to make a few promises to me."

She eyed him warily. "What kind of promises?"

"First, no matter what happens...you move onward knowing you did everything you could."

"You—"

"Let me finish, babe." Roman paused, looking as if he needed to catch his breath. His hand slid over hers, rubber gloves be damned. "Things happen for a reason. I need you to continue believing that. I need you to know that for the time I've had you in my life, you have made me the happiest I've *ever* been. I don't know what the hell I did to deserve you, but I'm sure as hell glad it happened. And I wouldn't change a damn thing...except to have more time with you."

Isa lost her battle with tears. Inside her hood, her mask fogged, but it didn't obscure her hearing. With every word, Roman's voice lessened until it was a faint whisper and, finally, he fell asleep.

Still holding on to his hand, she hooked her boot onto the nearby chair and dragged it closer to Roman's bedside...and then she sat. "I'm doing my best to make sure that happens, too."

And then she waited for a miracle.

CHAPTER
TWENTY-NINE

Roman was in a time warp…or what he imagined that to feel like. As he struggled to open his eyes, bits and pieces of the last few hours—or longer—flickered through his memory like a movie reel. He didn't even know if any of it had actually happened or if it was the effect of whatever drugs they'd been giving him.

He half-recalled hearing the hiss of the room's door lock, which was almost immediately followed by someone in a yellow hazmat suit. There were drugs and blood draws, so many he didn't know how he hadn't been drained dry.

He briefly recalled a snippet of a tear-stained Isabel as she stood over his bed—and his IV port—and said a prayer as she pushed a hot, burning liquid into his veins.

Now, after the passing of who knows how much time, Roman groaned at the effort it took to open his eyes. It's like they'd been glued shut, but when they finally obeyed, white light sent a stabbing pain through his head.

Fuck, had he been abducted by aliens?

He blinked, forcing his eyes to adjust, and slowly tilted his head to get a good look around the room.

Tru Tech's stark white walls slowly came into focus. Multiple sets of tubes and wires, all with different tinted fluids, went from the machines hanging on the IV pole and disappeared beneath his paper-thin gown.

He glanced out into the observation room beyond the wide window wall and saw *everyone*, all asleep in varying positions. Knox sat on a couch, Zoey nestled in his lap, and Cade and Grace looked to be in very much the same position on the other end. King sat propped against the wall with Nat's head resting on his shoulder, while Ryder served as a pillow for both their mother and Cade and Zoey's. And at some point while he'd been out of it, Jaz and Tank had returned from Texas.

His entire family... *almost*.

The last member sat in the same chair she'd fallen into who knows how long ago.

Roman didn't need to see through the top of the yellow hood to know the Minion-esque form alongside his bed was Isabel.

A thick black-gloved hand rested above his knee, as if she'd fallen asleep while touching him and had passed out cold. He covered her fingers with his bare hand, and Isabel startled as if he'd touched skin.

"Roman." Her gaze whipped to the monitors on the wall and back to him. She jumped up, sending her chair into the wall with a loud crash. "Oh my God! You're awake! How are you feeling?"

Forgetting about her bulky gear, she wrapped her arms around him and crashed her massive hood into his head.

His groan morphed into a low, rusty-sounding

chuckle. "Well, I was feeling okay, but now I have a bit of a headache."

"I am so sorry." She tried stepping back, but he wouldn't hear of it.

Latching onto her glove, he pulled her back to his side. "Nuh-uh. You stay right here where you belong."

Her pretty brown eyes roamed all over his face as if not knowing where to look, and he felt the same. He couldn't keep his eyes, or his hands, off her, even after hearing the slow awakening rumblings of his family.

Knox called out first, followed by his mother. Soon, everyone who'd previously been fast asleep now had their faces smashed against the thick window.

"Roman!" His mother cried, held by an equally weeping Gretchen.

"About damn time," Knox grumbled out his relief.

"I don't want to ever hear again I'm the lazy Steele who sits behind a computer," Liam teased with a relieved grin. "Because, dude, you laid on your ass *forever*."

Their mother smacked her youngest in the shoulder. "You leave your brother alone...at least until the IVs come out."

Roman chuckled as each of his family and friends made their sentiments known. All the while, he held tightly onto Isabel's hand.

"I'm guessing you figured it out." Roman squeezed her fingers, smiling proudly.

"With *a lot* of help from Maddy...but you did most of the heavy lifting. Your body was obviously not ready to let go any time soon."

"My heart, too." Roman gently tugged her closer

until her hood rested against his forehead. His eyes locked on hers, and he couldn't go another moment without telling this woman how he felt all over again. "I love you, Isabel Santiago. If there were thoughts I was holding on to, they were the ones of you. It took me this long to find you, and I wasn't about to let go without a fight."

Isabel sniffed. "Damn it, Roman. This suit doesn't come equipped with windshield wipers."

He smirked. "We could patent them and live high on the hog."

Isabel was already shaking her head. "I don't need to live high on the hog. Or have a white picket fence. Or a nine-to-five job with a steady retirement plan. All I need, Roman *Wallace* Steele, is *you*." Isabel's voice quivered. "If this whole ordeal has taught me one thing, it's that love isn't something that you should let pass you by. And I'm not letting you pass by. I love you too. So much."

In the observation room, their friends and family cheered, and there were a lot of *about damn times*. Roman relished the moment, and for the first time in longer than he could recall, he felt content.

Happy.

All he needed was his family and the woman in his arms...and he was complete.

EPILOGUE

In the days since Roman had finally taken that important turn for the better, Isa had never been busier. The inhibitor cocktail they'd given to Roman along with red blood cells from a healthy donor had worked with flying colors, and so she and Maddy had seen to its distribution in Beaver Ridge, where it had immediately been put into practice.

Infected patients were now turning the corner...even Tony.

There'd definitely be lasting effects, not limited to possible organ damage, but he'd live. And once he was back to his health, Nat was more than ready to put him in a jail cell near Blue Eyes, Connie, and the rest of their goon squad.

Isa should have been able to let out a huge sigh of relief, but her stomach knotted, too nervous to let herself enjoy the moment she'd been anticipating for the last week. She paced in the Tru Tech waiting room, which was filled to the brim with members of the Steele Ops family. Nat and King had come out for the occasion, and even some of the Tru Tech employees who'd been involved in Roman's post-FC-5 care had made an appearance. The only person not in attendance was

Maddy, and that was because Roman had requested she be the one to officially spring him from quarantine.

Isabel had wanted to argue, but she couldn't.

"Relax, cariño." Her grandfather brushed her arm in an attempt to soothe her nerves. "Your wait will soon be over."

Jaz chuckled. "And then you can kiss him straight on the lips instead of through the hood...because I got to tell you that was beginning to make me uncomfortable."

Isabel stopped pacing and smiled. "I can't thank you both enough for being here today."

Her grandfather brushed off the sentiment with a small wave. "You have no need to thank me for being here for you, or for the man who has stolen your heart."

And Roman had definitely stolen her heart...and she never wanted it back.

The double doors swung open and everyone turned as Roman, with Maddy walking by his side, swaggered into the room. His clothes hung off his broad shoulders, a little looser since he had lost quite a bit of weight, but now that FC-5 was officially out of his system, he was free to get back his normally scheduled life.

Roman's family clapped and cheered, and someone— most likely Liam—set off a pair of confetti poppers with flying streamers. The pink strands got caught in Ryder's hair, making him grumble.

But everyone hung back, not charging forward to wrap Roman in hugs like she expected, and it took a moment for her to realize why.

His gaze fell on her like an anvil, but instead of settling on her like a weight, Isa could breathe easier for the first time since forever. Roman took a small step forward, making her do the same, and after the first shuffle, she flew the rest of the way.

A foot apart, she launched herself into his arms, and he caught her easily.

Isa ran her hands up his arms and into his hair. She kissed what she couldn't easily touch, making him chuckle as he cupped her cheek and brought her lips back to his.

Another round of applause broke out in the room, mixed in with a few catcalls.

Isabel didn't care. This was exactly where she was meant to be...and she wasn't leaving anytime soon.

Or ever.

Someone is watching their every move.

After a lifetime spent in and out of hospitals, Zoey Wright is tired of playing it safe. She's ready to take charge of her own life and get out of her comfort zone, starting with a new job as a CSI agent. But when her childhood crush Knox Steele gets pulled onto her case, Zoey needs to put her feelings for him aside or more women will die at the hands of the serial killer preying on her hometown.

Former Army Ranger Knox Steele is back in Washington to help his brothers open an elite private security firm. He never expected to stumble onto a crime scene, or see his best friend's little sister working it. Zoey is all grown up now, and the attraction between them is electric, despite his best efforts to resist it. But all that changes for Knox when he realizes the victims have one thing in common...and Zoey might be next.

Keep reading for an excerpt from the first book in the Steele Ops series,

DEADLY OBSESSION

Available now

CHAPTER ONE

Chin up. Shoulders back. Breathe. Do not puke on the crime scene.

At her last position running the Washington, DC, crime lab, Zoey Wright had never needed a peppy mantra. There wasn't much that was nausea-inducing about Petri dishes and microfibers. But thirty minutes into her first on-site homicide and she'd already hit an even two dozen mental replays.

Repetition wasn't working.

Lieutenant Mason side-eyed her as they shouldered their way through a thick crowd of onlookers. "You look like you're going to blow any second, kid. If you need to go around the corner and puke, do it now. But you damn well better not contaminate my crime scene."

"I'm good." Zoey breathed in through her nose and out through her mouth.

The sixty-year-old police veteran lifted his bushy white eyebrows. "So good that you're the exact shade of green my wife made me paint our kitchen last week? Don't kid a kidder, Wright. If it gets too much for you, go take a breather. No one will think any less of you."

If she let an acute case of nerves derail years of hard work and her position as DC's only civilian crime scene investigator, *she'd* think less of herself. Not to mention the ammunition it would provide her hotshot detective brother in his quest to get her to return to the lab— if she'd told Cade about her job switch-a-roo in the first place.

She'd given herself until next week to break the news, but this assignment bumped the deadline up to tonight. As head of the Special Crimes Task Force Cade could— and would—turn the corner at any second.

Zoey cursed the ill-timed bacon maple doughnut that she'd inhaled on the ride from the station to M Street and spotted her brother's truck among the squad cars and unmarked police vehicles lining both sides of the street.

At one in the morning, most family-run businesses had long since closed, which meant the gathering crowd had come from the dance club down the block. Anyone who lived, worked, or played in the District during the last six months knew a police turnout of this magnitude meant one thing.

Another victim.

"Do you have any words of wisdom to lay on me before we get there?" Zoey tugged their collection cart behind her, giving it a little extra oomph when it lodged into a crater-sized crack.

"Yep. Don't inhale food fifteen minutes before being called to a homicide."

Zoey's glare fired off a small chuckle. She took the good-natured barb and followed the older man to the yellow police tape that cordoned off the alley from the rest of the world.

"You make sure everyone stayed out of our scene, Reed?" Mason stopped in front of the officer stationed at the mouth of the alley.

"Only ones who've been down that way besides your people is the guy who called it in. He's giving his statement to Detective Wright now," Officer Scott Reed mentioned her brother.

Zoey swung her gaze around, expecting Cade to pop up at any second. When he didn't show, she released a small sigh of relief...until Mason ducked beneath the rope, leaving her alone with Scott.

She'd barely cleared the tape when Scott stepped into her path. His tall frame and wrestler's build made him impossible to ignore, as did the gaze he skimmed over her body. It slid over her three times before his mouth lifted into a grin *he* probably thought sexy.

She considered it creepy.

Scott shifted a little closer. "You're all over the place these days, aren't you? I tried calling you a few times after our date. I even left a couple messages."

"Really? Huh." Zoey pushed her glasses back onto her nose, a nervous habit she'd acquired in grade school. "I've been having problems with my phone holding voice mails hostage. I'm looking into another model."

And another phone number. That "date" had been the worst she'd ever been on—and thanks to a romance app and one too many blind setups, she'd been on a handful of doozies.

"Maybe we can catch up tonight when this circus is all over. What do you say? You. Me. We can grab a bottle of wine and head back to my place...or yours. I'm not particular." Scott flashed her a suggestive wink. "We can have fun at either place, I'm sure."

Zoey barely suppressed a disgusted grunt. "Sorry, but I'm going to be here for a while. You know how thorough Mason likes to be. It's going to be a long night."

"Okay, sure. Maybe next time."

Unless they stepped into the Twilight Zone, there wouldn't *be* a next time. Someone's family member wouldn't make it home for another dinner or pose for this year's holiday card. One life ended meant dozens— and more—would never be the same, and he stood there, sensing an opportunity to fill a few empty hours—and her pants.

Before Scott made another play, she hustled over to where the lieutenant waited.

Mason chuckled as she approached. "Finalize your plans?"

"Thanks for the save. You could've thrown me a life jacket, a T-bone, or *something*...but no, you practically fed me to the wolves...er, wolf."

"Figured you'd gotten yourself into that mess all alone and that you'd get yourself out. But I can't deny being curious how the hell that happened. I always thought you were the smart Wright sibling."

"It happened because I hadn't been on a date in far

longer than I'm admitting aloud. It was *one* time, and I barely made it out of my apartment before I realized I'd made a mistake. Trust me, it's not going to happen again. I've proclaimed a moratorium on romance. It's career first from this point on."

"What did Romeo do to make you see the error of your ways?"

"Ogled the rear end of my sixty-year-old neighbor before we'd even made it to the car. Then the waitress's legs at the restaurant. And I don't want to know what went through his mind when he stared at the boobs of the barely-legal ticket-taker at the movies."

"What an ass." Mason snorted.

"Not going to disagree with you."

At five foot three, Zoey didn't possess the lithe body of a runway model, and her B cup had more wiggle room than she'd like. Girl-next-door *cute*. That's how one coworker had described her eclectic style to another. It wasn't a term with which every twenty-seven-year-old woman wanted to be linked, but it didn't bother her enough to give up her vintage Monkees T-shirts, either.

Zoey fidgeted with her shirt collar. As it did whenever she contemplated wearing something more revealing than neck-high cotton, the healed scar over her breastbone itched.

Those six inches of puckered skin definitely weren't *cute*.

Their debut appearance came with her first open-heart surgery when she was mere days old. A rerun surgery before her first birthday darkened them. Following a third operation at the age of seven, the scar widened, and then after she hit puberty, and underwent a fourth, it thickened.

Last year's emergent heart valve replacement brought her open-heart surgery grand total to a whopping *five*. Five times her chest had been cracked open. Five layers of gnarled, angry scar tissue loitered between her breasts, a physical reminder she'd skipped pajama parties and Spin the Bottle, and went straight to responsibility-laden adulthood.

Number five had been her wake-up call because some born with Tetralogy of Fallot didn't get a sixth chance.

Shedding the crime lab's cold isolation and joining scene investigation was the first step in redefining life on her own terms. Having lost his son a few years ago to a chronic illness, Mason got that, and had been a big reason why she'd stepped so far out of her comfort zone.

But the calm, laid-back man who'd taken a chance on her wasn't in that alley. The second they reached the site, he started barking orders. Crime scene techs bustled around the perimeter, not willing to incur his wrath for being too slow—or worse, sloppy.

Within the hour, the small four-flapped tent set off to the left would be filled with detectives and forensic scientists, all members of the task force who couldn't do their job until Zoey and Mason finished theirs.

She pulled the collection cart away from pedestrian foot traffic and kicked the wheel lock into position. On her right, a generator hummed to life. Overhead lights blinked once before flooding the entire alley into pseudo-daylight.

Zoey's lungs froze.

Having worked the string of homicides for the last six months in the lab, she thought she'd be okay, but pictures and written reports had nothing on the dark reality that rooted her feet to the ground.

Laid out on a pristine white blanket, as if her killer had wanted to make her comfortable, was the young victim. Her sleek blond hair had been meticulously brushed and fanned out over her shoulders; the wounds on her wrists, carefully bandaged.

The killer staged her resting place like he'd done the others—far enough from people so as to avoid detection himself, close enough for the woman to be discovered quickly.

"Wright." Mason's voice ripped Zoey from her trance. He watched her carefully, no annoyance or judgment on his face. Only concern. "You okay?"

Zoey forced her returning midnight snack back down her throat and let out a slow breath. "Yeah. It took me by surprise. I'm sorry."

"Hell, you don't need to apologize. When shit like this stops making your stomach roll it's time to get the fuck out...pardon my language."

"Do you apologize to all your trainees for swearing?"

"Not a damn one."

"Then don't start with me. Tonight, I'm the newbie grunt. Put me to work."

Mason didn't need to be told twice. He tilted his head in a slight nod and then immediately snapped orders. In the field, she wasn't Detective Cade Wright's little sister. She was the woman who'd hopefully replace Mason as lead CSI when he retired in a few years.

"You know the drill." Mason tossed her a Tyvek suit and gestured to the far right corner. "We start outside and work our way in. You photograph, drop a placard when needed, and log. Watch where you're stepping. Once that's all done, we'll start back at square one and begin the collection. Questions?"

"Not a one." Zoey shook her head.

Mason threw a fierce glare to the hovering technicians. "If any of you even think about doing something helpful, *don't.* Unless Wright or I give you the okay to breathe, you hold your breath. If you can't follow that simple rule, get off my scene now. Am I clear?"

"Yes, sir," a chorus of affirmations sounded around them.

Zoey secured her hair into a low ponytail, and after tugging her suit over her shorts and T-shirt, she donned her plastic booties. Satisfied she looked enough like a condom and wouldn't bring any contaminants into the crime scene, she grabbed her camera and got to work.

Picture. Placard. Log. Move onward. With her camera in hand, Zoey lost herself in the methodical pattern of canvassing and documenting, repetitive movements that never ceased to put her mind at ease. Before long, she stood two feet away from the victim.

Zoey counted to a long, drawn-out ten, then forced herself to examine the reason DCPD informally dubbed the monster responsible the Beltway Cupid Killer.

The *etching*.

Its top curves barely peeked out above the blue dress's sweetheart neckline, but it was there—a perfectly symmetrical heart carved into the flesh over the victim's sternum. Even without the medical examiner's report, she knew it would be the lone disfigurement other than bruised wrists and a single needle mark.

"I am so sorry this happened to you." Zoey battled welling tears.

Around her own age, or maybe a few years younger, the woman could've been a teacher or a nurse, maybe a college student from down the block like the last three victims had been.

No matter who she'd been in her life, she didn't deserve to have her hopes and dreams cut short. *This* was the difficult part of the job. There was no rewinding time and stepping in *before* someone got hurt.

There was only picking up the pieces and praying that one of those fragments helped put a loved one's mind at ease.

Mason crouched on the other side. "I always come in hoping to God that it's not another one."

Zoey chiseled her dry tongue off the roof of her mouth. "I didn't come across a purse or an ID. Did you?"

"Nah. Didn't expect to since he didn't leave them behind at the other scenes. The bastard's nothing if not predictable. We'll find out who she is and make sure to notify next of kin." The sky rumbled off in the distance. Mason glanced up and cursed. "That storm's coming in fast. We need to get this entire scene covered because I'll be damned if I'm going let a single strand of evidence wash away."

"I'll go get the tents," Zoey volunteered.

She backtracked toward the safe zone, careful not to disturb anything in the process. Less than five seconds into the arduous task of tugging off her protective gear, a familiar tingle formed at the base of her neck.

Her *Knox-dar*.

The strange, shiver-like phenomenon occurred whenever Knox Steele stood in close proximity, a sad reminder of the embarrassing level of interest she had for Cade's best friend. But it wasn't possible.

Knox hadn't stepped foot in DC in years—over two, to be exact.

"You're a little far from the lab, aren't you, angel? You get lost?"

Zoey's hand stalled on her zipper.

That voice. The impossible became reality because Knox Steele's low, husky baritone couldn't be replicated—except by the Knox who visited in her dreams.

Zoey turned on reflex, and came face-to-face with the man himself.

Sexily rumpled, Knox's dark hair curled over his ears as if he'd rolled out of bed a few minutes ago. Heavily worn blue jeans hung off his trim waist, and a leather jacket and dark cotton tee emphasized his broad chest and even wider shoulders.

Her heart stumbled into a double-time beat, and warmth rushed to her cheeks—and all points south. Under normal circumstances, she'd be ecstatic to realize her feminine parts hadn't dried up and turned to dust.

But there wasn't anything normal about Knox's presence, or the way his alert focus conjured life into her usually dormant libido.

Standing less than three feet away from her teenage fantasy, she'd never been more aware of the fact that with her Tyvek suit zipped to her chin and the hood pulled over her limp blond hair, she could've played the principal part in a live-action sex ed presentation. Knox, all six foot three inches of him, looked as if he'd stepped straight off the pages of *Bad Boy Weekly*.

She bumped her glasses onto the bridge of her nose even though they hadn't yet fallen, and forcefully put her attention back to shedding her suit. "I'm right where I'm supposed to be."

"You sure about that? This doesn't look like the crime lab—or your bed. Does Cade know you're here?"

"Are you sure about where *you* are? In case your cell doesn't have a map app, you're in DC. Thought you should know since you've made it your life's mission to avoid this place like the plague."

The muscle in Knox's jaw ticked wildly. If he'd been someone else, she'd apologize for hitting a nerve. Not with him. A former US Army Ranger like her brother, he could take that and a lot more.

"Hey, Wright!" Mason's voice shouted, garnering her attention. The older police officer pointed to the sky. "Put a little hustle into it!"

Saved by the grumpy lieutenant.

Without another word, or a glance at Knox, Zoey

deposited her suit into a large collection bag—in case any crucial evidence managed to stick on to her person—and handed it over to the tech to put with the others.

Walking back toward the CSI van, she fumed.

Unlike the rest of his brothers, Knox hadn't returned home after his discharge two years ago. He'd wiped his hands clean of everyone, not even gifting them an occasional I'm-Not-Dead text. And now he was going to stand there, naughty smirk in place, and make comments about her life decisions?

No thank you.

The Zoey Knox had known two long years ago *would've* been tucked into her bed, sound asleep, with her cat, Snuggles, curled next to her pillow. But last year, she vowed that if her bum heart kept throwing obstacles into her daily routine, the least she could do was enjoy life in between the chaos.

Her heart worked fine now, nearly all textbook characteristics of Tetralogy of Fallot resolved. Things that had at one time been a trial were now second nature. She even maintained a healthy exercise routine, and because of her once-a-week self-defense class, could *almost* throw larger assailants over her shoulder and onto the mats.

But that was something he wouldn't have known.

Because he hadn't been around.

Cue mic drop.

Zoey possessed a strength she'd never known before—and yet after one prolonged glance from the eldest Steele brother, breathing ceased being an automatic physical response.

She needed distance to pull her head back on straight.

She needed time to collect her thoughts—and keep down her food.

She needed Knox Steele messing up her life like she needed another hole in her heart.

ABOUT THE AUTHOR

April blames her incurable chocolate addiction on growing up in rural Pennsylvania, way too close to America's chocolate capital, Hershey. She now lives in Virginia with her college sweetheart husband, two young children, and a cat who thinks she's a human-dog hybrid. On those rare occasions she's not donning the cape of her children's personal chauffer, April's either planning, plotting, or writing about her next alpha hero and the woman he never knew he needed, but now can't live without.

To learn more, visit:
   AprilHuntBooks.com
   Twitter @AprilHuntBooks
   Facebook.com/AprilHuntBooks
   Instagram @AprilHuntBooks

DREAM MAKER
by Kristen Ashley

After years of being responsible for her family, Evan "Evie" Gardiner is pursuing her own dreams of an engineering degree. Working as a dancer seems like the perfect way to pay for tuition...until her family lands in yet another scrape—a deadly one. Since Daniel "Mag" Magnusson knows a thing or two about desperation and disappointment, he insists on offering Evie his protection. He has the skills to guard Evie's life, but as they grow closer, he'll need to come face-to-face with his demons in order to protect her heart.

FATAL DECEPTION
by April Hunt

When criminals break into Isabel Santiago's lab and steal a deadly virus, she's desperate to find the culprits before they turn her research into a weapon. But first she must put her trust in the brooding security expert who sees danger around every corner. As she and Roman race to track down the culprits, these two unlikely partners find there's more at stake for them than they ever imagined possible—but only if they stop the enemy in time.

I'LL BE WATCHING YOU
by Leslie A. Kelly

As a teen, Jessica Jensen had a ridiculous crush on Hollywood heartthrob Reece Winchester. When she meets him as an adult, he's just as charming, fascinating, and devastatingly handsome as she'd imagined. But her real-life Cinderella story is about to take a deadly turn...because someone knows the Winchesters have been hiding dark family secrets—someone out there just waiting to strike.

NOWHERE TO HIDE
by Leslie A. Kelly

The last thing LAPD detective Rowan Winchester needs is true-crime novelist Evie Fleming nosing around the most notorious deaths in L.A.—including the ones that haunt his own family. He's torn between wanting the wickedly smart writer out of his city...and just plain wanting her. But when a new killer goes on the prowl, Rowan realizes they must solve this case fast if they want to stay alive.

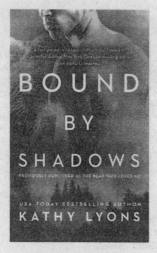

BOUND BY SHADOWS
by Kathy Lyons

As the leader of his clan, Carl Carman is surrounded by enemies. He's learned the hard way that keeping a firm leash on his inner beast is the key to survival, though his feelings for baker Becca Weitz test his legendary control. When danger stalks too close, Carl realizes he must unleash the raging, primal force within to protect everything he holds dear. But can Becca trust his grizzly side with her life—and her heart?